Six Summers to Fall

Six Summers to Fall

Copyright © 2023 by C.W. Farnsworth

All rights reserved.

No part of this book may be reproduced in any form or by any electronic or mechanical means, including information storage and retrieval systems, without written permission from the author, except for the use of brief quotations in a book review.

Published by C.W. Farnsworth LLC

Cover Design by Mary Scarlett LaBerge, M. Scarlett Creative

Edited by Jovana Shirley, Unforeseen Editing

Proofread by Tiffany Persaud, Burden of Proofreading

SIX SUMMERS TO FALL

Six summers. Six chances. One week spent pretending.

Ever since her younger sister's engagement was announced, Harper Williams has been dreading the wedding. What should be a joyous, sun-drenched affair is sure to be filled with plenty of awkward moments, thanks to Harper's strained relationship with her only sibling. Awkwardness enhanced by the wedding's location—a lake in Maine, swimming with painful memories of their late father.

Running into Drew Halifax—her childhood crush, who grew up to be the golden boy of hockey—is a surprise. Not nearly as shocking as his offer to be her plus-one is though.

She expects him to back out. He shows up. She's looking for a distraction from the past. He's killing time until his season starts and he can chase the championship. She's guarded yet outgoing. He's easygoing yet focused.

They hardly know each other. Until one week of sharing secrets, pretending to be in love, and sleeping in the same bed changes everything. Feelings that were supposed to be fake start to feel very real.

Problem is, neither of them is looking for a relationship. At most, they're meant to be a summer fling. Definitely not a happily ever after.

But when it comes to falling? You have no control. Once you start, it's impossible to stop. And sometimes…it takes six summers.

CONTENTS

Chapter 1	1
Chapter 2	17
Chapter 3	29
Chapter 4	41
Chapter 5	49
Chapter 6	58
Chapter 7	72
Chapter 8	82
Chapter 9	101
Chapter 10	106
Chapter 11	120
Chapter 12	130
Chapter 13	140
Chapter 14	159
Chapter 15	171
Chapter 16	187
Chapter 17	206
Chapter 18	217
Chapter 19	229
Chapter 20	235
Chapter 21	246
Chapter 22	251
Chapter 23	259
Chapter 24	268
Chapter 25	272
Chapter 26	284
Chapter 27	289
Chapter 28	297
Chapter 29	305
Epilogue	310

Acknowledgments	315
About the Author	317
Also by C.W. Farnsworth	319

SIX SUMMERS TO FALL

C.W. FARNSWORTH

CHAPTER ONE

HARPER

Rain slides down the windshield in steady streams, turning the house I'm parked in front of into nothing but a blob of yellow. Even blurry, I can picture the sunny structure perfectly.

White shutters. Crooked railing. Front porch swing.

The same bittersweet nostalgia of encountering any connection to childhood hits.

A feeling that's both familiar and reassuring. Also sad. It's looking back at a suspended remnant of time you'll never get back, tinged with the dissatisfied realization that you didn't appreciate simplicity when you should have. Coupled with the knowledge that everything you anticipated—adulthood, independence—isn't as glamorous or satisfying as you thought it would be.

Wipers swipe, clearing the water steadily collecting on the windshield. For a few seconds, every detail of the house's exterior is clear, its yellow paint and the neat row of blooming blue hydrangeas lit up by the bright glare of car headlights.

It looks friendly and cheerful.

A welcoming escape.

Proof that appearances can be deceiving.

I turn the key in the ignition, shutting off the engine. One of the upsides of living in lower Manhattan is how easy it is to navigate the city without driving a car. My ancient Jeep barely leaves the garage but runs reliably when it does, so I have no reason to replace it with a newer car that starts with simply the press of a button. Not that I would abandon this car even if it stopped running.

Metal teeth press into my palm as I grasp the key tightly, pulling in a final inhale of air-conditioning before opening my door. Damp humidity immediately seeps inside.

The wipers froze in the middle of the windshield. For a few seconds, I contemplate turning the car back on to switch them off in the correct spot, then decide it's not worth the extra effort of doing so. All it would be is a stalling tactic.

Steady drizzle saturates my hair as soon as I step out of the car onto the clamshell driveway. My hair clings to my temples as water starts rolling down my face and the exposed skin of my arms.

The cool glide of falling rain feels good.

Cleansing.

Grounding.

I inhale deeply, trying to suffuse my lungs with the scent of Port Haven, Maine. It's a melancholy smell. Sunny days and stormy nights. Easy flirting and unrequited crushes. Happiness and heartbreak. All mixed with pine and pure oxygen.

A growl of thunder rumbles in the distance.

I've always loved storms, especially in the summer. They have an energy to them.

A power.

An intensity.

My life lacks all three. Lately, it's been nothing but dread and predictability.

Rather than head in the direction of the house—or unpack the two bags stashed in the back of the Wrangler—I start walking down the sidewalk. Clamshells crunch beneath my Converse as I navigate around the puddles that dot the driveway.

Port Haven is a tiny town. When I was a kid, traveling here from a subdevelopment in suburban Connecticut, arriving always felt like an overflow of character.

Every house I walk past is something different, not an endless stretch of cookie-cutter colonials. I'm surprised by how many of the residences haven't changed at all from my teenage memories.

The McNallys' cottage, three doors down, is still painted a shocking shade of red. It stands out like a shiny apple against the backdrop of a stormy gray sky. Across the street, three bikes lean against the picket fence that separates the Garretts' front yard from the pavement. No locks in sight—another indicator that I've left the bustle of the city behind.

I shove both hands into the front pockets of my jean shorts, cringing at the uncomfortable chafe of damp denim against my knuckles. But the scrape anchors me in the present, which is what I was hoping for. This stop is about moving forward, not reminiscing about the past.

But just being back in Port Haven makes that nearly impossible. It transports me to a time that appeared practically perfect, but was nothing more than a pretty illusion.

This used to be my favorite place on earth. That familiarity and happiness are still here. They're just cloaked with darker emotions that are too easy to drown in. Storminess similar to what's swirling in the sky above me.

Maybe Port Haven hasn't changed in the last decade.

But I have.

Walking down the quiet, peaceful street is like ripping off a bandage to assess the wound underneath. Mine should look scarred yet healed. But now that I'm actually peeking underneath, it still appears pink and raw.

Time only heals if you acknowledge its passing.

Grief has no finite measure.

The end of Ashland Avenue dead-ends into the unoriginally named stretch of Main Street—the center of Port Haven's small downtown section.

My destination sits right on the corner, fluorescent lights shining through the rain and darkness like a lighthouse's beacon. Main Street Market serves as the town center. Memories of purchasing Popsicles to suck on down at the lakeshore and picking up hot dog buns for a cookout creep into my mind as the automatic doors slide open. Happier, simpler times.

Harsh lighting and the acrid scent of chemical cleaner greet me as my wet sneakers squeak across the linoleum.

Port Haven's only grocery store hasn't changed the arrangement of its aisles since I was last here. Produce is up front, the waft of additional refrigeration raising goose bumps on my skin. The meat counter is located in the very center, mostly displaying cuts of fish and emanating a continual gurgle from the lobster tank. All the alcohol is tucked against the far wall, so you have to cross the entire store to reach it.

I grab a couple of limes from the basket of green citrus set up beside the bananas before weaving my way down the chip aisle. Following a brief debate between cheese puffs or potato chips, I pick up a bag of salt and vinegar potato chips to serve as a late dinner. Then, I beeline toward the back of the store and make a quick selection.

One bottom-shelf bottle of tequila later, I'm in line for Express—the only open checkout lane. The market is close to empty, which is hardly surprising. It's past what most of Port Haven's residents would consider appropriate shopping hours and too late in August for there to be much of a tourist influx lingering in town. There's only one man in line in front of me.

Water drips from my soaked clothes as I study the final flecks of coral still sticking to my toenails and wait for the other customer to pay. No doubt my mom and my sister, Amelia, will have something to say about their chipped state.

I'd rather endure comments about my poorly polished nails than have them delve deeper than the surface level of my appearance. That's always been my strategy when it comes to interacting with my family. The more obvious I make our differences—my shortcomings—the more civil our conversations are. The more superficial subjects there are to discuss, the less likely painful topics will come up.

A fading pedicure is nothing in comparison to my lack of wedding date or disappointing choice of career.

I'm twenty-seven years old. Long past the point where my family should dictate my life choices. And I know their comments come from a place of love—it's just heavily disguised by judgment and dismay. By my mother mentioning which of her friends have single sons and my sister saying many of her former law school classmates are in their mid- to late-twenties. I have as much interest in dating an investment banker or attending law school as I do in leaving this store empty-handed.

None.

My phone begins vibrating in the back pocket of my jean shorts. I'm guessing it's my best friend and roommate, Olivia—there's no one else I can imagine calling me this late. She's an ER nurse with a hectic schedule that I can't keep track of even though we live together.

I fumble for my phone, dropping one lime in the process. The green fruit rolls away slowly, like it's taunting me with its departure.

"Shit," I mutter.

I can't lean down without dropping either the chips or the tequila—precious cargo I'm not willing to part with. So, I ignore my ringing phone and step closer toward the register, stopping next to the guy who's taking a ridiculously long time to pay for groceries that have already been scanned and bagged.

"Is it okay if I just—"

My intention is to ask the cashier if I can set my items on the empty stretch of counter next to the credit card machine. But for some unknown reason, mid-question, I decide to glance at the guy holding up the line.

Or maybe the reason *isn't* unknown.

Maybe it's a remainder of the urges my thirteen-, fourteen-, fifteen-, sixteen-, *and* seventeen-year-old self fought for the five summers he lived next door.

Just as stubborn as an adolescent, I was bound and determined not to be the cliché who lusted after the hot guy every girl had a crush on. The guy who went for a shirtless run every morning. The guy who turned out to be more interested in my younger sister than he ever was in me.

Drew Halifax smiles at me from beneath the brim of his beat-up ball cap, and my silly heart skips a few beats. A collision of nostalgia and hormones can cause palpitations, I guess. My throat goes dry and my palms turn sweaty.

I swallow, suddenly intensely aware of my ragged appearance. Faded T-shirt that could possibly be see-through now that it's soaked, muddy sneakers, and wet hair. Never have I imagined what running into Drew as an adult might be like. But an ideal scenario would look nothing like this—clutching cheap liquor and dripping water, like I just took a shower while wearing clothes.

I try and fail not to feel self-conscious about my appearance as water continues to streak down my face like tear tracks. If my hands weren't full of alcohol and junk food, I'd attempt to make improvements to my appearance. But it's probably a lost cause at this point.

"Hi," he says. "Remember me?"

With another guy, I'd play dumb. Call this a self-absorbed power play. A *look at me now* way to get me to acknowledge I know who he is. So I can stroke his ego by admitting, after ten years, I still recall too many details, including that brief moment we shared—once. So I can admit that I'm aware he's now a famous athlete who graces magazine covers and makes millions.

He takes my stunned silence to mean I don't. "Drew. Drew Halifax. My parents own the place next to yours."

My head nods automatically, the motion jerky and uncomfortable. Stiffened by surprise. I wasn't expecting to run into him here —or ever. And I absolutely wasn't expecting him to recognize me.

I clear my dry throat. "Yeah, I remember."

Drew was seventeen the last time I saw him in person. Even if I hadn't searched his name and scrolled through some articles over the years, usually after a drink too many, I'd recognize him. His hair is a dirty shade of blond that used to be shaggy and is now just long enough to run fingers through. All the shorter length does is emphasize the way Drew's features have hardened and sharpened. All man, no boy.

His eyes haven't changed at all—magnetic and mossy. They pull me in as successfully as they used to.

He's *stupid hot*, as Olivia would say.

I clear my throat again, in some hasty attempt to regain my composure. "You're sort of famous, you know."

I say it as a test, wondering how much of the guy who used to shift in response to praise remains, following years of fame and adoration.

Drew grins, an easy expression that simultaneously manages to put me at ease and make my heart race. The smile creases the corners of his eyes and exposes a devastating pair of dimples. "Only *sort of*?"

He's looking at me like he's happy—*elated* even—to see me, which is strange and unexpected. Drew and I were never close as teenagers. We simply coexisted as part of the same group of summer kids whose parents had transplanted them to Port Haven from early June until the end of August.

Both before and after his ill-fated romance with Amelia fizzled out, Drew and I spent barely any time together. Nothing significant ever transpired between us.

Time around him was memorable—only because of my stupid crush on him. A stupid crush that never fully faded, apparently, because I feel his smile *everywhere*. It douses me as effectively as the water falling from the sky did, charged awareness skittering across the surface of my skin.

"How have you been, Harper?" he asks, *still* looking happy to see me. It doesn't falter the way fake masks do.

"Fine," I answer quickly, expecting that to be that. Pleasantries exchanged, moving on with our separate lives.

Drew was always a genuinely nice guy. Sincere in a way few guys I knew in high school were. Sincere in a way few guys I've *ever* encountered were.

My teenage self was drawn to more than his good looks. It's nice to know fame hasn't changed that about him. Comforting, the same way this town seems to be stuck in time.

"Are you here for long?"

To my surprise, Drew seems interested in extending our conversation beyond the obligatory acknowledgment. Which wasn't even obligatory. He could have said nothing to me.

I shake my head. "Just tonight actually."

Drew's eyes skim my expression and drop down to my outfit. There's no interest or disapproval on his face. It's more like he's searching for something.

A more robust answer maybe. On why I'm back and why my visit is so short. If he's visited Port Haven with any regularity since high school, he must know I haven't. And why.

It's depressing, I guess—how I assume everyone I encounter is only interested in the bare minimum exchange. Even sadder how it's almost always the case.

"Are you?" I ask, shifting my grip on my groceries. It feels rude to only answer his questions and not ask any in response. "Here for long?"

"Not sure. I got in a week ago and still have some time before preseason starts up. Was hoping my folks might be able to come up like old times, but..." Drew rubs his forehead, knocking his ball cap up and then tugging it back down. "My dad had a stroke a year ago, so it's harder for him to get around. He and my mom basically stay put in Boston now."

"I'm so sorry about your dad," I say.

My memories of Aiden Halifax are fuzzy at best. But what I do remember of him, he was always jovial and smiling. A bright, happy presence and as hockey-obsessed as his son. Drew's mother, Rebecca, was always just as cheerful. She was the type of parent who baked chocolate chip cookies and made homemade lemonade. The polar opposite of my mom.

Foolishly, I feel like I should have known about his dad's health. But it's a misguided notion.

Drew and I haven't kept in touch. It's a private family matter he's obviously chosen not to share with the rabid fan base obsessed with his slap shot and his six-pack. He never posts anything personal on his social media. And my mother basically cut this town off years ago. I'm certain she hasn't kept in close touch with Mr. and Mrs. Halifax.

"Thanks." Drew rubs his jaw with one hand, drawing my attention to the sharp angle and dusting of stubble there. He's uneasy with sympathies. We have one thing in common, I guess. "And...I'm really sorry about your dad. I wanted to go to the funeral, but I was at school and—"

"It's fine. Thanks," I cut him off, distantly aware of how my voice has turned sharp and brittle, nearly cracking in the middle of *fine*. I mistook his uncertainty as being associated with his family, not mine. And while it's *not* fine, it's also nothing I want to discuss with him. Especially not here.

Drew nods once. For someone sincere, his serious expression is difficult to interpret. I can't tell if he's uncomfortable or understanding.

I exhale. "Sorry. I just—"

"It's okay. I shouldn't have brought it up."

A large lump forms in my throat as I manage a nod. What I'm acknowledging, I'm not really sure.

A decade after his death, Drew's condolences still sting like my dad passed yesterday. But they don't bother me the way some people's do. Or did. Most people seem to assume there's an expiration date for grief. That after a set amount of time, you should no longer experience it. Nothing in Drew's expression says that.

"Your total is sixty-three forty-five."

I jerk, having totally forgotten we're standing in the checkout of the supermarket. Mostly alone, but not entirely. Drew recovers more gracefully, nodding at the cashier as he pulls out a credit card from his wallet and taps the machine to pay.

The cashier—a gangly guy who looks to be in high school—alternates between glancing at the computer screen and at Drew. I steal a look as well, only to find out Drew's eyes are already on me.

Quickly, I glance away, my cheeks warming without permission.

He's just nice, I tell myself. I got my hopes up about Drew Halifax once before. Then, they crashed as I watched my little sister hang all over him. Being back here is messing with my head.

"Thanks," Drew says as his receipt is handed over.

"Can I get an autograph?" is the response. The question comes out more like *can-I-get-an-autograph*, a rushed exhale that sounds like a burst of courage. And that also explains the slow speed of the line.

"Of course."

I'm unsurprised by Drew's answer. He seems like the sort of celebrity who would see fans as a responsibility instead of an inconvenience.

I watch as Drew grabs the pen from the weekly specials clipboard and scribbles his signature on the back of the receipt. "What's your name?"

"Dustin."

Drew adds *To Dustin* above his signature before handing the slip of paper back to the boy.

The cashier takes the receipt like it's a breakable object. "Thank you *so* much."

Drew smiles before leaning down. Too late, I realize what he's reaching for.

The wayward lime that I forgot about as soon as I saw him.

"I can get—" I step forward at the same moment he straightens.

Suddenly, we're close—*too* close. I can find the small freckle just to the left of his bottom lip. Spot the slight bump on the bridge of his nose that, if I had to guess, was put there by a hockey puck. Smell his cologne, some heady combination of sandalwood and cedar.

Drew sets the lime on the counter. I hurriedly step away from him and glance at the green fruit. I doubt the linoleum floor is cleaned very often, but the citrus appears unscathed. Winding my way back through the store to grab a new one doesn't sound appealing. Tequila will get me drunk either way.

"Thanks."

Drew nods, the corner of his mouth curling up as he takes inventory of the other two items I'm clutching. His purchases are already bagged, so I can't return the favor. I doubt *he's* just buying alcohol and junk food, though.

I don't know much about hockey.

I *do* know it's not played professionally during the summer.

But despite being out of season, Drew's physique is impressive. He's wearing a pair of mesh basketball shorts, a T-shirt, and sneakers. None of it covers the definition of his calves or the bulge of his biceps, which make it obvious he's in excellent physical shape.

I add the second lime, bag of chips, and bottle of tequila to the lime already set on the counter. The cashier rings up my items slowly, distracted by glancing at Drew, which is terrific for my ego.

Drew picked up his bag of groceries, but hasn't walked away. I steal peeks at him while my purchases are scanned. He's looking at his phone, which he must have pulled out of his pocket, brow furrowed as he swipes at the screen.

And...*waiting* for me? Maybe?

I can't come up with another explanation for why he's loitering around—unless he thinks the guy working is looking for a second autograph.

The cashier cards me for the tequila. I'm tempted to roll my eyes. There's no chance I could pass for twenty or younger, even if I am dressed like a sloppy teenager. But I hand my driver's license over without comment and pay before grabbing the brown bag.

Drew follows me outside. Rain is still falling steadily from the dark sky, dripping off the store's overhang and bouncing off the pavement.

We both linger outside the store, but it's not awkward, like I expected. More unfamiliar. Uncertain. I have no idea what Drew is thinking.

"Did you walk here?" Drew asks.

His voice and question are both casual. Unaffected, like us running into each other at the Main Street Market is a normal occurrence. It soothes my anxiety. Removes the inclination toward making up some excuse to leave. Stopping here was the start of a lot of unknown, and any glimpse of normal—even feigned—is welcome.

"Yeah. You?"

"Yeah." Drew tilts his head toward the left, in the direction of Ashland Avenue—where we are both headed—green eyes drilling into mine in a silent question.

I nod and shoot him a small smile, tightening my grip on the bag I'm holding as I walk into the rain.

It's not that I don't want to spend more time around Drew—the opposite.

But I'm apprehensive about the prospect.

I'm in a melancholy mood, lost in the past and worried about the future. No part of me is prepared to flirt or to smile or to act like I have my life together in the present.

Normally, I have no problem appearing bubbly and poised and assured.

Not tonight. Not here.

Exhaustion weighs me down as we walk along the rain-drenched sidewalk. All I really want to do tonight is drink tequila in my pajamas without worrying about how my hair looks. I know that won't be possible around Drew. His presence is impossible to ignore. It lingers like a silent shadow next to me as we start down the street, walking side by side over cracked pavement.

Drew says nothing as we stroll.

I'm the one who speaks first. The falling rain prevents total silence, but it still feels strange to walk with someone I hardly know without speaking a word.

"I don't know a lot about hockey. But one of my friends from work is a big fan. She was super impressed to hear that I swam out to a floating dock with you when I was fourteen."

He glances at me. Half-smiles. "What do you do?"

"Hmm?"

"For work. What do you do?"

"Oh." I tighten my grip on the bag I'm carrying. God, do I hate this question. "Answer phones and pick up coffee, mostly. I'm trying to figure out what else to do with my life." I force out a light laugh.

"You need to do something else?"

I don't do a great job of keeping the surprise off my face. I've gotten that response before. But only from people I've given the bright and shiny version of my responsibilities to. The ones who have heard, "I'm an executive assistant at Empire Records, managing artists and tracking album sales," and imagined me rubbing shoulders with celebrities and having a say in their careers. And none of them have achieved an iota of the success Drew has.

"Some people seem to think so." *Including my family.* Bitterness seeps into my tone.

"Seems like *your* opinion is the one that should count."

"Yeah, it should," I respond.

Spoken like a multimillionaire, I think.

It's awfully simple to follow your heart when you don't have to worry about paying bills.

Not that I resent Drew's success. It's just easier to be brave with a safety net in place. One I don't have and he does.

Our steps slow until we stop in front of the yellow house. My eyes trace the familiar outline of the cottage my parents bought when I was in seventh grade. Lots of summers in rentals—mostly on Lake Paulson—and then five here.

It's annoying—how easy it is to recall what we're hoping to forget, but how hard it is to remember what we're desperate to. I tear my eyes away from the cheerful yellow, glancing at the Halifaxes' blue house next door and then at Drew.

"My evening plans begin and end with drinking tequila." I blurt out the sentence. "If you feel like hanging out, I have plenty…" My voice trails as I glance down, watching water as it continues to drip from my hair in a steady stream onto the bits of gray and white shells.

"I need to put these groceries in the fridge. Then, I'll come over." Drew's response is immediate. And sincere, it seems.

But I try not to focus on those details. I try to act like his response doesn't matter to me one way or the other, even as I feel relief erase uncertainty. Drinking alone no longer sounds like the ideal evening, if the alternative is his company.

"Okay," I say.

"Okay," Drew echoes.

Then, he's walking away, toward the blue house next door.

I trudge toward the yellow cottage, in no hurry despite the ongoing downpour. Walking toward a moment you've actively avoided isn't an easy task. I've been dreading this as much as

Amelia's wedding. For years, I've known there would be a moment where I'd walk inside 23 Ashland Avenue again. I'm just unprepared for it to be *this* moment.

I pass my parked car and approach the front stairs, my steps slowing the closer I come until I'm at a standstill a few feet from the first step. I study the front door for a few minutes, barely aware of the rain dripping down my face and soaking my shirt. The paper bag I'm holding is damp, liable to disintegrate soon.

But I don't move.

CHAPTER TWO

HARPER

Logically, I know I can't stand out here all night.

One final sigh, and I step forward, climbing the stairs and stopping under the cover of the porch.

The spare key is still hidden beneath the pot of geraniums. It's those little things—the preserved things—that make facing big changes so hard. They make it too easy to pretend nothing is different from the last time I was here.

The front door opens without a creak. If anything, the house is better-maintained than when we actually stayed here. I force myself to keep walking.

Everything is exactly as I remember it, as soothing as old grooves in wood. Ancient yet sturdy.

I move through the quiet, lifeless house like a ghost, flipping more lights on as I explore until the whole first floor is illuminated. The bulbs cast an eerie glow over the white-sheet-covered furniture, making the fabric look luminous.

The kitchen appears normal and functional. It's the only room that looks like someone lives here. I set the bag of groceries on the counter and carefully unload it, setting the tequila, limes, and potato chips down on the spotless marble.

After a little rummaging through cabinets, I come up with a bowl, a knife, and a cutting board. I open the potato chips and shove a handful into my mouth, savoring the saltiness, paired with the sour tang of the vinegar, as I chew and swallow. Then, I wash the limes and start cutting them.

The sound of the front door opening a few minutes later startles me. So does the echo of the same voice I used to imagine saying my name.

"Harper?"

"Kitchen," I call back.

The door shuts. My heart takes off like a racehorse leaving the gate.

I should have taken a shot before he arrived.

I focus on the cutting board instead of the erratic drum of my pulse, sectioning the lime with precision a surgeon would be proud of. Neat wedges get dropped into the bowl, one by one.

"Hey."

His voice is closer than I expected.

I startle, knocking the other lime off the counter with my elbow.

I make a wild grab for it, but Drew is faster. He catches it and hands it to me. Our fingers brush, and I squeeze the citrus too tight in a useless attempt to quell the spark of electricity that travels through my body with the speed and power of a lightning bolt.

"Nice reflexes."

He grins, leaning against the countertop in a casual, relaxed pose. "Played goalie for a bit back in elementary school."

"Not since then?"

He shakes his head, still smiling.

"What happened?"

"They figured out I could score." He doesn't say it like an innuendo, but that's exactly how it sounds in my head. My grip tightens around the lime to the point of bruising before I set it back on the counter.

Drew reaches into his shorts pocket and pulls out a plumed ceramic figurine that's painted with streaks of turquoise. He sets it on the counter in front of me.

I squint at it. "What's that?"

"Saltshaker."

"It's...a bird?"

I catch his nod out of the corner of my eye.

"A finch, yeah. My mom has a thing for them. She told my dad she liked birds, so he took her to an aquarium for their first date to see penguins. She still gives him a hard time about it. I guess the smell of fish wasn't overwhelmingly romantic."

I smile. "Still, that's sweet."

"Yeah. It worked out for them, obviously."

"Your mom still likes birds? Sorry, *finches*?"

A smile tugs at one corner of Drew's mouth. "Yeah. If I'd been a girl, I would have been named Sparrow."

"Narrow miss."

He chuckles. "Anyway, I wanted to contribute to the evening."

I glance at the blue bird. "With salt?"

"I knew you had the tequila and limes, so..."

A smile pulls at my mouth as I meet his dancing eyes. "I, uh, I'm surprised you still come up here."

"Why? You love it here as much as I do."

I swallow and look away.

Drew is right.

I *do* love it here. I always have.

Facing this house was always going to be hard. Staying away was easier than missing it.

Love enhances other emotions—for better or for worse.

"Let's go out to the porch," I say, grabbing the bottle of tequila and bowl of limes. "Bring the salt. And can you grab a couple of glasses?"

"Sure." Drew studies me curiously but does as I requested.

The hem of his T-shirt rides up a few inches as he reaches toward the cabinet, exposing a sliver of skin, carved with muscle.

Low in my belly, something clenches.

I swallow, look away, and start walking toward the front door, only stopping at the basket in the mudroom. There are a few blankets tucked inside.

My mother hired a management company to take care of renting this place out over the summers after we stopped coming up. They didn't change much in terms of interior decoration, and I'm glad and also annoyed about that fact. Just like I'm relieved and irritated the cottage is never rented in August. It just sits unoccupied. Alone.

Moist summer air coats my skin and hair as I step outside. The rain has stopped, but the pure smell of it still fills the breeze that swirls my hair around my face.

I wrap the blanket around my shoulders and take a seat on the swing, running a hand through my damp hair as I watch water drip off the railing and into the hydrangeas. All I hear is the soft *plink*.

Drew appears a few seconds later. There's another clench in my stomach as he sits beside me, carefully setting the glasses and saltshaker on the seat between us.

His T-shirt is damp in spots, clinging to his impressive musculature. And I *look* because it's right there and nice to stare at. I watch him settle on the swing beside me, absorbing the dip of his weight before I focus my gaze out on the front yard again. The darkness and mist in the air make it hard to see far past the sidewalk. There are no streetlights, just the moon's glow and the light spilling out of Ashland Avenue's houses. The asphalt of the road is barely visible.

This is a tiny bubble.

This town, this porch, this moment.

I count sixty-eight drops falling off the rim of the roof before Drew speaks.

"Have you been back since?" he asks.

"Nope." I tuck my knees up under my chin, certain he already knew the correct answer. "I'm surprised my mom hasn't sold it."

Part of me really wishes she would. It would make everything easier. Instead, it lingers like a puzzle piece that doesn't fit with the rest, preventing the end of a chapter. Just sitting here. A house that's cleaned and cared for and *empty*.

Drew leans back and rests a foot on the railing. I stop staring at the street and side-eye his profile instead. Up close, I thought there might be a flaw in his appearance. But I can't find one.

Five summers.

That's how long we "knew" each other. But all I really know about Drew, aside from the facts that he plays hockey and has nice parents, is that his favorite drink used to be Dr. Pepper and that he's allergic to peanuts. On the spectrum of strangers to friends, we're a lot closer to the former.

The muscles in his calf clench and relax. The swing starts to sway, the motion nothing more than a slight rocking.

I unscrew the tequila and pour generous splashes of alcohol into the two glasses before I pick up a wedge of lime and shake some salt onto it.

Drew raises a brow, but doesn't comment before doing the same.

"Cheers." I tap my salted wedge against his.

An easy grin unfurls, those lethal dimples appearing right on cue. "Cheers."

Looking for a distraction from Drew's lips, I bite into my lime. Sour saltiness explodes in my mouth. Hastily, I reach for my glass. Drew reaches for his first and raises it, tapping lightly against mine with a subtle *clink*.

"To summer."

"To summer." I wash the nostalgia down with the smoky burn of tequila.

Warmth spreads through me as the alcohol sears my stomach before it begins trickling through my veins, lazy and relaxing.

"Fuck." Drew coughs. "That's terrible."

I grin and take another sip. "Main Street Market's finest."

"College trick?" Drew asks, dropping his lime back in the glass.

"My roommate and best friend worked as a bartender for a bit. Some guy she worked with would always salt the limes for tequila shots."

"More hygienic than licking a stranger, I guess."

"Speaking from experience, Halifax?"

He grins, and that smirk really ought to come with a warning label. Suddenly, I'm not sure if the light, loose sensation I'm experiencing is from tequila...or from *him*.

"Nah."

"Liar."

You don't look like him and not have girls lining up. Not to mention, the whole rich-and-famous thing isn't exactly a turnoff.

Drew chuckles as I pour myself another drink and pass the bottle to him. My dirty Converse land on the railing beside his sneakers as I sink into the blanket wrapped around me. Gradually, fresh air replaces the musty scent of no use.

"Is that what it's like, playing professionally? Wild parties and puck bunnies?"

He looks over at me, eyebrows raised and green eyes surprised. "Puck bunnies?"

"Yeah." I take another sip of tequila.

Drew's right; it's bad. Cheap. But it's also effective. I don't know if it's sitting on this porch again or the liquor or Drew or the blanket my grandmother quilted, but I feel lighter—happier—than I have in months. Years maybe. The exact opposite of what I thought this night would be.

"Isn't that what you call girls chasing after a hockey player?"

"I'm familiar with the term, Harper. I just wasn't expecting you to know it."

"I know things," I tell him.

Drew shakes his head, a soft chuckle slipping out of his mouth before he takes another sip of tequila.

"This singer I worked with dated a hockey player. I'm also familiar with the terms *hat trick* and *offsides*."

"Familiar, as in you know they exist or know what they mean?"

I roll my eyes. "First one."

Drew laughs again. I like the sound of it—his laugh. It's the first time I've really registered the way someone's laugh sounds. I tuck it away for safekeeping, like a secret to remember.

"So, you're a singer?"

"God, no. I just work with them."

"Answering phones and getting coffee."

I'm annoyingly, overwhelmingly pleased he remembered my job description from when I rattled it off earlier. "Exactly."

"Do you *want* to be a singer?"

It's my turn to laugh. "No."

"Why not?"

I debate on telling him what I sort of *do* want to do. But instead, I reply with, "I can't sing."

"Yes, you can."

"You're only saying that because you haven't heard me sing."

Instead of agreeing or laughing, Drew says, "I've heard you sing."

"What? When?"

It's not bright enough to tell for certain, but it almost looks like Drew is embarrassed. There's a darker flush to his cheeks as he rubs his thumb along the outside of the glass he's holding. "There was that summer we hung out on the Duxburys' dock a lot. Before Jeff left for college. You would sing at the firepit."

"I can't believe you remember that. *I* barely remember it."

Vaguely, I recall dancing on pine needles with Katherine Eddings and Sophie Stewart. We'd try to choreograph our moves and then immediately forget them. Singing was meant to be a distraction from that.

Meanwhile, Amelia would sit off to the side, sipping seltzer instead of beer, often with her best friend, Savannah, who would come up here with us sometimes.

"I doubt there's a single guy who was there who's forgotten about it."

I raise both eyebrows as I study his expression. There's no longer any trace of embarrassment. Something heavy and significant passes between us. Some whisper of what-ifs. I knew those existed on my side. I acknowledge them every time I get drunk and search his name. But I never ever had any sense Drew Halifax might have been interested in me until right now.

"Hmm," is my only response.

This trip doesn't need the complication of a hookup with a famous hockey player. No matter how hot or nice he is.

SIX SUMMERS TO FALL

I'm trying to grow up. To reject the inclination toward burying my feelings and insecurities with attention and cheap thrills.

And maybe it's vain of me to think he's talking about me at all. Maybe he had a secret crush on Katherine or Sophie and would have said the same thing to either of them if he'd run into them at the grocery store earlier.

We lapse into silence, both taking the occasional sips, but it's not uncomfortable. It's peaceful—something I never thought being back here might be.

I'm not sure how long we sit and sway before Drew speaks. Time always passes differently in happy moments. It becomes sand slipping through your fingers. Clouds blowing away and out of sight.

"So...you wanna tell me why you came back for one night?" he asks.

I exhale and glance at the tequila bottle resting between us like a barrier. It's half-empty, which means more is a bad idea. Drew is drinking slower than I am. Probably because he's rich and famous and attractive and he isn't hiding from his problems for the night.

"Pity party, basically."

He nudges my knee with his. An electric current zips upward, racing along my nerve endings. "I'm a good listener."

I know he is. The one and only other time Drew and I spent any time alone together was a night when I was seventeen. It could have been the same one he just mentioned. He was in the Duxburys' kitchen, grabbing chips, when I went inside to use the bathroom. We talked for a few minutes. I can't remember what we talked about, but I remember the giddy sensation—remarkably similar to what I'm experiencing right now.

A week later, Amelia announced she was going out on the Halifaxes' boat for the day. As soon as I found out it was just her and Drew going, I knew I needed to get over the boy next door. So, I went out with Freddy Owens the following weekend and tried to pretend I'd never looked twice at Drew until we left for the summer. My dad died a few months later, and we never came back here.

I tug the blanket closer around me. The later it gets, the colder it becomes. I forgot how Maine summers are like this—humid days and chilly nights. The city isn't like that. The blacktop absorbs sunbeams all day and radiates the heat all night.

"Amelia is getting married next Saturday." I finally answer his question. "Her fiancé's aunt and uncle own a family camp on Lake Paulson. Rather than have individual bachelor and bachelorette parties, they invited the whole wedding party to spend a few days there before the rest of the guests arrive on Friday. Not only could I not get out of it, but I'm also the only bridesmaid showing up alone. And since I was already driving up north, I decided to stop and spend a night in Port Haven. Delay the inevitable, I guess."

Face the past, I add silently.

He knows what I'm avoiding, even if I don't say it.

Drew doesn't respond right away. I pass the silence by fiddling with my glass and pulling in a deep breath of damp air. He asked. But my answer was sad and pathetic; neither of which is an adjective that is pleasant to be associated with.

Right as I'm draining the rest of my drink, he speaks. "I'll go to the wedding with you."

I start coughing mid-swallow. Clear my throat, then fix him with an incredulous expression.

Drew is smirking, obviously amused by my dramatic reaction. "*What?*"

"I said, I'll go to the wedding with you," he says with the

exaggerated enunciation of someone who knows you heard them the first time.

If I hadn't, my sinuses wouldn't feel like they're on fire right now.

"Why would you do that?"

He shrugs. "It sounds like fun."

"You got *fun* out of what I told you?"

"You asked if playing professionally is wild parties and puck bunnies. It's not. It's skating until you puke and early mornings and a ton of travel and…I love it. I'm fucking lucky to have made it. But the off-season is long. Most of the guys don't stick around Seattle. I visited my folks and a few college buddies, and now, I'm just here. I'm bored. So, yeah, a week on the lake sounds fun."

"Everyone will assume we're a couple."

"Yeah, so?"

"Won't it be weird? Because of you and Amelia?"

"Me and Amelia?" Drew's eyebrows rise, followed by a low laugh. "We hung out a couple of times in high school, mostly in a group. Kissed…once, I think? Maybe twice?" He shrugs, then tugs on the brim of his ball cap as he relaxes against the back of the swing. "It wouldn't be weird."

My head spins from a lot more than liquor.

Drew's nonchalance is an extreme departure from everything I remember Amelia giggling about that summer, gushing, "Drew is such an amazing kisser," and, "Drew is so hot," and, "Drew can't keep his hands off me."

I'd usually snap my gum or roll my eyes in response. But there was always a twinge in my chest when Amelia talked about Drew, a pang that never appeared whenever she mentioned any other guy.

"You two haven't gotten any closer?"

When I glance over at Drew, he's studying me closely.

"Yeah…nope."

Just another failure on my part. In addition to being single and only marginally successful by most people's measures, I'm also a shitty big sister. I can't even manage to go to my sister's wedding without having an existential crisis.

"Well, the offer still stands. You can even call me mid-week, and I'll show up."

I believe him.

I like to manage expectations. To be surprised rather than disappointed. But I believe Drew would show up.

"Thank you," I tell him. "Seriously. For drinking and for talking and for offering."

Drew smiles and then tips his glass toward me again. Amusement fades from his face. "To Paul."

I pull in a shaky breath as our glasses tap. "To Paul."

His lips quirk up in a sad smile before closing around the rim of the glass. I pour myself more tequila, down it like a shot, and then bite into another salty lime. Rather than set it on the floor like a normal person, I hurl it into the front yard.

"Fuck," I exhale.

Drew reaches over and squeezes my knee.

"Fuck," I repeat, softer.

He doesn't offer any empty words of comfort. He just sits next to me, his grip tight and grounding. And we sit like that, side by side, watching water drip off the roof onto the hydrangeas, on the porch of the house where my dad killed himself.

CHAPTER THREE

DREW

A pounding headache pulls me out of unconsciousness. I groan and roll onto my back, roughly rubbing a palm across my face and swallowing in a sad attempt to get rid of my dry throat. All it does is emphasize how parched my mouth is. I need water, coffee, and another two hours of sleep. Preferably in that order.

When my eyes squint open, the harsh glare of sunshine makes me want to pull a pillow over my head. Instead, I focus on my surroundings, trying to figure out where the hell I am.

Waking up in an unfamiliar place is nothing new. Common actually. But this room doesn't contain the standard hotel decor I see on road trips. Or the blue and green color scheme of my parents' lake house, which is where I've woken up for the past week.

All the furniture, besides the bed I'm lying on, is draped in white fabric that blends in with the bare walls. The floors are a honey-hued wood. My shirt and shoes are gone, but I'm still wearing my shorts, sprawled across light-blue bedding that's the only color in the room.

I sit up, immediately closing my eyes when the motion worsens my headache to a painful pounding.

I don't drink much during the season. Or during the off-season. I don't drink much, period. But I'm experiencing all the symptoms of an epic hangover, so I obviously drank last night.

A lot.

Voices drift under the door. One that sounds familiar—that was my soundtrack late into the night—and I suddenly realize *exactly* where I am. I remember seeing Harper in the grocery store. Walking over to her parents' place in the rain. Talking on the front porch. Tequila—lots of tequila.

The end of the evening is a blur that apparently ended with me passed out in here.

I slide off the bed. My T-shirt is a crumpled heap on the floor. I pull it on and glance around. No sign of my shoes. I head for the door, yawning as I walk. I should force myself to go for a run and then take a shower. Eat something greasy too.

"Can't believe you showed up here!"

I hesitate, my hand freezing around the doorknob.

Harper's voice is high and upset. She said she wasn't bringing anyone to her sister's wedding last night, so I assume she's single. But maybe an ex followed her here and is attempting to make amends?

The thought bothers me more than it should.

I shove the misplaced annoyance aside as I open the bedroom door and step into the hallway, determined to confront any awkwardness and get out of here. Up until last night, I hadn't seen Harper Williams in ten years. Her love life—*anything* about her life—is none of my damn business. So what if I thought she was hot in high school and she's gorgeous now? It doesn't matter that she intrigued me then and fascinates me now.

After today, I'll probably never see her again.

"I'm leaving this morning. I'll be up there by noon," Harper says as I walk down the short hall, turn the corner, and approach the connected living room and kitchen.

The Williamses' cottage has an open layout, same as my family's.

"You were supposed to be there last night, Harper. I called Olivia, and she said you left right after work."

I glance at Harper, who's standing with her arms crossed, in the same outfit she wore last night. Her dark hair is piled in a messy bun on top of her head. Then, I look at the woman standing next to the stove, wearing a trench coat and heels.

I recognize her immediately. Francesca Williams was well known in Port Haven for the five years my family's summer vacations overlapped with hers. While her husband, Paul, puttered around the property and her daughters hung out down at the nearest lakeshore, Francesca was famous for spending most of her time indoors, preparing for her next high-profile trial and commuting back to Connecticut.

Based on our conversation last night and the tension swirling in the air, Harper and her mother are no closer now than they were when the Williamses lived here. I'm ridiculously relieved it wasn't a guy who showed up, but this will still be plenty awkward.

"I just decided to stop here for one night. I knew the house was empty, like it usually is. I didn't think it would be a problem." Harper sighs. "How did you even know I was here?"

"Mrs. Hanover called me last night. She said there were lights on and a strange car in the driveway. I drove up first thing this morning since I'm not due in court until this afternoon."

Harper's shoulders slump. "You could have just called," she mutters.

"I tried to, last night. You never answered. Which was also concerning."

"I was...distracted." The slightest tint of pink flushes Harper's cheeks. "And then I..." She shakes her head. "Never mind. It doesn't matter. Am I not allowed to come here? You should change the locks then. Or better yet, sell this place so it doesn't have to sit like some sick shrine."

I take a step back. Harper and her mother are too busy facing off to notice me yet, and this definitely isn't a conversation I should be eavesdropping on. Resentment and anger are so thick in the air that they're practically tangible.

Francesca sighs. "There is no need to always be so dramatic, Harper. You want to stay here? You should have asked. Better yet, you should *not* have pulled a stunt like this a week before your sister's wedding. You don't think I have enough going on? You thought I should have to drive two and a half hours to check up on my adult daughter for trespassing?"

"*Trespassing*? You're unbelievable, Mom. And I didn't *ask you* to check up on me. How many times do I need to tell you to butt out of my life before you listen?"

"I haven't heard from you in *weeks*, Harper! I had to call your *roommate*—whom I've only met once—to find out what your plans were. How do you think that made me look? You haven't expressed any interest in Amelia's wedding. I ran into Marcy Evans last week, and she said you never reached out to Ransom! He was all excited to accompany you to the wedding."

"I told you to stop trying to set me up with your friends' sons. I told you I was happy to go alone. That I would *rather* go alone than show up with a guy who irons his shorts and considers golf a sport."

My lips tip up at that comment.

"Problem is, you *don't listen*," Harper continues. "I figured you would be happy I'm showing up alone. All the focus will be on Amelia, like always."

"That is not true, Harper. And don't talk about your sister like that."

"You're on her side," Harper drones. "Shocker."

Silently, I move another step away. Except, instead of encountering smooth wood, my heel slides onto rough fabric. Half of the white cover protecting the couch is pulled away, landing on the floor in a heap.

When I glance up, Francesca and Harper are staring at me.

Fuck.

I focus on Harper's mother first. "Hi, Mrs. Wil—" Midway through, I realize Francesca probably doesn't go by Williams any longer. She got remarried. "Hi. It's nice to see you again."

Francesca's thin eyebrows nearly reach her hairline as she appraises me standing in the living room. She has the type of commanding presence that can make anyone—regardless of their actual age—feel about ten years old. Her expression is schooled quickly as she gives me a quick nod of acknowledgment.

"Drew. What a surprise."

Her remembering my name is also a surprise. I sincerely doubt Francesca is a hockey fan, and she was the least present of her family members when I lived next door.

"Same here. Harper didn't mention you were stopping by."

"It was last minute." Francesca gives me a tight smile before glancing between me and Harper, obviously trying to figure out what I'm doing here.

Harper is staring down at the kitchen counter, her cheeks flushed with embarrassment or anger or both.

I spot my sneakers lying on the floor next to the kitchen island and walk toward them, pausing next to Harper.

"Good morning." I press a kiss to her temple, inhaling the

lingering scent of lime and rain. "Offer still stands," I whisper to her, tugging gently on one of the strands that's fallen out of her bun before continuing to my shoes.

My memory of her choked response to me saying I'd accompany her to Amelia's wedding is one of my clearest from last night. It's also a good indication she won't take me up on it. But especially after hearing what I just did, I wish she would. And I don't iron my shorts or play golf, so she could do worse.

I slide my sneakers on and head toward the front door. "See you later," I say, not glancing at Harper as I do. Maybe she's pissed at me. Maybe I overstepped just now—in multiple ways.

"Nice to see you." I nod at Francesca, still unsure of how to address her.

"Bye, Drew," she responds.

I step out onto the Williamses' front porch, sparing a glance at the swing that's moving slightly in the morning breeze. There's a desiccated lime peel lying on the wood boards beneath the swing, stripped of pulp and dried out. I stop to grab it, tossing it into the row of hydrangeas below the railing before continuing down the steps.

Clamshells crunch as I walk across the Williamses' driveway and over the short stretch of grass that separates the two properties.

My mother opted for gravel for our driveway. A new load is delivered every spring to cover up the weeds that crop up between the small stones, even though my parents hardly come up here anymore. My mom broached selling it last Christmas, which is partially what inspired this trip. A last hurrah, possibly a final goodbye.

But Port Haven is not the town I remember. Sure, it looks the same. Even smells the same. But it lacks that feeling I used to experience here.

Or it *did*—until I turned around in the grocery store and saw Harper Williams. All my favorite memories of this place—sneaking beers and lazy days on the lake and s'mores and stupid dares—include her.

When I step inside the front hall of the cottage, I wince. It's even more of a mess than I remember. I rushed through unloading the groceries last night, more eager to head over to the Williamses' than to store food in cabinets that I'd just end up pulling back out. A waste of time, in other words.

All I bothered to store were the perishables. The counters are covered with boxes of cereal and loaves of bread and canned soups. Dirty dishes are piled in the sink.

The living room doesn't look much better. There's an empty water bottle on the coffee table, and one of my hockey hoodies is tossed over the back of the couch.

I keep walking past it all, down the hallway and into the master suite. It's cleaner in here, mostly because it's where I've spent the least amount of time. My sneakers get kicked off in the corner before I head into the en suite, popping two painkillers from the cabinet above the sink and washing them down with a gulp of water from the tap. I strip off my shirt and shorts, then step under the stream of the shower.

The warm water and the pills help my headache. By the time I step out of the shower and towel off, the pounding has dulled to a slight ache.

I pull on a clean pair of shorts, not bothering with a shirt, and pad back into the kitchen to survey the fridge contents. Better than yesterday, thanks to the trip I took to the store last night. I pull out a package of bacon and a carton of eggs, then begin brewing coffee.

My phone rings right as the saucepan begins sizzling. I pull it out of my pocket, glance at the screen, and answer before flipping the bacon and eggs.

"Hey, Crawley."

"Hey," my best friend, Troy Crawley, replies.

We play on the same line for the Washington Wolves. He lives three floors down from me, in the same high-rise in Seattle that's close to the stadium. Both bachelor pads. While I'm single because I prioritize hockey over everything else and have yet to meet a woman who's okay with being mostly ignored for more than half of the year, Troy just has a short attention span when it comes to women. When it comes to most things, actually. But he's a hell of a hockey player and a loyal friend.

"What's the crackling sound?" he asks.

"I'm frying bacon."

Troy groans. "Fuck, that sounds so good. Now, I want bacon. Nina is on vacation this week, so I've been eating like shit."

I snort. "Sounds like you should get a *second* private chef as a backup."

"Says the asshole with a cleaning lady."

"It's so someone looks in while I'm gone on road trips!" I tell Troy for the thousandth time.

He's not wrong though. And it's partly why the cottage looks so terrible. I've gotten lazy.

Troy laughs. "Whatever, man."

A loud sizzle from the pan draws my attention back to the stove. A spot of oil leaps out of the pan and onto the granite counter, making me question the judgment of not bothering to put on a shirt before I began cooking.

I quickly turn off the burner and start toward the bedroom to grab one. "So, what's up?"

Before Troy has a chance to respond, the doorbell rings.

"Hang on, man. Someone's here. Can I call you back in a bit?"

"Yeah, sure," Troy replies.

I drop my phone on the coffee table and pivot, heading toward the front door instead of the bedroom.

It's probably just a neighbor, I tell myself.

Mrs. Owens down the street brought me a batch of peanut butter cookies a few days ago. I felt too bad to tell her about my peanut allergy, so I offered to look at her rain gutters as penance for immediately throwing the homemade baked goods out. I'm supposed to go over there at some point this week.

And Chris Albertson, the other next-door neighbor aside from the Williamses, stopped by two days ago, asking if he could borrow a basin wrench. I called my dad, who didn't answer, of course, and then stood out in the garage with him for twenty-five minutes while he sorted through my dad's tools and told me about his lobster business.

Maybe he's back today for something else. I got the sense he was eyeing this yard as a spot to store some extra traps. Must be weird for everyone else on the block, seeing these two houses sit empty most of the time.

But when I open the door, it's to the one neighbor I want to see.

"Hey." Harper smiles, but it doesn't reach her eyes. She's showered, too, her brown hair almost black, just like it was last night. It hangs loose, reaching just past her shoulders.

"Hey," I respond, leaning against the doorframe and studying her closely.

Her eyes dart down to my abs, then quickly back up to my face. I chew the inside of my cheek, not reacting to the appraisal. You can't skate five miles a game without winding up in great shape. I'm used to women checking me out. But it feels different with Harper, who met me as a scrawny thirteen-year-old.

She fiddles with the hem of her shirt and bites her bottom lip before fully meeting my gaze. "How much did you hear this morning?"

I'm honest. "Most of it, I think."

Harper sighs and looks down at the doormat. It's a cheery weave of sunflowers. She kicks once against the slight lip that separates the doorframe from the front porch. "Yeah, that's what I thought."

"I wasn't trying to eavesdrop. I just heard voices and then…"

"I know." She's still staring at the ground.

After a few seconds, she looks up. Something tightens in my chest when our eyes connect. There's lust, yeah. Harper is gorgeous. Always has been. Freddy Owens bragged about his date with her for weeks while I resisted the urge to punch him in the face and tell him to stay the hell away from her.

But there's something else too. Something protective and compelling. Something that doesn't really make sense when it comes to a person I haven't seen in over a decade.

"I still don't get why *you'd want* to come to the wedding. But *I* want you to come with me. You know, if you still want to. If the offer still stands. And if it doesn't, that's totally fine."

I blink at her. Part of me was fully convinced I'd made a fool of myself by offering to go with her—twice.

I'm not even sure why I made the offer in the first place, honestly. There are plenty of other things I could do to entertain myself for the next week that don't involve attending the wedding of a girl I shared a sloppy make-out and awkward outing with in high school.

Going to Amelia's wedding has nothing to do with Amelia and everything to do with Harper. I got the strong sense last night and this morning that Harper doesn't have a whole lot of people in her corner. And I have the unexpected urge to stand there.

I cross my arms, enjoying the way Harper's eyes dart down again. "Offer still stands."

Harper exhales, and it sounds a lot like relief. She wasn't sure if I would agree, and it throws me off. Confidence is what I associate most with her. She was the girl who did what she wanted; opinions and consequences be damned.

"Thank you, Drew."

"Don't thank me yet. If your mom tries to prosecute you for trespassing, I'll cause one hell of a scene."

Harper huffs out a rough laugh. "Yeah. It's…well, it's what you saw. Anyway, I've got to leave shortly. There's some garland I'm supposed to pick up in Hayden for the wedding planner to test out. I can text you the address. It's on Lake Paulson. I can't remember if I mentioned it last night."

Her cheeks flush, like perhaps she didn't mean to mention last night.

I reply as if I didn't notice, "I've got some stuff to take care of here, but I can be up at Lake Paulson this evening. It's an hour away?"

"Unless you hit traffic, it should be more like fifty minutes."

I nod. "Even better. One sec. Let me grab my phone." I turn and walk toward the living room, grabbing my phone off the coffee table and then returning to the open door.

Harper smirks, glancing around at the mess behind me. "You redecorating the place?"

"It's a mess, I know. Working on it."

I hand her my phone. She taps at the screen for a few seconds, then holds it out to me. "The camp is called Basswood. If you search for it, the address should come up. Text me if you have any problems finding it. And if you change your mind, no hard feelings."

I take the phone and pocket it. "You don't have a lot of faith in me, huh?"

"Nothing to do with you, Drew. I don't have a lot of faith, period." She shoots me a tight smile. "I'll see you later. Or not."

I roll my eyes. "You will."

Harper nods and turns away, only to pivot back and complete the circle. She looks like the girl from last night again. Cheeks flushed, hair a little wild.

"Nothing…happened between us last night, right?"

I grin. "You'd remember if it had."

Then, I close the door and hunt down a shirt so I can finish making breakfast.

CHAPTER FOUR

HARPER

The drive to Lake Paulson takes me well over an hour. There was an elderly man at the flower shop in Hayden who was picking out flowers for his wife, and I felt guilty about rushing him along in his selections. They've been married for fifty-three years, he told the salesclerk. That length of love is hard for me to comprehend. It feels like all the relationships I witness are uneven and fleeting. Lacking love and passion.

Once I'm off the highway, I put the windows down for the rest of the scenic trip. It's a perfect August day—breezy, dry, and warm. The beautiful weather is almost enough to help me forget about the nausea I'm battling, thanks to the amount of tequila I imbibed last night.

I steal sips of the iced latte I bought from a sweet woman named Darcy at Hayden Coffee as I weave along the pine-lined roads. Fleetwood Mac blares from the Jeep's speakers, the wind that's combing through my loose hair carrying the sound away. I sing along to "Dreams" when it comes on.

"I've heard you sing."

That sentence appears in my brain without warning, letting me know I memorized Drew's words without meaning to.

"You'd remember if it had," is also engraved in my memory now. Not to mention how Drew looked when he said it, one shoulder propped against the doorframe, dimples out in full force, and shorts slung low enough to show off the V carved between his hips.

Hastily, I drink more iced coffee. I wanted a distraction this week. Now, I'm worried Drew might be *too* distracting. Despite being pitched as a relaxing lead-up to the wedding, I very much doubt this week will be much of a vacation. There will absolutely be last-minute tasks to complete, and Amelia will undoubtedly find offense with even my full attention.

I brake and flick on my left blinker as I reach the bait shop. I avoid looking at it, but I can picture it perfectly. While I inherited my creative, wild side from my dad, one thing he didn't pass along to Amelia or me was a love of fishing. Not for a lack of effort on his part. One of my dad's favorite things was pulling us out of bed before the sun had fully risen, shoving travel mugs of hot cocoa in our hands, and heading down to the lakeshore to take the boat out.

Down to *this* lakeshore.

Before they bought the house in Port Haven, our parents would bring us to Lake Paulson in the summers. We wouldn't spend the whole two months, only a week in a rented cabin. It's where my dad would come with his family when he was younger and an experience he was adamant about giving Amelia and me.

In some twist of karma or fate or maybe just an uncomfortable coincidence, Amelia's fiancé, Theo, spent his summers at his aunt and uncle's camp on this same lake. It was one of the things they bonded over after meeting at law school in Boston, I guess.

And now, it's where they're getting married.

Once I pass the bait shop and the convenience store—basically the extent of any downtown section—I spot the sign for Camp Basswood almost immediately. I turn off the asphalt and onto the dirt driveway that winds through the pines until I reach the main house—a gray-shingled structure with white trim.

At least a dozen smaller cabins are visible past it, nestled down closer to the water's edge. There's a sand volleyball court, a covered pavilion, and a firepit off the path that leads down to the dock. A shed stands right next to the beginning of the dock and a speedboat is bobbing at its end.

Past it all is the breathtaking sight of dark blue lake water that meets with the light-blue sky on the horizon.

I step out of the car and stretch, running a hand through the tangled mess that's my hair and using my sunglasses to keep it out of my face before opening the back door to retrieve my bags and the box containing the garland. Arms full, I slam the car door shut with my foot and then turn toward the entrance, not bothering to lock the Jeep.

I know Theo's aunt and uncle closed the camp reservations early this summer to accommodate the wedding, but the grounds are even quieter than I expected. I should be the last to arrive.

But the only sign of activity is a scampering squirrel that startles and darts away when I have to drop one of my suitcases in order to open the screen door.

I walk into a massive living room. There's a huge stone fireplace tucked against one wall with three couches boxing it in. My attention is immediately drawn to the far wall, which is almost entirely constructed of glass. At least twenty panes offer a dazzling view of the sunbeams sparkling off the surface of the lake. I set my bags and the garland down before I take a few steps closer, standing and staring out at the lake.

A few seconds later, an unfamiliar female voice jolts me from my reverie.

"Hi! Can I help you?"

I turn to see a woman about my age walking toward me, smiling widely, an open door that leads into what looks like an office behind her. I can make out a desk with a computer and an open filing cabinet in the corner.

"Hi," I reply, smiling back. "I'm here as part of the wedding party."

"Oh! Welcome!"

Impossibly, the wattage of her smile grows brighter. Mine probably dims.

"Thank you." I glance toward the stairs. "Are the rooms assigned? I also have this garland—"

"Harper!"

I spin to see Savannah Lewis approaching, a brown-haired man trailing a few steps behind her. She's added highlights to her hair since I last saw her in May at Amelia's law school graduation party, but otherwise looks the same as the bubbly blonde who's been best friends with Amelia since kindergarten. I've known her since her pigtails phase.

Savannah throws her arms around me, squeezing me tightly. She smells like expensive perfume and sunscreen.

"Hi, Sav," I greet, returning the hug.

"How have you been?" she asks me, lively and perky as ever.

"Oh, you know, just…thriving." I drawl the last word.

Savannah smiles and waves her manicured fingers toward me. Unlike mine, hers have no chips. "There's the famous Harper humor."

"Famous, is it?"

Savannah laughs and winks at me before turning toward the guy with her. "This is my boyfriend, Jared."

"Nice to meet you, Jared," I say, shaking his offered hand.

"You too." Jared gives me a small smile, then shoves his hands into the pockets of his jeans. He's a bulky guy—broad, tall, and muscular. Quiet too, it seems.

"Such a bummer you got held up at work yesterday," Savannah says.

I nod in response, my stomach flipping uneasily. That's what I told Amelia, that I wouldn't be able to arrive until today instead of yesterday, like I was supposed to. Thanks to my mother, she'll now know that was a lie. Sure to get what was already going to be an awkward greeting off on the wrong foot.

Savannah glances at Jared. "Harper works at Empire Records. She gets to meet all sorts of music superstars. And gets paid for it!"

"It's not as glamorous as you're making it sound," I say.

"Well, it's definitely more glamorous than my job. Are you saying you didn't meet any singers this week?"

I sigh, then admit, "Sutton Everett came in for a meeting yesterday morning."

"See! I *love* her music! She sings 'Heartbreak for Two,' remember, Jared? I love that song."

"Yeah, great song," Jared replies.

I hide a smile. I'd bet money he has absolutely no idea what song Savannah is talking about.

Savannah catches it too, rolling her eyes. "Jared likes *sports*," she informs me.

"Ah," I reply, not sure how else to respond to that.

Most of the guys Savannah has dated over the years have been as outgoing as she is. She and Jared seem to fit better despite his more reserved personality and athletic interest. But I'm far from a relationship expert.

"Theo and Amelia are meeting with the wedding planner,

Daphne. She's great. You'll love her. Everyone else is out on the lake, waterskiing. Jared and I decided to nap instead. We just got back from Paris, and I'm still jet-lagged." Savannah glances over at the woman who's patiently waiting, watching our exchange. "You met Sara?"

"Sort of." I send Sara a smile. "Nice to meet you, Sara. I'm Harper."

"Nice to meet you, Harper. You're in room six."

I nod and glance down at the box stamped with the flower shop's logo. "Um, I picked up this garland. Any idea where I should put it?"

"I can take that for you."

I exhale a relieved sigh and hand the box over before picking up my luggage. "Thank you." I look over at Jared and Savannah. "I'm going to go get settled. I'll see you guys later?"

"For sure," Savannah chirps. "We have all week to catch up!"

With one last smile, I head for the wide staircase that leads upstairs. The banister is smooth and shiny. My fingers trail up it as I climb the steps to the second floor, pulling my luggage behind me.

Vintage-looking framed photos of the lake line the cream-colored walls as I walk until I reach the white door with a black six affixed to it. I wonder if the rooms are always numbered or if they were added just for the wedding. I wouldn't be surprised in a house this size. I also wouldn't be surprised if they were just for this week. The house where my mother and stepfather, Simon, live only has three guest rooms, yet my mother decided to name all of them. Numbered doors sound like something she'd suggest.

I turn the knob and step inside, my jaw dropping.

I know Theo's family is wealthy. And I looked up the photos of the camp online, so I knew the cabins weren't rustic huts with an outhouse and no electricity. There weren't any photos of the main house's interior on the website, probably because this is technically their private residence. And, I'm realizing, because it makes the cabins look somewhat shabby in comparison.

The space I walk into is more of a suite than a bedroom. I gape at it for a few seconds before dragging my bags inside and shutting the door behind me. The same view of the lake from downstairs is visible here, except elevated—literally.

Three large windows let in streams of sunlight through the tall pines that stretch upward and out of sight. The lake is visible in the gaps between them, but the shore and ground aren't. It feels like I'm in a tree house, floating above the water.

The bed is around the corner and tucked under the eaves to the left, neatly made with a striped woolen blanket folded on the end. Twin nightstands are on either side of the bed, one with a fresh vase of flowers.

I drop my bags on the leather couch that faces the wall across from the bed. There's a low bookcase, which partially covers the wall, with a television on top. Aside from that, there's not much to pull attention from the view. The walls are white shiplap, simple and clean.

There's an attached bathroom, accessed through a sliding door. I step inside, glancing at the toilet and shower before focusing on the sink. Specifically on the mirror above the sink.

"Jesus." It looks like several birds nested on my head and then I went through a wind tunnel.

I comb my fingers through a few of the tangles, but it doesn't help much. I head back into the bedroom to grab my brush from the dopp kit. It only takes a few steps to be back at the couch. My legs brush against the bedspread as I rummage through my dopp kit.

The room feels large because of the expansive view through

the windows, but it's not really that large. And it's hitting me that I'll be *sharing* this space.

Unless Drew backs out.

I pull my phone out of my pocket and glance at the screen. There are a few messages from Olivia, but nothing from anyone not in my contacts. I gave Drew my number, but didn't think to ask for his. He has a way to contact me, but I can't reach him.

Which is probably for the best. I already got drunk and then got accused of trespassing in front of him. Any version of *hey, you still planning to show up so we can pretend to date* seems like it'd be best unsent.

And I'm concerningly certain that he'll show.

Concerning because I *want* him to show. I've gotten alarmingly attached to the idea of having not just company, but *Drew's* company to get through this week and the wedding.

I find my brush, tug it through my hair a few times, and then tie the strands back in a low ponytail. After going to the bathroom and washing my hands, I pull a sunhat out of my suitcase and then stack the bags in the corner of the room before I leave.

Time to face the inevitable.

CHAPTER FIVE

DREW

I've heard of Lake Paulson, but this is the first time I've ever been here. The closest lake to my parents' house in Port Haven is Fernwood Lake, about a ten-minute drive without traffic.

Fernwood Lake is smaller and more secluded than Lake Paulson, which is a major tourist attraction. Lake Paulson is a destination people who have never been to Maine would probably recognize. Real estate on the lake itself runs into seven figures, easily. All the houses I pass before the navigation directs me to turn down a dirt driveway are large and ostentatious. The Camp Basswood sign is impossible to miss.

It's still light out when I park in front of the largest building. Harper's old Jeep is parked two cars down, so I know I'm in the right place. I remember the summer she got it, cruising around Port Haven with the windows down. Usually with Katherine Eddings and Sophie Stewart, the two girls she hung out with most. I also know the Wrangler was a gift from her dad. I'm not surprised she still has it.

I stretch as soon as I'm out of my car. I spent the rest of the morning and most of the afternoon cleaning. Cleaning the cottage and cleaning Mrs. Owens's gutters. Then, I had to take a second shower and pack.

By the time I got on the road, it was after four. And after adding a stop in Portland to pick up a suit, I hit plenty of traffic. Most of the local vacation rentals run Saturday to Saturday, making it the worst possible day to travel.

I grab my duffel out of the trunk and sling it over one shoulder, taking in the scenic view as I walk toward the front door.

This place is even nicer than I expected.

I grew up more than comfortable. My dad worked as an accountant until he retired, and my mom was on the board of a huge corporation. Money was never tight. And now, I get paid a ridiculously high salary to do what I love most in the world—play hockey.

But I have simple tastes, for the most part. When I drink, it's usually mainstream beer. Ever since our season ended in May, I've lived in shorts and T-shirts. I bought the condo in the same building as Troy because it was close to him and the stadium, not because it was the most expensive high-rise in Seattle. And I have a cleaning lady because she worked for the former tenants and I felt bad letting her go.

I've never stayed anywhere like this before.

I knock on the door once, but there's no answer. I peer in through the screen at what looks like the living room. The *empty* living room.

I pull my phone out of my pocket, deciding I'll text Harper and tell her I'm here. Maybe we're staying in one of the cabins down by the water instead of in the main house.

When I tap the screen, I discover that my phone is dead. I usually charge it overnight, and I spent last night passed out in Harper's parents' house guest room.

With a sigh, I open the screen door and step inside, taking in the soaring ceiling and stone fireplace.

One wall is almost entirely made of windows. Must make heating this place a pain, but I'd probably do the same if I lived right on a lake. It's one hell of an unobstructed view—water reflecting the dapples of sunset streaked across it.

Everything is spotless. There's no sign of people or any bags or belongings. I turn around, deciding I'll walk down to the water and see if I can find anyone to ask where I should go.

The screen door swings open right as I step toward it. I narrowly miss getting smacked with a face full of woven aluminum.

"I'm so sor—" The woman who just walked in the door glances at me and freezes. "Holy shit. You're Drew Halifax."

There are times when I expect to get recognized—mostly in Seattle, during the season. When my face is plastered on billboards and the side of the arena. But there are times like this when it's totally unexpected.

I was drafted in the first round and have had a solid career. But I'm not the flashy star. I've never been the guy photographed while stumbling out of a club with girls draped over him or who brawls on the ice. I'm the reliable role model, and I never thought that would garner the attention it has.

I paste a pleasant smile on my face. "You're a hockey fan?"

"Yes. No. I mean, sort of. My dad is. You're his favorite player. And he loves *a lot* of players."

I chuckle at that, relaxing. "I'm honored. Tell your dad thanks."

"I will." She flashes me a shy smile and holds out a hand, which I shake. "I'm Sara. The property manager."

"Nice to meet you, Sara. I'm looking for the wedding party

that's staying here. I hit some traffic driving up, and no one seems to be around now."

"Oh. They're down at the pavilion, eating dinner. I can show you?"

"Yeah, that would be great. Is it cool if I leave my bag here?"

"Of course. Leave it wherever," she tells me.

I drop my duffel down next to the couch and follow Sara outside. She leads me in the opposite direction of the parked cars, past a row of cabins.

"Have you worked here long?" I ask as we walk.

"This is my third summer. Michael and Jane are terrific. I'll stay here as long as they'll have me."

I figure Michael and Jane must be the owners. Amelia's fiancé's family. "I don't blame you. This place is awesome."

"Yeah, it is." After a brief pause, she asks, "So, what do you do?"

I glance at Sara, trying to figure out if she's kidding. I'm not egotistical enough to expect most people automatically know who I am. Except Sara already made it clear she *does* know.

Pink stains her cheeks as she comes to that same realization. "Shit. Sorry. I know what you do. Obviously." Sara laughs nervously. "How do you know Theo?"

"I've never met him, actually," I reply. "I'm dating his future sister-in-law, Harper."

I don't consider myself a great liar. But there's no false note in my voice. It's easy to lie about something you want to be the truth, I guess.

Not that I want to *date* Harper. I'm winding up for a season that I hope will end in finally winning a Cup. If there was ever a time to have a serious girlfriend, it absolutely wouldn't be now, when I'm about to return to Seattle and throw myself into training, which will hopefully last until the finals next June.

But I definitely don't mind everyone thinking I have a claim to Harper Williams. I'll have no issue sticking to the fake dating story around Amelia, her friends, or anyone else.

"Oh. That's cool."

There's a note in Sara's voice that sounds a little like disappointment before another silence stretches between us.

"Do you host a lot of weddings here?" I ask, grasping for a different topic to discuss.

"This is the first, actually," she replies. "We've hosted a couple of corporate retreats and one family reunion. None of them rented out the whole place like this, though. I've never seen the camp so quiet while it's still summer. Usually, it's chaos around here. Although this week will shape up to be plenty busy, I'm sure."

We pass three more cabins and then I see the pavilion. It's tucked to the left of the dock, a stone path leading to the first pillars and continuing in a square shape. Four picnic tables are set up underneath the cover. Three of them are packed with people, and the last one is laden with food.

I spot Harper right away. She's nodding along to something a redheaded woman next to her is saying and sipping from a can of seltzer.

One by one, people notice us approaching until everyone is looking this way.

"Hey, everyone," I say as we reach the end of the path, sending a smile around.

The stares don't really bother me. I'm used to being the center of attention in some way or another. I'm an only child and a people pleaser. There are plenty of events or clinics in Seattle I go to where I'm greeted with the same shocked awe that seems to be lingering in the air right now. I'm just not sure if it's because I'm a stranger crashing what appears to be a small, close-knit group or because I skate around and score goals for a living.

I glance at Sara. "Thanks for being my tour guide."

She blushes and nods as a woman at the nearest table stands.

Amelia Williams walks toward me. Her hair is a lighter shade of brown than her older sister's, her features more severe. Harper looks like a mix of her parents while Amelia favors their mother. In manner, not just appearance. The same assessing gaze Francesca aimed at me in the kitchen this morning appears again now.

"Drew? Drew Halifax?"

I grin and nod. "Hey, Amelia. How are you?"

"I'm good," she answers carefully, then looks at Sara. Presumably for some explanation about why we're here.

Sara clears her throat. "I'm headed out for the night. Just was helping Drew find his way down here for dinner."

Amelia's eyebrows climb her forehead. "For dinner?"

"You should stay and eat with us." A tall man with a hint of stubble approaches, resting a hand on Amelia's lower back while looking at Sara. "Assuming you haven't eaten. There's plenty."

"I don't want to impose…"

"You're not imposing, Sara. Stay." The man, who I assume must be Theo, smiles at her and then looks at me. He holds out a hand. "Theo Madigan."

I shake it. "Drew Halifax. Nice to meet you."

"I know who you are, man." Theo chuckles. "That was a hell of a series against San Diego."

"We'll get them next year," I tell him. "Is it okay if I grab some food?"

Theo nods. "Yeah, of course."

He and Amelia exchange a look, and I hide a smile. They obviously have no clue why I'm here and are too polite to outright say so. I figured Harper would at least mention I *might* be coming, but I'm also unsurprised she didn't.

I feel eyes on me as I walk toward the food.

Harper is sitting on the inside of one bench, meaning I'll have to walk right past her to get to the food.

I stop behind her spot and gently tug on the ponytail her hair is tied back in before dropping a quick kiss to the top of her head. She smells like sunshine and fresh air.

"Told you I'd show up," I whisper, then keep walking.

Behind me, someone gasps. Again, I have to hold back a grin. This fake boyfriend stuff is fun. None of the second-guessing or the stress that comes along with actually dating someone.

I pile a plate high with food. There's mac and cheese, cornbread, salad, and barbequed chicken, all of which smells amazing. I pass over the beer and grab a seltzer instead. My headache is finally gone, and I'd like to keep it that way.

Quiet chatter fills the pavilion as I walk back toward Harper. The redhead next to her sees me coming and scooches over, leaving an open spot. I shoot her a grateful look as I set down my plate and squeeze into the opening.

"Aren't you going to introduce us to your *boyfriend*, Harper?" the redhead asks, leaning forward to look at the woman to my right.

The blonde sitting across the table beams at me. "Claire isn't a sports fan."

"Not true," the redhead protests. "I love watching tennis." She glances at me. "Do you play tennis?"

I smile and crack open my seltzer. "Not well."

"Nice to see you again, Drew," the blonde woman says.

I search my brain for some recollection of her and come up empty.

"Savannah grew up in Fayetteville too," Harper says. "She visited us in Port Haven a few times."

"Oh, right." I smile back at Savannah, pretending that prompted some recognition. "Nice to see you again."

Savannah's smile turns into a sly smirk. "You didn't mention you're dating last year's Sexiest Athlete Alive, Harper."

Harper chooses to take a bite of chicken instead of answering. I hide my amusement behind the can of seltzer.

"Hard to get a word in edgewise around you sometimes, Sav," the redhead, Claire, says.

Savannah rolls her eyes. "Whatever. You know, Drew's parents owned the cottage next door to Harper and Amelia's." She grins at me. "All the girls in the neighborhood would get up early to watch you run around, shirtless."

"Really?" I glance at Harper, who's studiously focused on the remains of her dinner. "*All* the girls, huh?"

The small section of her cheek that I can see turns pink.

The guy sitting next to Savannah holds a hand out. His smile is wide and genuine, his expression eager. "I'm Jared. So cool to meet you, dude."

"Nice to meet you, Jared," I reply, shaking it.

"My best friend was in Boston for college. Used to go to every one of your games. He knew you'd go first round. He's going to lose it when he hears I've met you. Are you staying all week?"

"Yep."

Jared's face lights up. "Awesome. We should go running together."

"Sure," I agree, taking a bite of mac and cheese.

Savannah glances at Jared. "Babe, you weren't this excited the *entire* time that we were in Paris."

Harper snorts, then tries to cover it with a laugh, followed by a sip of seltzer. I shovel more pasta into my mouth as the conversation picks up around me. I finish the mac and cheese and start cutting up my chicken.

"So…you came."

I glance to my right. "Uh-huh."

Slowly—steadily—her lips curve up. "Cool."

Without consciously deciding to, I smile back. "Cool?"

"Yeah."

My hand finds her knee under the table. I give it a quick squeeze, registering her surprised inhale as I stab a bite of chicken. "Cool."

Harper rolls her eyes before turning back to her salad. But she's still smiling.

CHAPTER SIX

HARPER

When I wake up, Drew is gone. Probably out on the same morning run he used to take in high school, which Savannah unhelpfully mentioned last night. I could have gone a lifetime without Drew knowing I used to wake up early just to see him run, shirtless. Based on his smirk at dinner, it's not the last I'll be hearing about it.

I climb out of bed and put on a pair of jean shorts and a T-shirt over a pink bikini, not bothering to do anything with my hair or makeup. I just quickly use the bathroom and then head downstairs.

Everyone went to bed around ten last night, but no one is in the kitchen when I walk inside. Either they've already passed through or they're still asleep. I find a yogurt in the fridge and granola in the pantry. The camp's chef is preparing lunch and dinner this week, but we're on our own for breakfast.

Someone already brewed coffee, so I pour a mugful to go with my food and head out onto the deck with my bowl.

It's another beautiful day. Clear and sunny. The blue sky is unmarred by a single cloud, and the surface of the lake looks like glass. No whitecaps in sight.

I take a seat at the long table that stretches about half of the deck. Three lounge chairs take up the rest of the space.

Theo's aunt and uncle are gone until the wedding. He mentioned at dinner last night that they're staying with his parents for the week and that they haven't left the lake over the summer for years. I don't blame them. If this were my house, I would never leave either.

I'm almost finished with my yogurt and granola when the screen door leading into the kitchen opens and closes again. I glance over one shoulder and take an uneasy swallow.

Amelia looks as poised and perfect as always, in a seersucker sundress and a pair of leather sandals that slap against the wooden deck as she approaches.

She takes the seat directly across from me, setting a mug of tea and a glass bowl of strawberries down on the table. "Morning."

I rub a finger against the rim of my cup of coffee. "Morning."

Amelia moves the bowl of strawberries closer toward me. "Sara brought these over this morning. They're from her garden."

"That was nice of her."

"It was."

We linger in silence, which is common between us. Conversations between Amelia and me usually vacillate between long pauses and sharp words. We've only spoken on the phone once since I last saw her in May at her law school graduation party in downtown Boston. Before that, it was at Christmas at our mom and Simon's. Most of the communication about the wedding has come through group texts and email chains that haven't consisted of any direct conversation.

I grab one of the strawberries and take a bite.

"So…you're dating Drew Halifax."

Red juice dribbles down my hand. I lick it away, and Amelia makes a face before sipping her tea.

"Yeah." It wasn't really a question, but I answer anyway. "I figured Mom mentioned it."

"*Mom* knows?"

"Um, yeah. He was at the Port Haven house when she… stopped by."

"You were at the Port Haven house?"

The open communication I thought my mother and sister shared starts to look a little narrower.

"I stopped by on my way up."

"Why?"

"Because I—I don't know. I wanted to."

Amelia stares at me for a minute, then lifts her mug again and blows on the steam rising from her tea.

We're tiptoeing dangerously close to a subject we don't discuss.

Unsurprisingly, she chooses to change topics. "How long have you been dating?"

I cough to kill a few seconds. "Uh, not very long. We're just, you know, hanging out."

"Right. Of course you are."

Amelia scoffs, and I know exactly what she's thinking and not saying—*Typical Harper. Flighty, reckless, and finicky*.

Based on her tone, you would think I was the least reliable person to ever exist. I've worked at Empire Records ever since I graduated from college—*five years ago*—and she acts like it's a summer internship I'll move on from any day. My track record with men is admittedly terrible, but I don't consider that a character flaw. Just high standards.

"Was I not allowed to bring a plus-one?"

"You were. You just told me you *weren't*."

I grab another strawberry because they're delicious. Supermarket fruit imported from Mexico might be ruined for me. "If it's a problem, I can ask him to leave."

"It's fine. He's already here."

I'd be offended on Drew's behalf, but I know Amelia's attitude doesn't have anything to do with him. Drew was the most popular attraction at dinner last night. Everyone wanted to talk to him, to be around him. It's somewhat comforting to know his charisma isn't something I'm especially susceptible to.

Amelia's issue is solely with me. She's annoyed I changed a part of her plan without her permission.

"Good morning!" Savannah sashays out onto the deck, closely followed by Claire.

Theo emerges a few seconds later, carrying a platter of scrambled eggs. One by one, the rest of the wedding party filters out from the house. Surprisingly, it looks like I was one of the first to get up.

Savannah takes a seat beside me, distracting Amelia with a question about bouquets. Savannah is who Amelia asked to be her maid of honor. I'd be lying if I said her choice didn't sting, but I refuse to admit it caused any injury.

Aside from me, there are three other bridesmaids—Cristina, Willa, and Claire. Cristina is a friend of Amelia's from law school. Her husband, John, came down with a stomach bug the day before they were supposed to leave and stayed at home. Willa is here with her boyfriend, Luke. All I know about him is that he works in construction and says little. And Claire is engaged to Rowan, some finance hotshot who has been on his phone every time I've seen him.

Theo's younger brother, Alex, is his best man. He's missing right now, along with Drew and Jared.

Since Amelia will have five women standing up with her, Theo was obviously required to have five guys, for symmetry's sake. The rest of the groomsmen are Austin, Lincoln, Silas, and Colton, each of whom I've only exchanged a few words with. Austin was at the joint party Amelia and Theo had to celebrate graduating law school, but I'd never met Lincoln, Silas, or Colton before yesterday. Only Lincoln is here with a girlfriend, a petite woman named Tatum, who's missing from the deck. Silas is married, but his wife couldn't get the full week off from work and so is only coming for the wedding.

Claire plops down beside Amelia and opposite me. Her red hair is down and loose, blowing across her freckled face in the subtle breeze coming off the lake. "Where's your hot hockey player, Harper?"

"Uh, he's out on a run."

I think. Honestly, I'm not sure where Drew is.

"I can't believe you're dating *Drew Halifax*."

"I can't believe you know who he is," I reply, smirking.

Before Drew arrived last night, Claire was talking about how annoyed she gets when Rowan watches sports. She and Savannah had a long bonding session over it, during which I stayed silent. Being with someone who shares your exact interests sounds sort of boring.

"I didn't." Claire grins as she stabs at a piece of egg on her plate. "I looked him up last night. He's a big deal."

"I guess," I reply.

I probably know as much as Claire does about hockey. That is to say, not much.

Stalking Drew occasionally over the years has ensured I know what team he plays for—the Washington Wolves. And based on the millions of followers and likes he has on social media, I know he's well known in the sports world. But that's about where any insight ends. My dad didn't watch sports. And I've never cared enough about a guy to mind if he watched sports, let alone taken an interest.

"How did you guys meet?" Claire asks, resting her chin on one hand and staring at me expectantly.

"Um..."

Why did I think no one would care that I showed up with a guy who was apparently voted the Sexiest Athlete Alive? I didn't even know that detail until Savannah mentioned it last night. After meeting Claire, Willa, and Cristina before—not to mention practically growing up with Savannah—I didn't think they'd care about Drew's choice of career. I failed to consider their significant others or Theo's friends. Or the fact that, athlete or not, Drew is a ridiculously attractive guy.

"We've known each other for a long time. Recently, we reconnected...and things just happened from there."

I don't look at Savannah or Amelia as I answer Claire. It's not a total lie. Not the full truth, either.

I glance toward the lake, admiring the way it glints in the sunshine. Three figures appear from the woods, walking up the path toward the house.

"I'll be right back." I stand and start toward the steps, abandoning my empty dishes and heading toward the stairs.

Alex reaches me first.

"Hey, Alex," I greet.

"Morning, Harper," he replies, shooting me a quick smile before he passes me.

I keep walking toward Drew, hoping I'm imagining the way it feels like lots of eyes are watching me.

"Hey."

"Hey." Drew stops walking, using the bottom of his shirt to wipe at his sweaty face and blinding me with his abs.

Suddenly, the sun feels a thousand times hotter, especially once he drops his shirt and fixes me with his unwavering attention.

Jared walks past, flashing me a quick smile before continuing toward the deck.

"Good run?" is all I can manage to come up with.

"Uh-huh." Drew runs a hand through his hair, making the blond strands stick up in every direction. "You should come tomorrow. The trails around here are beautiful."

"I'm good, thanks. I'm not really…athletic."

Drew uncaps the water bottle he's carrying and takes a long sip, his eyes never leaving mine as his lips quirk upward. "Uh-huh. Okay."

I kick a pine cone off the path. "I wasn't sure where you went."

"I thought you knew I went on morning runs? Rumor is, you used to get up early…and watch." He grins.

I roll my eyes, ignoring the way my stomach flips in response to his dimples making an appearance. "Congrats. You went less than a day without mentioning that."

He chuckles, unrepentant, then mercifully changes the subject. "Alex said they're taking out the boat this morning to do some waterskiing. It's a perfect day for it."

I look past him, at the smooth surface of the lake. It *is* a perfect day for it. "Yeah, it is."

"So, you in?"

I shake my head. "I don't think so."

Drew tilts his head, gaze too inquisitive and searching. "Too athletic for you?"

"Honestly, yes. I haven't waterskied since I was…seventeen."

I'm pretty sure Drew was on the boat the last time I waterskied, now that I think about it. We used to go out a lot as a group on Fernwood Lake. Our parents collectively decided there was safety in numbers.

A misguided theory. We mostly just egged each other on.

Drew's teasing expression melts into something more understanding. "It's just like riding a bike, Harper."

"I haven't done that in a while either."

"More of a saying than a requirement, Williams."

I hum in response and glance at the lake, not sure what else to say.

Drew throws me off-balance. No better evidence of that than last night. I took first shift in the bathroom, then crawled under the covers and pretended to be asleep while he got ready for bed and then climbed in beside me. What little sleep I got was while hugging one side of the queen-size mattress. Sharing a bed with a guy was a foreign experience. Sharing a bed with a guy of Drew's size? Even in a queen, there wasn't a whole lot of room.

"It's okay to move forward," he says softly.

I glance toward him, hackles immediately rising in response to the innocent sentiment.

That's what my mom and Amelia would say in the months—years—following my dad's death. Acting as if everything had to return to normal on a set timetable. Acting as if sadness was something to be afraid of. And I know why, even if neither of them ever said it. They *were* afraid of my sadness. Searching for signs they had missed with my dad.

Emotion sharpens my tone to a razor's edge. "I don't need you to *fix* me, Drew."

I'm expecting him to flinch away from the acid. Instead, he steps forward and tilts my chin up, so I have no choice but to look at him.

"I'm not trying to fix you, Harper. I'm trying to spend time with you." The earnestness in his voice drains my anger more effectively than a sieve. Drew holds my gaze for a beat before he drops his hand and keeps walking.

I spin around, surveying his steps away. "Drew," I whisper-shout. "Drew!"

He doesn't stop, long strides eating up the path that leads to the deck stairs. Either he can't hear me or he's pretending not to.

I suck in my bottom lip and stare after him, briefly glancing at the group sitting on the deck. Most of them are looking this way, though they quickly glance away when they notice I've spotted them. Amelia and Savannah are the only two who don't.

I exhale.

Fuck.

For the sake of Amelia's wedding, I hope I didn't manage to mess everything up on day one. Drew's exit would undoubtedly cause a stir. Among the wedding party and for the wedding itself. Cristina told me on the walk from the pavilion back to the house last night that her husband is a huge Wolves fan and can't wait to meet Drew on Saturday.

But the main reason I don't want him to leave? Is just that.

I don't want him to leave.

As someone very comfortable being alone, it's a terrifying thought.

Twenty minutes later, I stand at the edge of the dock, staring out at the water. A pair of Jet Skis flies by, excited shouts carrying across the water. A small family of ducks—six ducklings and one adult—float by the edge of the dock and disappear past the shiny speedboat tied to two cleats.

I keep staring across the broad expanse of water. Up until yesterday, it had been years since I'd been anywhere with memories of my dad. Been anyplace that I knew he'd been. My mom no longer lives in the same house I grew up in. My dad died before I left for college and then I moved to New York.

Maine is the place I most associate with him. And all of a sudden, I'm staring out at a body of water I know he visited—because I was here next to him. If I squint, I can pretend to see the yellow canoe he used to rent for fishing.

Voices drift down the path.

I glance over one shoulder to see Theo, Alex, and Colton grabbing life jackets from the boathouse. They all look surprised to see me.

"Hey, Harper," Theo says. "You want to go out?"

"If there's room."

"Of course. Let me grab you a life jacket."

Theo turns and heads back toward the small shed that stores the boating supplies. I watch him go.

Amelia and I might struggle to get along most of the time, but none of my reservations about this wedding have to do with Theo. He's an amazing guy who treats my little sister like a queen. I'm happy Amelia found him.

I just wish his family didn't own property on *this* lake.

Theo returns with an ugly orange life jacket and hands it to me.

"Thanks," I tell him, holding the life jacket at my side in an attempt to ignore the mildew smell. "Uh, is Drew coming?"

"He said he'd be right down," Alex says.

"Oh. Great," I reply, not missing the look Theo and Alex exchange.

They're probably thinking I'm the one who should know that and likely wondering if I'll manage to ruin this week with some dramatic breakup. Here's to hoping not.

Drew appears with Jared while Colton is loading the skis on

the boat. He looks surprised to see me, but doesn't comment, just shoots me a small smile. He's shirtless, wearing nothing but a pair of navy swim trunks, and it's a struggle to focus my eyes on anything else but his abs.

The only hockey game I've ever attended was in college. Olivia dragged me to a game because she had a crush on one of the players, and we left after about ten minutes. I still remember the amount of gear they wore. How they all looked like color-coordinated blobs on the ice. No tight baseball pants or short-sleeved football jerseys. Just bulky blurs skating around.

I kind of like knowing all of this is hidden when Drew plays. That the view of tan skin and chiseled muscle I'm taking in right now isn't one many women get to see.

And that makes absolutely no sense, because I've never felt possessive toward a guy in my life. My default setting is staying detached.

It's not intentional.

I'm just *good* at it.

Detachment is cleaner. Easier. Safer.

"You tow out from here?" Drew asks Theo.

"Yeah. Sure. You want to go first?"

Drew looks to me. And somehow, I know exactly what he's silently asking. He knows that I'm nervous and unsure. That I want to do this and also don't. That the longer I think about it, the more uncertainty will grow.

I nod.

"Nah. Harper's going first." Drew doesn't ask; he declares.

Maybe it's a famous athlete thing, having the innate inclination to lead while others follow. I'm more of a lone wolf. I'm brave enough to do my own thing, but I don't expect others to copy it. I'm always surprised when they do.

Drew doesn't look the least bit surprised when no one argues with his statement.

Immediately, Colton unloads the skis he just put on board. Drew climbs onto the boat and attaches the tow rope before jumping back off.

"Start it up," he tells Theo.

Theo nods, immediately realizing what it takes me a few seconds to comprehend—Drew is staying behind with me.

Colton and Alex exchange a glance.

"No worries if you can't get up, Harper," Colton says. "Usually takes a few times."

I shoot Colton a tight smile, resisting the urge to flip him off. Competitiveness eats away at some of my nerves.

"Can you spot her, Jared?" Drew asks.

"Yeah, of course," Jared replies, puffing up with importance.

If I wasn't so nervous, I'd smile at his obvious crush on Drew. Colton scoffs.

I'm not used to people going to bat for me. I have amazing friends. And I know my mom and Amelia love me despite our dysfunctional communication most of the time.

But I've gotten used to being independent. To advocating for myself. The fact that Drew is advocating for me is unexpected. Not that it's uncharacteristic coming from him. More that I'm accustomed to no one bothering to, which is a decidedly depressing thought.

The boat chugs away from the dock, leaving me, Drew, and the skis behind on the dock.

Drew nods toward the life jacket I'm holding. "Put that on and jump in."

He slips the skis into the water and then dives, swimming after the skis with quick, efficient strokes. My tally is still at zero for things Drew is bad at.

I snap the life jacket on and jump. Cold water soaks my swimsuit and surrounds my skin. I emerge from the lake with a gasp, my life jacket yanking me to the surface, and then start swimming toward where Drew is treading water, holding the skis.

The motorboat has stopped about twenty feet away, Alex visible in the rear to toss me the handle. Jared is right next to him, his gaze lasered onto me as if I'm already upright and his job has begun.

I take one ski from Drew and slide it onto my left foot, then tighten the strap until it's snug. I bob awkwardly in the water as I slip the second boot on as well, trying to keep the first ski vertical while I pull the strap taut on the second.

"Toss it," Drew calls.

Alex swings the rope like a rodeo star, throwing it across the expanse of water until it drops a few feet away. I barely hear Drew's quiet scoff over the rumble of the engine. He swims the short distance, grabs the plastic handle, and then hands it to me.

I glance at Drew. In the bright glare reflecting off the lake, all I can really make out is his profile. "Thanks. And...I'm sorry about this morning. I didn't mean—"

Drew shakes his head once. "Just shut up and ski, Sunshine."

I raise a brow. "Sunshine?"

"Yeah. It's a reference to your cheerful optimism." Drew grins.

"Apology officially revoked," I tell him, snapping the rope so it hits the water with a loud smack.

Drew chuckles. "Lean back," he reminds me. "Let the boat do the work. Keep your balance behind you. If you get ahead of yourself, you'll crash."

I nod.

"It's calm enough that you should veer out from the wake. It'll be a smoother ride."

Again, I nod.

"Boots are loose enough to get out, right?"

I wriggle my toes. "Yeah. I'm good."

"Okay." Drew flashes a thumbs-up at the boat.

The engine roars as Theo engages the throttle, sending out a stream of exhaust. The rope tugs taut, slowly pulling me out deeper into the lake.

I pull in a deep breath as I hold my skis perfectly straight, water rushing past faster and faster. My shoulders strain, my thighs tense, and adrenaline floods my system. I feel like a kid again.

"Hit it!" I call, my voice echoing across the flat water.

The boat lurches, and I go with it, a violent yank jerking me upright and out of the cool water. It flies off of me and then gets lost back in the lake as I skim across the surface.

Behind me, there's a shout of, "Hell yeah!"

A broad smile stretches across my face as I lean to the left, careening out of the engine's wake and gliding out to the side. Wind whips through my wet hair and dries the droplets clinging to my skin. A burn begins in my hands and works its way up my arms. I ignore it, focusing on the blue flashing by instead.

This is how I imagine flying must feel.

Thoughtless.

Weightless.

Happy.

CHAPTER SEVEN

DREW

"I've been brainstorming group activities," Savannah announces toward the end of lunch. "And I think we should do a canoe race this afternoon."

"A *race*?" Claire replies dubiously. Then, she glances at her fiancé, Rowan, who's busy typing something on his phone.

Every time I've gotten a glimpse of the guy, it's what he's busy doing. It'll be difficult to paddle a canoe one-handed, so I get Claire's concern.

"Yeah. Winner gets bragging rights," Savannah says.

"That's *it*?" another one of Amelia's bridesmaids questions. I think her name is Willa.

"There's nothing better than bragging rights," Harper comments, taking the final bite of her turkey sandwich and echoing my thoughts.

I finally let myself look at her—something I've been avoiding the entire meal because I'm not entirely sure where we stand.

I'm not the least bit taken aback by Harper's response. I already knew she had one hell of a stubborn competitive streak.

Savannah gestures toward Harper. "That's the spirit!" She glances around. "Everyone else in?"

There's grumbled agreement around the table as everyone finishes eating.

"Are we doing teams?" Amelia asks.

I glance at Harper. She's talking to Alex now, her sunburned nose scrunched. She lasted three laps around the lake before letting go of the handle, and I don't think I've ever been prouder of anyone in my entire life.

"Of course," Savannah responds. "Couples paddle together, and Theo's two playboy—I mean, *bachelor*"—she grins at Austin and Colton—"friends can go together. Alex and Cristina can team up. It sounded like Silas will be a while."

One of Theo's groomsmen headed inside to talk to his wife about ten minutes ago.

"Okay." Claire stands. "Let's go now, before everyone has to go to the bathroom or grab something, and then it's basically dinnertime."

A few minutes later, the whole group has migrated to down by the water. One by one, the green canoes are pulled down from the rack next to the shed that serves as a boathouse and dragged down to the sandy stretch of shore to launch. Each couple climbs in and then paddles toward the small inlet that's been chosen as the starting point. The first boat to reach Snake Island will be crowned as the winner.

I'd guess it's about a mile from the shore to there.

Since I'm helping to launch the canoes, Harper and I end up in the last one.

"We can win this, right?" she whispers to me as we wade into the shallows.

When I glance at her, those blue eyes are dancing. I can make out every single fleck of color—navy and cyan and sapphire.

Filled with excitement and delight, none of the apprehension that clouded them earlier. Or the anxiety when she attempted an apology after.

"Absolutely, we will win this," I assure her.

Her arms must be dead from waterskiing earlier. But I have no doubt she'll be the one paddling the hardest. And even if she's not, I'm confident in my own capabilities.

Harper grins. "Good."

I hold the boat steady while she climbs in, then get in myself. It rocks a few times before settling. I extend the metal handle of the paddle as we move toward the inlet, where everyone else is waiting.

Savannah is waving around a bullhorn. Where she got it, I have no idea. It works well, projecting her voice across the water as we all line up in a row.

Amelia and Theo both look focused. So does Jared, but I ran with him this morning and know his conditioning could use more work. He admitted he hasn't worked out since the start of the summer. Rowan is on his phone, Claire staring out into space. Willa and Luke are wild cards. So are Austin and Colton. Lincoln and Tatum appear bored. Alex looks uncomfortable, fiddling with his paddle behind Cristina.

"And...*go!*"

I dig in immediately, uninterested in waiting to see how everyone else responds to the start. I pretend they're all right beside us as I start paddling toward the distant shape of Snake Island.

Harper does the same, the muscles of her shoulders flexing as she dips the paddle into the water over and over again. The hem of her T-shirt rides up, exposing the twin divots on either side of her spine, just above the hem of her shorts.

I thought I'd be focusing on the glide across the smooth

stretch of lake. The dip of the paddle into the clear water and the satisfying burn of exertion in my muscles. The sunshine filtering down from the sky that illuminates the gray rocks and greenery lining the shore.

But no matter where I look, my gaze quickly returns to that strip of skin. Snags on the two dimples above Harper's ass and ends with me paddling even faster, like I'll manage to get closer to them.

We're whizzing across the surface of the lake with no sign of anyone on either side of us. But I keep up the same speed, and so does Harper. She's contributing, not just along for the ride, which adds to the healthy respect I already have toward her. A strong work ethic says a lot about someone's character.

Snake Island grows closer and larger, rising from the midst of the lake like a welcome beacon. According to Theo, it's uninhabited by humans, nothing but trees and birds living on it.

I don't stop paddling until we're close enough to the island that I can see the rocky bottom of the lake, only a few feet deep this close to the shore.

When I look behind, I laugh. The closest canoe looks to be Savannah and Jared. And they're several hundred feet away still, faceless blobs in a green canoe.

Harper follows my gaze, a wide smile stretching across her face when she realizes we won.

"Told you we would," I say.

Impossibly, Harper's smile brightens. And I somehow just *know*, the way I know my name and that Dr. Pepper is superior to other sodas and the right second to shoot the puck, that Harper Williams beaming at me while sitting in a canoe is a sight I'll never forget.

The glow of the fire brightens when Theo tosses another log of wood onto it. It's after eleven, and I was ready for bed an hour ago. My run is routine. But my body isn't used to waterskiing or canoeing, and muscles I didn't know I had are currently aching.

Dinner was later than usual. Everyone wanted to shower after the canoe race. And once dinner was over, it was already dark. We ended up down at the firepit, roasting marshmallows that have long since disappeared and slapping at mosquitoes. Mojitos were also passed around.

"We're headed to bed." Savannah stands and stretches, Jared following her lead.

Everyone else has slowly dispersed over the past hour.

Once Savannah and Jared disappear from sight, it's just me, Harper, Amelia, and Theo left. Harper tucks her feet beneath her, probably in response to the increasing chill in the air, leaning back in the chair. She's wearing a pair of green pajamas with a blue tiger pattern on them. Not attire I ever thought I would consider sexy...but here we are.

All day, I've been trying to get Harper out of my head. To stop noticing small details and gravitating toward her. So far, it's been a useless effort. And I'm about to spend all night lying less than a foot from her.

"We should head up too," Amelia says. "I'm exhausted after all that canoeing. I can't believe Savannah came up with that."

"Isn't coming up with activities part of her maid-of-honor duties?" Harper asks.

"And...there it is." Amelia laughs, but it lacks any amusement. It's an ugly, unpredictable sound.

"There *what* is?" Harper asks, a dangerous note sneaking into her voice in response.

In seconds, the peaceful atmosphere changes, becoming tense and volatile.

Theo and I exchange an uncomfortable glance.

"There's the first passive-aggressive comment about you not being my maid of honor." Amelia sips her drink and glances at the glow of the firepit. "Savannah is my best friend, Harper. She's been there for me through *everything*. Grades and boys and the stress of law school. She called me halfway through my first date with Theo to give me an out if I wanted it. You showed up here a day late! Is it really a surprise I wanted her to be my maid of honor?"

"Nope," Harper replies. "Not a surprise *at all* actually. The only shock was that I was even invited to be in the wedding party. Maybe I should just plan to sit in the audience and pretend to dab at my eyes instead?"

Amelia scoffs. "If you didn't want to be here, you should have made up some excuse, like you usually do. Some trip with Olivia that *just happened* to coincide with my wedding, maybe?"

"You picked your wedding date two years ago, Amelia. Nothing could *just happen* to coincide with that amount of advance warning."

Theo decides to intercede. "Let's head up to bed, honey."

"Fine," Amelia agrees, standing and swaying slightly. "Good *night*." She emphasizes the second word with a sharp edge, aimed mainly at her older sister.

I can see the insecurity and uncertainty hovering in Amelia's expression, but I'm not sure Harper can. Because I've seen it on Amelia before, and I don't think Harper ever has.

She and I sit in silence as Theo's and Amelia's shapes head back toward the house and disappear inside.

"Is it safe to leave this?" Harper finally asks, looking at the fire.

"Probably." It's a stone pit. But I don't want to be responsible for burning a property worth millions down. "I'll put it out, just in case."

There's a bucket by one of the chairs, presumably for this exact purpose. I walk down to the lake and fill it with water before walking back toward where Harper is now standing. Orange flickers cast shadows across her impassive expression.

I toss the bucket of water on the fire, extinguishing the flames with a low hiss.

The buzz of mosquitoes accompanies us on the short trek from the pit back inside the house. There's no sign of anyone else as we ascend the stairs and walk down the hall to our room.

Harper says nothing until the door is shut behind us. She kicks off her flip-flops, resting a hand on the wall to keep herself steady. "Bet you're regretting coming, huh?"

"Nope."

She looks at me, eyebrows raised. "Either you're a liar or you're a psychopath who thrives on family drama."

"Either you had too much rum to remember I *offered* to come or you're forgetting that I knew you and Amelia in high school, so I had a pretty good idea exactly what this week would be like."

Harper gifts me with one of her rare full smiles. We're close enough that I can count every freckle on her nose. Trace them together like a map of constellations.

"Sorry," she whispers. "I'm embarrassed you're seeing all this."

"Don't be. Siblings argue all the time. It's normal."

"Not like this. Amelia was right. She and Savannah are way closer than we've ever been. I don't know why...I shouldn't have been surprised she asked her."

"She asked you to be in the wedding, Harper. That counts for something."

"I guess." Harper starts unbuttoning her shirt.

"What are you doing?" I ask, my brain slow to catch up with my mouth.

"Uh, changing." She gives me a *duh* look as her shirt separates, the green and blue print falling apart and revealing a whole lot of tan skin. And that she isn't wearing a bra. A strip of skin runs interrupted from the curve of her collarbone to the band of her pants.

"You're already in pajamas."

"These are my public pajamas, not my actual pajamas."

I feel the furrow between my eyes appear. "I have no idea what you're talking about."

"These"—Harper gestures to her blue tiger-patterned pajamas—"are what I wear when I know I'll be seen in them. Girls' night, delivery guy bringing takeout, firepit at my sister's wedding, for example. This"—she leans down and grabs a T-shirt and a pair of shorts I'd be surprised to learn cover her entire ass—"is what I *actually* sleep in."

I have no response ready for that. And no idea what Harper wore to bed last night. By the time I took my turn in the bathroom, like we were randomly assigned college roommates, she was already under the covers. And she was fast asleep when I got up this morning.

Sharing a room last night wasn't awkward, but it felt stiff. I'm glad we've made the leap to being comfortable enough to change in front of each other, partly because the bathroom is *tiny*, but it's definitely going to complicate things where my dick is concerned.

I'm attracted to Harper. I was when we were younger, and it hasn't changed since. When I offered to come to this wedding as her date/fake boyfriend, I didn't think this part through. The *sleeping in bed together, sharing a small room* part.

Harper pulls a couple of other items out of her suitcase and then shuts it.

"Do you want me to go into the bath—okay." I glance away as soon as Harper pulls her top the rest of the way off. It's like a reflex—of what, I'm not sure.

Probably me knowing seeing her topless would shred away at my self-control.

Harper laughs at my averted eyes, the sound low and throaty. "Such a gentleman."

My dick twitches in my shorts, protesting that statement.

It's difficult to judge how tipsy Harper is. She's always a little wild and a lot unpredictable. But beneath it all, there's the vulnerability I got a glimpse of a few minutes ago.

I head into the attached bathroom to get ready for bed, giving her the privacy she didn't ask for.

Harper strolls in while I'm brushing my teeth, snagging her toothbrush from the counter and doing the same. She grins at me through a mouthful of white foam, wearing what are her *actual* pajamas, apparently.

The hem of the shirt ends about an inch above the bottom of the shorts. And I was right about the shorts not covering her entire ass. As she finishes brushing and washes her face, it looks like she's wearing nothing beneath the shirt at all.

By the time we're both in bed, I'm worked up with no outlet. The bathroom is approximately six feet from the bed, so it's not like I can go take care of matters myself.

I close my eyes, intent on willing away any arousal and ignoring the half-naked woman lying next to me. Harper is quiet and still, probably already asleep, thanks to the two mojitos she drank.

Two minutes later, the pounding starts. It quickly picks up in volume and frequency, paired with the high tenor of a female voice.

"Yes, Rowan! Yes! Oh, yes!"

"Wow. Claire said she was *so* exhausted," Harper says after about a minute of the noise, startling me.

"Guess she knew what was coming later," I reply.

A giggle escapes Harper's mouth. I can't see her in the dark room, but I can picture her amused face perfectly. The dancing, widened eyes and the way she's probably biting down on her bottom lip to keep the laughter in.

The pounding and the cries continue, remaining steady in volume and frequency. It sounds like the soundtrack of an adult film is blasting on the opposite side of the shared wall.

"Jesus," I mutter, pulling the pillow over my head in a useless attempt to block out the noise.

Harper laughs, for real this time. And then she does something that shocks the hell out of me.

"Yes, Drew! Fuck me harder, Drew!"

The pillow gets whipped off my face and flung onto the bedspread. "What the fuck are you doing?" I hiss.

"Yeah, baby. Right there. Oh, yes!"

Holy fuck. "Harper!"

"I'm reminding them how thin the walls are," Harper whispers. "Relax, Halifax. I'm making you look good." Her white teeth flash in the dark, and that's about all I can make out of her expression.

Before I can reply, she's off with another round of sex noises and shouts that include my name and end with, "I'm coming!"

I'm torn somewhere between arousal and amusement as I listen to her theatrics. About a minute after the sounds on the other side of the wall die off, Harper stops moaning.

"Night," she tells me, then flips over and appears to fall asleep immediately.

I, on the other hand, am left lying here with a raging hard-on, knowing I won't be able to fall asleep for a long time.

CHAPTER EIGHT

HARPER

I'm out on the deck, eating breakfast alone, when Drew returns from his run. His T-shirt is damp with sweat, and his blond hair is tousled from the wind. I try my best not to trace with my eyes the spots where his shirt sticks or imagine running my fingers through the wayward strands, but it's a half-hearted attempt at best.

"Morning," I say as he takes a seat across from me.

"Hey." He takes a long drink of water, the muscles of his throat contracting and loosening in tandem.

I look down at my half-eaten muffin. "Did you eat already?"

"Yeah."

"Good run?"

"Eh, not great. I'll probably go out again later."

"Are you feeling okay?"

One corner of Drew's mouth tips up. "Yeah. Just tired. Not the best night's sleep I've ever had."

Up until now, I'd successfully repressed the memories of last night's events. Suddenly, it's all I can think about. I seem to be on an endless streak of embarrassing moments where Drew is concerned.

I clear my throat. "Yeah…sorry about that."

He shrugs, still half-smiling. "It would have been *hard* to fall asleep, regardless."

I tilt my head to the side, trying to figure out if I imagined the emphasis. Drew holds my gaze, amusement sparking in his intense expression.

A warm flush that has nothing to do with another day of bright sunshine slowly spreads across my body.

There were *moments* between us yesterday. Lots of moments. Skiing in the lake. Winning the canoe race. Toasting marshmallows by the campfire. They all felt different with him here.

Drew was supposed to be my buffer. Instead of seeking him out as a distraction, I've started craving time around him for that reason alone.

I'm not sure how to feel about it. This week was supposed to be uncomfortable, not enjoyable.

"We could do that for real."

I choke a little on my last bite of muffin. "Do what?" I strive for indifference and land somewhere close, I think.

"Have sex."

I blink at him. Once. Twice. Three times. For once, my mind is totally blank. Lights off. I'm fumbling around in the dark with nothing to grasp on to. "What?"

"Just an idea," Drew says, taking another sip of water, like this is a normal conversation to be having.

We're still alone out on the deck.

I lean closer, lowering my voice. "What, uh, what gave you that idea?"

I'm not expecting for him to say *I've always been wildly*

attracted to you, although I wouldn't hate hearing those words coming out of his mouth. Especially considering he's caught me checking him out plenty of times.

But what I'm *really* not expecting him to say is, "It was listening to you shout, 'Fuck me harder, Drew!' last night, actually."

All I can choke out is, "Oh."

I can't be sure what shade of red my face is, but based on the way my entire body suddenly feels like a furnace, I think somewhere in the range of ripened tomato is accurate.

I glance longingly at my empty glass of iced coffee. All that remains are a couple of ice cubes. My throat is dry, and my mind is spiraling in a thousand different directions. "Um, I was just acting. Trying to make it sound realistic, you know?" I busy myself by pouring more coffee from the pitcher set out, adding a splash of oat milk.

Drew is smiling. I can *feel* it somehow even though I'm not looking at his expression. "Uh-huh. Well, you're a talented actress. Made me wonder what you say when you're *not* acting."

To that, I have absolutely no response.

Drew Halifax is in a league all his own. My younger self never experienced what the full focus of his attention was like. My older—debatably wiser—self is used to sorting men into clear categories.

Categories Drew doesn't fit into.

And that scares me, honestly.

I'm used to knowing what to expect from people. From my mom, from my sister, from my friends, from my coworkers. From guys.

Drew is constantly surprising me.

I wasn't expecting him to wait for me at the market. I wasn't expecting him to offer to come here with me. When I said I wasn't waterskiing, I thought he'd drop it. He challenges me in a way I've come to expect from no one.

The screen door slams.

"There you guys are!"

I glance behind me to see Savannah hurrying this way, with Jared right behind her.

"We're all going hiking up to Larson's Peak. Hurry up. Everyone is waiting!"

I glance down at my athletic shorts and sneakers, wishing I'd chosen to get dressed in a dress and sandals this morning.

After waking up with a hangover, thanks to both alcohol and embarrassment, I lounged around in bed until I thought most people would have finished eating and then threw on the most comfortable clothes I could find.

"Hiking? I don't know if…"

"You're coming," Savannah states firmly. "Everyone is."

I sigh. I won't be able to avoid Amelia indefinitely. "Okay, fine."

Savannah smiles, victorious, then turns to Drew. "You're up for a hike, right, Drew?"

I narrow my eyes at the suspicious shift in her tone. Conviction has melted away, leaving sweetness behind.

"As long as Harper is," Drew replies.

I glance toward him, then quickly away when I find his eyes on me.

"Yay!" Savannah claps her hands, way too much excitement for this hour and this activity saturating her tone. "Do you mind driving, Drew? We need a few more seats."

"Sure, just let me grab my keys." Drew stands and heads inside.

Jared follows him.

Savannah stays where she is, studying me.

"What?" I ask, standing and grabbing the remnants of my breakfast.

"You're blushing. Or sunburned. But I'm pretty sure you're blushing."

I roll my eyes as we walk into the kitchen. "It's warm out." *Miserable weather for a hike*, I think, but don't say. It's only going to get hotter and more humid the closer we creep toward noon.

"I've never seen you flustered over a guy before," Savannah comments, following me over to the sink and watching me rinse the dishes. "It's cute."

"I'm *not* flustered."

The fork I used to eat my fruit slips off the plate and clatters to the floor. Savannah raises one eyebrow. I roll my eyes as I retrieve the wayward utensil and stash it in the dishwasher.

"If you say so," Savannah sings, following me through the living room.

I try to think through anything I'm missing as we pass the stairs. I'm dressed in appropriate hiking attire, my sunglasses are perched on top of my head, I put sunscreen on after washing my face, and my phone is in my pocket.

No excuse for how to get out of this comes to mind, so I push open the screen door with a resigned sigh.

Everyone is standing around in a loose circle beneath the pines that shade most of the property.

I glance at Amelia first. She's leaning against someone's sedan while talking to Theo, expression smooth and unruffled. No sign of the derision she shot my way last night.

That's always been Amelia, though. She's better at faking

emotions—especially positive ones—than I am. My mom is the same way. If she doesn't want you to know she's irritated or upset, you won't. It's probably part of why she's such a respected attorney.

And why I would have made a terrible one, if I'd gone to law school, like she'd expected me to.

Amelia's eyes flicker to me and away, squeezing the ball of anxiety in my chest.

I need to swallow my pride and apologize to her. Smooth everything over. I know I do. This is her week, her wedding. Maid of honor was her choice.

Usually, after an argument, we simply don't speak until enough time has passed that it's easier to pretend nothing ever happened. That's not an option this time, unfortunately.

Drew and Jared walk out of the house and toward the group. They were the only two missing.

"Let's go, gang!" Savannah calls out.

Amelia climbs into the backseat of the sedan she was leaning against with Theo right behind her. Everyone else begins to climb into cars as well.

I heave a sigh and start after Drew. He's walking toward the nicest car in the row, which I'm surprised by.

I know Drew has money. His parents are well-off, and I have a general sense of what professional athletes make—a lot. But Drew isn't flashy. If I'd had to guess, I would have assumed he drove a truck or an older SUV. Not a sleek *tank*, so shiny that I can see my reflection in the black paint as I approach.

Other people are staring at the car too, specifically the guys.

This is the first time any of us have left the property. Theo's aunt and uncle might be gone, but they left their staff here, running the place.

Preparations for the wedding have been constant, with caterers and florists and cleaners coming and going to drop items off or to begin setting up for the end-of-the-week festivities. Sara, the property manager, has come by every day. And the camp chef has been making most of the meals and providing groceries. None of us have had any reason to go anywhere.

"I'll ride with Drew," Rowan announces, peeling away from Claire.

Rowan wouldn't have been my first choice of carpool buddy. I'm careful not to look at Drew as I climb into the backseat of his fancy Mercedes, memories of last night too fresh in my mind. Maybe I should buy some earplugs while we're out today. If I do that and build a pillow fort between our bodies tonight, maybe I'll finally get a decent night's sleep. It's too overwhelming, knowing he's *right there* when I'm trying to fall asleep. Close enough to touch.

"We could do that for real," gets added to the list of things Drew Halifax has said to me that I can't forget.

Jared and Savannah climb into the back of Drew's car with me, filling the car. Doors slam all around, the purr of engines interrupting the quiet that usually permeates the pure air around here.

Drew pulls out of the spot and begins rolling down the dirt driveway, toward the main road.

"How far is this place?" I ask Savannah.

"Ten minutes," she replies.

I sigh and lean my head against the glass. Drew turns the air-conditioning on full blast, which I appreciate. The sticky heat clinging to my skin slowly begins to dissipate, chased away by cold air.

Today would be a perfect day to be on the lake, but no one

consulted me about the plans, and things are too precarious between me and Amelia for me to back out. I can only imagine what she'd have said if I'd chosen to go off and do my own thing today. More ammunition for her that I don't want to be here. Which isn't even true.

Do I wish she were having her wedding somewhere unconnected to our father? Yes.

Am I apprehensive of all the ways she and our mom will pick me apart this week and this weekend? Yes.

Would I have *chosen* to miss her wedding? No.

"You and Amelia get into it last night?"

I glance at Savannah, who's studying me closely. "What makes you think that?"

Savannah sighs. "Come on, Harper."

"I'll talk to her."

Another sigh. "I told her to ask you."

"Ask me what?"

"About being maid of honor."

"It's fine," I mutter. I'm not sure if it is, but I'm not sure what else to say either.

"She thought you'd say no."

"Typically, that's why you *ask* someone something. To find out what they'll say." The bitterness in my voice leaks out into the silent car. I regret the words immediately. They're words I shouldn't have said at all. Or only said to Amelia. "It's fine," I repeat.

Savannah drops it, although I can feel her eyes on me as I stare intently out the window, watching the bait shop pass by.

Rowan is the one who breaks the quiet, surprisingly. Aside from last night's late-night activities, which I'm trying hard *not* to think about, he's been the most reserved member of the group.

"What made you go with the G-Wagon instead of the Maybach?" he asks Drew.

"Uh," Drew starts.

"This car isn't nice enough for you, Rowan?" Jared asks.

Savannah swats his arm.

"That—that's not what I meant," Rowan replies. He glances at Drew. "You just seem like a guy who'd consider all of his options. You probably test-drove the Maybach, right?"

"Um, no, I didn't," Drew replies.

I can't see his expression since I'm seated directly behind him, but it sounds like he's smiling.

I'm glad he's enjoying himself. I'm not. Between the extra tension with Amelia, the looming hike, and the boring car talk, this is shaping up to be my idea of a terrible morning.

"They might not have had any on the lot," Rowan says. "A buddy of mine had to wait six months for his to come in from the factory."

"That's some serious dedication."

Rowan nods, missing what I think is sarcasm in Drew's voice. "Yeah. Patrick is crazy when it comes to his cars. He'll be so jealous when he hears about this. I mean, you even have the chrome finish. Was that custom?"

There's a pause before Drew responds, "Honestly, I have no clue. They gave me this car after I did an ad for them."

Rowan's profile provides me with an unflattering view of his agape mouth. "They...*gave* this to you? For *free*?"

"Yep."

The car turns, pulls into a gravel parking lot, and comes to a stop. The lot is mostly empty. A minivan and a truck are the only vehicles that don't belong to our large group.

"Great. We're here!" I sing, jumping out of the car before

Drew has even turned the engine off. Maybe acting excited will end with actually feeling that way.

Humid air coats my skin and curls my hair as soon as I'm outside the air-conditioning. I start toward the wooden sign that marks the bottom of the trail and study the map displayed, mostly just for something to do as everyone else moves more slowly toward the start of the hike. The sooner we start, the sooner we'll finish.

I trace the lines and squiggles on the map, deciding the route is fairly straightforward. There's one main path you can take up or down the mountain with several offshoots that are less direct or steeper.

Bored with the map, I let my gaze wander. The wooden posts holding the sign upright are littered with writing. Messages from years—decades—of visitors. I scan the array of initials and dates the way you look at the menu for a restaurant you've been to many times before, not planning to see anything unexpected.

But my gaze snags on a name I'm stunned to see.

Snags on *my* name. With Amelia's right below it.

Hot air constricts around me, feeling suffocating. All the oxygen has been sucked from my lungs. Breaths are hard to pull in and impossible to exhale. My head swims from shock and panic.

I'm drowning on dry land.

Focused on the scribble of *Harper Williams*.

"Harper!"

My head jerks to the left, nothing more than a reflex. I'm no longer looking at the sign, but the black writing is still all I can see. Little by little, I refocus on Claire, who's waving me over.

Almost everyone else has stopped by a bench closer to the parking lot. I suck in a deep breath of air, relieved my lungs have decided to function normally again for the time being. My steps are quick as I walk away from the sign, as if my speed will affect how fast I recover from the realization that I've been here before.

Drew is still in the parking lot with Rowan and Jared. Rowan is studying the car like there will be a test on its appearance later. Jared is talking with Drew, a broad smile on his face. Claire calls them over as well, waiting for everyone to assemble.

"Amelia, take a seat on the bench so I can figure out the spacing," Savannah instructs, standing with a fancy-looking camera. "Harper, you sit too."

Amelia settles on the metal bench, her posture stiff. I know exactly what Savannah is doing. If I hadn't walked ahead and seen the sign, I probably would have been more receptive to it.

After our father died, he became the biggest wedge between Amelia and me. She—and our mom—made Paul Williams a taboo topic. He was slowly and methodically erased as something "too hard to talk about." His clothes and books disappeared. Older family photographs were replaced with recent ones.

I wanted to cling. To talk about him with the two other people who had known him best.

And every time I tried to, my mom and Amelia would resent it a little more. Until I was all alone in an ocean of my own grief.

I clear my throat. I doubt Amelia remembers coming here with our parents. And I *know*, if she does, she won't react well to me bringing it up now.

So, I sit down, and staring straight ahead, I say, "I'm sorry about last night."

"I am too." Amelia's tone is as stiff as her posture when I glance over to look at her. Back straight, shoulders back, eyes focused forward.

"We're good then?"

"We're good," she responds.

And it feels like we are. This is more resolution than most of our tiffs end with since, typically, we act like nothing ever happened.

But for the first time in a long time, it doesn't feel like enough to revert to our dysfunctional form of normal.

I want to dig deeper instead of gloss over.

I want to ask Amelia what she remembers of our family trips to this lake.

Whether she wonders what our father would have said about her wedding being here.

Most of all, I want to ask her when this animosity between us became a permanent state instead of a phase.

But now is not the time. Everyone else is gathering around us, squeezing closer for the photo Savannah is asking a passing hiker to take. He's here with his wife and two daughters, and that detail is all I can focus on as he tells us to smile and snaps some pictures on Savannah's camera.

She thanks him profusely before our group gets moving, separating into smaller clumps as we approach the start of the trail. Theo passes out bottles of water from the backpack he's carrying.

No one besides me casts more than a passing glance at the map marking the entrance of the path. But I pause, my eyes easily finding the same spot as before. With a shaky breath, I cradle the cold bottle of water in the corner of my elbow so I can pull my phone out of my pocket and snap a photo.

I'm not sure if I want a permanent reminder, but I'm equally uncertain I won't.

"What are you doing?"

I spin, surprised, and immediately feel the gravel ground beneath me shift. Drew grabs my arm before I can windmill, steadying me before I fall.

"Thanks," I say, feeling my heart gallop as adrenaline spreads and my center of gravity recalibrates.

He's already let go of me, but I can still feel the phantom burn of his touch.

"Uh-huh." Drew's gaze is as hot as the sunbeams filtering down from the blue sky.

I can't figure out why his attention has such a powerful effect on me. I'm equally unsure if I like or hate it.

I hook a thumb behind me. "I was just checking out the map."

"In case we get lost?" Drew glances between me and the wide, well-groomed path packed with tourists, a small smile tugging one corner of his mouth.

"Yep, exactly."

"Well, in that case, you'd better lead the way." He sweeps one arm to the right.

I follow the movement to the rest of our group steadily approaching the first bend in the trail.

Looks like I'll be bringing up the rear, and I thought I'd be doing it alone. Most of the couples aren't sticking together. Willa, Claire, Savannah, and Amelia are all walking together with Theo, Rowan, Alex, Austin, and Colton a few paces ahead of them. Tatum and Cristina walk behind with Jared, Luke, and Lincoln trailing after them.

But Drew—undoubtedly the most in shape out of all of us—is right next to me, way behind, patiently waiting for me to begin walking first.

So, I do. The longer we stand here, the more likely Drew is to inspect the sign closely.

Our climb up the mountain is mostly silent.

Occasionally, Drew will point out something we pass—a chipmunk or a patch of poison ivy. And *a lot* of birds. He immediately knows every species, both ones I've heard of, but I couldn't identify and varieties totally foreign. Woodpeckers, chickadees, wrens, sparrows, warblers, cardinals, and starlings all fly by us, according to Drew. It feels like a lifetime ago we stood in the kitchen, discussing his mom's interest in birds, but I remember it. And it obviously transferred to Drew.

I barely say anything as we hike, and I can tell it catches Drew off guard. Because I usually have plenty to say, have spent this whole week so far spouting almost everything that's popped into my head.

I guess my life theory is the more you show people to start, the less likely they are to try to look beneath the surface. And I'm not sure what it is about Drew—maybe that I'm continually embarrassing myself in front of him—but the thought of Drew *looking* doesn't terrify me.

I'd actually like to think *he thinks* I'm more than a mess.

By the time we make it to the top, I'm tired and testy. And sweaty. My T-shirt is sticking to the middle of my back, and I can feel the perspiration coating my face. My stomach grumbles with hunger, the muffin I ate for breakfast a distant memory.

But the incredible view is *almost* enough for me to forget about everything else.

Lake Paulson looks like a puddle from up here. A vibrant blue puddle with a few dots near the center, one of which must be Snake Island. Pines surround it like a blanket spread in every direction, the sharp points of the tree needles waving in the wind and creating a ripple effect similar to the surface of the water. Roads snake through the forest, the occasional peak of a house or jut of a chimney interrupting the endless green stretch.

"Wow," I breathe.

The word doesn't seem to do the scenery justice.

Savannah talks another tourist into taking a group photo of us once again. This one is less pleasant since I'm not the only one who broke a sweat on the trip. There's a breeze blowing at least, which slowly cools the temperature of my skin.

"There's a second lookout," I say as Savannah and Amelia take a seat on a flat section of the rock.

Willa and Luke are just past them, snapping selfies, and I don't register the location of anyone else.

"I'm going to walk over there."

Savannah responds with an, "Okay," busy shading her phone with one hand to look at the screen.

Amelia half-smiles in acknowledgment before sipping some water.

I glance at Drew, raising one eyebrow in a silent question. He nods and follows me toward the next section of the path.

"Oriole," Drew says as a flash of orange zooms by.

"Like the baseball team?"

The wind carries the sound of his chuckle straight to me. "You follow baseball, but not hockey?"

"Who said I didn't follow hockey?"

"Just a hunch."

"I don't know a lot about any sport," I admit. "My dad—" Words stall on my lips. I might be the dictionary definition of a hypocrite because I judge my mother and sister for not mentioning him while doing the same thing.

There are clear distinctions in my life between people who know about that part of my past and people who assume I don't mention my dad because of an estrangement or disinterest.

And regardless of whether they know my dad is dead or not, I never bring him up in casual conversation the way I just did with Drew.

"My dad didn't really follow sports," I finish.

"I remember. He was always reading or fixing something by breaking it worse."

I laugh, the sound surprising us both. "Yeah, he did do that."

He would fiddle with a faucet for a day before it sprung a leak and forced him to finally call a plumber.

The path opens again as we reach the second overlook, which is much less crowded. The mountainside is steeper here. If you walk closely enough to the edge, where we are, the mountain disappears. It's just the view, spread below without any interruption.

"Guess looking at the map paid off," Drew teases, stopping next to me and staring out.

"I wasn't looking at the map. I was looking at my name."

I keep my eyes looking straight ahead, feeling his on me without needing to look over.

"I've been here before. About fifteen years ago. Before my parents bought the Port Haven house, we'd come to Lake Paulson in the summers. Rent a little cabin, whatever was available for a week. My dad would wake us up early in the morning for fishing trips. We'd stop at the bait shop on our way into town and go out in a yellow canoe at sunrise. And we came here once, I guess. I don't remember it, but we must have."

I pull in a deep breath as the wind blows strands of hair across my face.

"It's hard to remember him sometimes. I feel like it's all slipping away, and the harder I try to remember him, the easier I forget. There's so much he's missed. So much he *chose* to miss, you know? That's the worst part."

Another breath, this one less steady.

I sniff, the wind burning my wet eyes. "Sorry."

"Don't—fuck, Harper. Don't *apologize*." Drew's fingers weave with mine, tugging me toward him until our bodies collide.

"I'm sweaty," I protest.

"So am I."

I relax against the solid support of his body.

"A guy I played with in college took his own life sophomore year," Drew says quietly. "It was over the summer, so the administration sent out an email to the whole school. I had a group chat with the guys, and no one knew what to say. The last time I had seen him was right before finals. He was doing a keg stand at this party in the backyard. He wasn't the guy you'd ever think would…" His chest shifts as he exhales. "It's a tragedy, Harper. And tragedies never make any sense. They're just weights we have to live with."

I look out over the trees and the lake, something in me settling with the knowledge my dad got to see this view. That he glimpsed some beauty amid darkness.

Drew squeezes the hand he's still holding. His thumb traces a light circle.

I want him to kiss me.

I've *wanted* him to kiss me.

When we were teenagers. On the porch, drinking tequila. In the lake, when he was reminding me how to waterski. When we won the canoe race. At the firepit last night before everything got awkward.

But now, I manifest it, watching Drew's gaze drop to my lips before darting back up to my eyes.

I can see the indecision written across his face, wondering if I'm upset and this is the wrong moment. Questioning why we'd kiss when the romantic aspect of this week was supposed to be feigned. I've considered sex with him, and he's done the same, based on his comment this morning. But kissing on a mountain in the middle of the day is not usually part of a random hookup. This would be something else entirely.

"Are you going to kiss me?" I put it right out there, certain we're both thinking it.

"Depends," he answers.

"Depends on what?"

"Is it part of this *fake date to the wedding* thing, or is it just us?"

He doesn't wait for a response, probably because the answer is written all over my face.

There's no one to see this. Whatever we say here—whatever we do—is a secret between us.

Drew's mouth lands on mine, his lips commanding and seeking as his tongue slides inside my mouth. I whimper, grasping handfuls of his shirt in an attempt to anchor him to me. To ensure this sensation never ends. This wet, delicious glide that I can feel everywhere at once. A throb settles between my legs, sparks of electricity pulsing through me. One hand slides into my hair, pulling most of it out of the ponytail. The other lands on my waist, slipping under the hem of my T-shirt. I'm sweaty and gross, and I don't even care. I'm way too overwhelmed to feel self-conscious right now.

Unsurprisingly, he's a good kisser. The perfect amount of pressure. The slightest tease of tongue. A skilled rhythm that turns my heartbeat into a series of stutters.

I forget about the breathtaking view. I forget about the soreness in my muscles.

I lose myself in Drew, and it feels like being found.

"Harper! Drew!"

Reluctantly, I pull away, glancing over one shoulder to see Savannah and Jared smirking at us.

"We're leaving," Savannah adds.

"Okay," I call back, my voice raspy and distracted.

Drew grins knowingly before dropping his hand from my waist, threading our fingers together instead and pulling me toward where Savannah and Jared are waiting.

They probably thought nothing of our kiss. A normal activity between a couple.

But I'm thinking everything about that kiss. Because it felt extraordinary, not normal.

It felt like a beginning.

Like a world-wrecker.

Like a final first kiss.

And I've never, ever thought that before.

CHAPTER NINE

DREW

I steal another glance at Harper in the rearview mirror. She's nodding along to something Claire is whispering to her, a small smile curling up the corners of her lips.

Lips I kissed earlier. Lips I would have *kept* kissing if Savannah and Jared hadn't shown up.

I knew this week would partially be spent battling attraction. I offered to come here with Harper as an ally. As a buffer. As a friend.

Making a move felt like a betrayal of that mission. I don't want her to think I had ulterior motives involving sex all along. And I'm worried that's the exact impression she has now, after our conversation this morning and the kiss I can't stop thinking about.

I knew we had chemistry. Up until we kissed, I never realized how combustible it was. How it contained sparks I can still feel every time I catch a glimpse of her.

Rowan asks me another question about my car, distracting me from the backseat.

I'm shocked he hasn't realized I know basically *nothing* about cars yet. I drive a beat-up Chevy in Seattle. The only reason I'm behind the wheel of this brand-new Mercedes is because they gave it to me when I was already on the East Coast and it seemed silly to continue driving a rental. How I'll get it to the West Coast is a detail I haven't ironed out yet.

We stop at a seafood shack for lunch on the drive back to the lake. The smell of fried food fills the fresh air, making my stomach grumble. The shack is crowded with other tourists enjoying the tail end of summer, but we're served fairly quickly, our larger group cramming together into two picnic tables. Every time I take a bite of lobster roll or a sip of Dr. Pepper, my arm brushes against Harper's.

It's incredibly distracting. I've never been so aware of another person's proximity before. Never been so desperate to kiss a girl. Do more than kiss her.

Silas and Jared are sitting opposite me, discussing baseball. Aside from hockey, it's the sport I follow most closely. My dad and I went to a game in late July. As soon as I mention that they begin pelting me with questions about Boston's team, which is currently sitting at the top of the standings.

I'm finishing the last of my lobster roll when Harper's arm nudges mine in a way that feels more purposeful than accidental.

I glance down, fully prepared for the jolt as our gazes connect. Her blue eyes widen as they do. For a few seconds, we simply stare at each other.

"Um." Her nose scrunches, which makes me grin. The pink has faded, leaving a few new freckles behind. "Are you going to eat your chips?"

I glance at the unopened bag of potato chips that came with my lunch, then back at Harper. Shake my head, slowly, still smiling.

"Can I have them?"

"What are you offering in exchange?" I tease.

"My undying gratitude."

"Don't I already have that?" I ask, low enough no one else can hear.

Before Harper can answer, her name is called from across the table. We both look at Willa, who's pointing a French fry between us. "How did you two get together? Did I miss the story?"

I glance at Harper, who's reaching toward her lemonade.

Immediately, Willa's question has captured the attention of the entire table. Everyone has been focused on Amelia and Theo. On details about the wedding this weekend and enjoying the lake. Jared has asked me a few questions about hockey, and Rowan made a scene about my car costing six figures, but since the night I arrived, it's never felt like the focus is on me. On *us*.

Until now.

At possibly the worst time, since it feels like there could be more to us than just a fake story.

Harper takes a sip and sets the glass bottle down. "We've known each other since middle school. We just…reconnected."

I'm guessing Willa won't let that vague answer be the end of it, and I'm right.

She turns to me this time. "Did you always have a thing for Harper?"

"Yep." My answer is immediate. And…honest. Some people grow on you over time. Some people make an impact the second you meet them. Harper is in the latter category for me.

Harper elbows me, then winces as she hits solid muscle. "Shut up. You did not."

"I did. Wanted to break Freddy Owens's nose after he bragged about kissing you."

Harper's eyes are wide as she searches my face, likely looking for some sign I'm joking. We didn't plan what we'd say if this subject came up. This definitely wasn't part of our planned arrangement for this week. But it's the truth, and it feels good to say it to her.

"That is so sweet," Willa coos. "What about you?" She looks at Harper, and my gaze never leaves her. "Did you always have a crush on Drew?"

"Look at him," Harper drawls. "What do you think?"

There's laughter around the table. Harper's eyes dart to me and away, more emotions than amusement or lust evident swimming in the blue.

I thought the real answer would be no. But her reaction suggests the opposite. And that's something I can honestly say never occurred to me before. I dedicated most of my free time to hockey when I was younger. I missed parties and school dances because I was playing on two travel teams in addition to the local one. I don't regret it—that dedication got me exactly where I wanted to be.

But there are moments like this, where I feel like I missed out on something important. That continuing to prioritize hockey over everything else in my life has had a cost higher than any eight-figure salary.

"You'd better invite us all to the wedding, you two," Willa says, picking up her beer and pointing it toward us.

"Wouldn't want to be Simon," Lincoln adds from his spot next to her. "Losing two daughters back to back? Not to mention the cost of two weddings."

Lincoln laughs. Harper stiffens.

And if anyone else at the table had been talking, I have a feeling they would have stopped.

It's obvious who knows the full story behind Harper and Amelia's late father and who's assumed their stepfather, Simon, took over for an absentee dad. Or maybe even thinks Simon *is* their biological father.

Uncomfortable glances are exchanged all around.

"Simon won't have to worry about paying for my wedding," Harper says before taking a bite of her lobster roll.

Lincoln doesn't know what to make of that response or the strange energy coursing around the table. Wisely, he opts to shut his mouth and finish his lunch.

Conversation picks back up slowly, but the awkwardness doesn't entirely dissipate.

Theo starts talking about a boat trip when we get back to the lake. Savannah leans over and asks Harper a question about a country singer that I gather is related to her job. I nod along when Jared asks me about going on another run tomorrow morning. Colton overhears and starts asking me about my training plan. I polish off the rest of my soda, then slide the bag of potato chips in front of Harper.

She notices immediately, tearing the bag open with the ferocity of someone who hasn't eaten in days.

I laugh under my breath before refocusing on Colton. He's asking me about sprints versus distance conditioning when I feel warm fingers brush my palm beneath the picnic table. My grip tightens around the can I'm holding as Harper threads her fingers with mine.

We sit like that, holding hands, for the rest of lunch.

CHAPTER TEN

HARPER

I let out a long breath as soon as the door to our room swings shut behind me. It feels like years since I hid under the covers in here this morning.

Everyone else headed down to the lake after we got back from the hike and lunch. I claimed a headache and exhaustion, both of which were true, and came upstairs.

After mindlessly scrolling on social media for a few minutes, I end up calling Olivia. We've texted back and forth since I left to come here, but we haven't spoken on the phone.

"You're alive!" Olivia exclaims dramatically.

"We texted yesterday," I remind her.

"That's different than talking. I miss you. The apartment is too clean when you're not here."

I laugh, lying back on the couch. It smells good. Wood and leather. Also a hint of smoke and spice. I trace the scent to the gray hoodie flung over the back of the couch. Like a total creep, I pull it closer and sniff.

"Harper?"

I drop the sweatshirt, heat flooding my cheeks—which, thankfully, no one is here to see. "Yep. Still here."

"Is everything okay?" Concern carries through Olivia's voice.

"Yeah." I sigh. "It's beautiful here. Savannah is great, and all of the other bridesmaids are nice too."

"How are things with Amelia?"

"Fine, for the most part. She took something I said last night the wrong way and went off a little. But generally, we're fine. Better than I was expecting, honestly."

"Any cute groomsmen?"

"Ha." I force out a laugh. "No."

This is where I should tell Olivia about Drew. Out of everyone, she's least likely to judge. We've had plenty of crazy times together. I was there the time she got a heart tattoo of a guy's name she had met that night and never saw again. And for all the subsequent removal appointments. If there's anyone I can admit this to—that I brought a guy I hardly know and who happens to be very famous—it's Olivia.

But I'm known for being secretive when I should be open. And I'm also very confused about where things stand between me and Drew after our conversation and kiss on the mountain. I want to talk to *him* and figure out where things stand before inviting anyone else's input. Even if there are real feelings there, on his end or mine or both, it won't change how this is a temporary arrangement.

"Your mom called on Friday night, said you hadn't made it to the lake."

"Yeah." I run my fingers across the smooth fabric of Drew's hoodie. "She mentioned it when she showed up to the house in Port Haven."

"You went to the house, huh?"

"Yeah. It was stupid."

"It's not stupid, Harper. I think it's good that you went.

Great."

"Everyone else thinks I'm stuck in the past."

Olivia exhales, the breath echoing through the phone speaker. "Look, I'm a nurse, not a psychologist. But avoiding the past isn't healthy either. You should do whatever feels right. If that includes revisiting the past, then do it. That doesn't mean you're *stuck* there."

There's a pause.

"Your mom sounded really worried."

"She accused me of trespassing when she showed up."

Olivia snorts a laugh. "She did not."

"She did. And I wasn't even surprised."

"It does sound like something she'd say," Olivia admits. She's only met my mother once, a couple of Christmases ago when her parents were visiting her older brother in Africa for the holidays, so she spent the day with us.

"Yeah."

"Everyone handles things differently, Harper. Expecting someone to react to something the same way you would is setting them up for disaster. Especially when it comes to…what happened."

Suicide sounds like a taboo word. I'm not sure I've ever spoken it aloud. I always say, "He took his own life," or, "He lost a battle," or I don't provide a cause of death. But at lunch earlier, I wanted to stand up and scream it. I wanted to stop all the hushed tones and wide eyes that suggested struggling was something to be ashamed of and lay the truth out in the open. Shout my dad had committed suicide when I was seventeen and I'll never know why because he didn't even leave a note.

"Tragedies never make any sense."

At the rate I'm collecting them, soon, I'll have an endless loop of Drew Halifax's words running around in my head. He somehow manages to pierce past the ordinary and the mundane, hitting exactly what I need to hear like an arrow finding the precise center of a target.

"Enough about me," I say. "What's new with you?"

"Well…" Olivia's tone shifts from understanding to uncertain. "I kind of met someone."

"What? Where?"

"At the hospital. Where else?"

"Ooh, a workplace romance. Is he a nurse?"

"Uh, no. He's, um, he's actually the chief of surgery."

"Really?"

I've heard Olivia talk about her job enough to know that's basically the top of the hierarchy. And based on how often she gossips about the politics at the hospital, this is out of the ordinary.

"Yeah. He just transferred here from Los Angeles last week. A huge deal—he invented all these new surgical techniques. He's insufferable, honestly."

I laugh. "Uh-huh. You must *hate* him if you're sleeping together."

"Well, we don't do a whole lot of talking."

"So, it's not serious?"

"No! Not at all."

"You're not going to have him meet Mama C when she visits this weekend?"

"Absolutely not. She'll scare him off with her *I'm desperate to be a grandmother* schtick. Carson is too busy saving starving children to knock anyone up, so it's all on me."

I smile. Olivia and her mother have the type of relationship I wish my mom and I shared. They're more like best friends than mother and daughter. But Olivia isn't exaggerating about her mom's desperation for grandchildren. Every time her mom has visited us in New York, the topic has come up. And since Olivia's older brother is a doctor who works in Nigeria as part of a humanitarian organization, Olivia bears the brunt of her nagging.

"Aside from crushing her dreams of having grandchildren anytime soon, what do you have planned for her visit?"

We talk restaurants, museums, and shops until Olivia has to get ready for work.

After we hang up, I lean off the couch and pull my laptop out of my bag. When I open the screen, the Word document is there, waiting.

I'm not exactly sure when this became more than a jumbled mass of musings. Every time I type more, I'm surprised all over again by how much is written. And I just keep adding to it, accumulating words like drops of rain form a puddle.

I get lost in the quiet tap of keys, writing and writing, until I finally register how low the sun has sunk, golden light illuminating everything with a flattering glow.

With a groan, I close my laptop and roll off the couch, standing and stretching. I need to shower and change before dinner. There's a chance I offended Amelia by hiding away for most of the afternoon. Another apology is probably in order. The prospect doesn't even bother me. I feel more relaxed than I have since arriving.

I pull off my T-shirt and toss it in the corner, making a mental note to ask if there's a washer and dryer I can use here. Doing laundry in the basement of my building is a pain, and I can only imagine how much worse that shirt will smell by the time I'm back in the city. I should have showered right when I got back to the room.

I lean down and untie both sneakers, then pull my socks off too. I'm reaching for my shorts when the door to the room opens. I still, watching Drew walk in, carrying a beach towel, T-shirt, and a glass of water. He uses his foot to shut the door and then turns, freezing when he spots me standing here.

"Hey."

Drew swallows, eyes darting down to my bare stomach before they return to my face. "Shit. Hey. Sorry for barging in. I, uh...I didn't think you were in here. Everyone headed up to get ready for dinner, and I—" His eyes drop from my face again.

He's seen me in a bikini that's way more revealing than my sports bra and shorts. But we've never been alone in a bedroom any of those times. And all I can think about is, "*We could do that for real,*" and, "*Wanted to break Freddy Owens's nose after he bragged about kissing you.*"

On Sunday, he'll be gone. This weird week will be over. What used to be a relieving thought now holds a tinge of melancholy. When this week is over, we will be too.

"It's fine. It's your room too." I take a couple of steps closer to Drew, registering how his chest heaves with an unnecessary extra breath. That small reaction makes me bold. "Did you mean what you said at lunch?"

"About what exactly?" He tosses the wet towel on the floor and the T-shirt on the couch where I was just lying. The water gets sipped and set down on the bookcase.

"You had a crush on me when we were younger?"

I wait for him to deny it. To tell me he was selling the fake narrative of us being an actual couple.

Instead, he says, "You knew that."

I shake my head. "I didn't know that. If I had, I would have..."

"You would have what?" Drew takes a step this time.

The distance between us has shrunk down to inches.

"I would have done this," I whisper.

And then I kiss him. It's a match tossed on gasoline. Water

hitting a live wire. Lightning splitting the sky in half.

Either Drew was expecting it or his reflexes are superior. There's no hesitation or awkwardness or fumbling. Our mouths fit together like two puzzle pieces, hasty and desperate and searching.

The backs of my knees hit the edge of the mattress, and then I'm falling, back onto the bed where we've slept together the past couple of nights.

Drew hovers over me, the green of his eyes all I can focus on in the mostly white room. "You wore a red bikini all summer when we were sixteen. Every fucking time I saw you in it, I'd imagine touching these."

His hand slides up my side to cup my left breast through the flimsy nylon of my sports bra. I moan, arching to allow him better access.

"Fuck," he rasps. "You're perfect."

I'm not. I'm so far from perfect that it's laughable. I'm insecure and messy and broken, and I have a tendency to do or say the wrong thing.

But I still feel a warmth blossom in my chest. Coming from Drew, it doesn't sound like a lie or a line. It sounds true. And I *care* what he thinks of me. Care more than I've ever considered anyone else's opinion about anything, let alone me.

"Roll over," I whisper.

Drew listens, shifting off me and over to his side of the bed. I follow, straddling him and lining up our bodies. We both groan as the bulge of his erection settles between my legs, brushing against the spot that's soaked for him.

I reach up to tug off the sports bra, wishing I were wearing something lacy and sheer instead. The constricting polyester sticks to the dried sweat on my skin, leaving the imprint of a band around my rib cage.

It shouldn't be sexy. But the way he's looking at me? I've never felt this admired or desired.

Drew's hands settle on my waist as he stares at my boobs like they're the first pair he's ever seen. I feel his dick react, thickening against my thigh.

I shift away so I can tug at the hem of his swim trunks, exposing the rest of the V that's taunted me since I caught my first glimpse of him shirtless. The nylon material is light blue, patterned with tiny red sailboats. The print makes me smile—until I yank the shorts low enough that Drew's cock bobs free.

It's my turn to stare.

Excitement and nerves swirl with anticipation. It's *obscene*, seeing Drew like this. There are the carved muscles I've admired all week, chiseled biceps and broad shoulders and the stacked ridges of his abdomen. Muscles meant for action. For movement. For beautiful brutality.

And then there's the thick, heavy penis I can't look away from, the broad head an angry purple color.

Drew watches me take him in, his eyes trailing over me like the brush of a flame. There's no trace of uncertainty or politeness in his expression now. Just raw heat and hunger.

Each time our eyes collide, I feel the tug of something tangible. Something that feels like history and fate and *right*. Something I've never felt before.

I want to spend hours studying every inch. I want to remember exactly how he looks naked, the same way I memorize his words.

I trace a throbbing vein with one finger before attempting to close my fist around his sizable length.

Drew hisses as I grip the hot, hard skin, the muscles of his abdomen clenching impossibly tighter as his head tilts back with a groan. It's a heady rush of power, feeling and seeing him react this way to my touch.

I lean down and trace the flared tip with my tongue, my entire body flooding with heat when he moans my name.

There's a loud knock on the door.

"Harper! *Harper*! Harper, open up! I know you're in there."

I freeze, the reminder the rest of the world exists as irritating as my sister's loud voice.

"Harper!" Amelia calls again.

"Fuck," I mutter, rolling off Drew and looking for my sports bra.

I can't find it, so I just pull on my T-shirt sans bra. Drew takes one look at my breasts, nipples prominently pebbled, and rubs a hand across his face before averting his eyes and tugging his swim trunks back up. The bulge of his erection is still noticeable.

Drew follows my gaze. "Staring at it isn't going to help, Sunshine."

I roll my eyes. "Don't call me that." I stride toward the door and open it. "What?"

Amelia smooths the front of her yellow sundress. Unnecessarily. Unlike me, her appearance is fresh and clean. She clearly just showered, hair still damp and skin faintly pink. "Finally. Can I come in?"

"It's actually not the best time…" Not only is the room a disaster, but I was really hoping this would be a brief visit that ended with Drew and me resuming what we were doing.

Amelia pushes past me anyway, obviously considering it a rhetorical question.

Droplets of water fly from her wet hair and land on my arm as she walks toward the couch, carefully stepping around the clothes, shoes, and suitcases that litter the hardwood floor.

"Look, I know you're mad about—" Amelia stops talking as

soon as she sees Drew sitting on the edge of the bed.

He's pulled on a shirt at least, but his hair is a mess. So is mine probably.

Amelia glances between me and him, a darker hue of pink staining her cheeks as she realizes what she interrupted.

"Oh. Sorry. I thought all the guys were still down at the lake."

"I said it wasn't a great time," I remind her.

Drew stands and grabs a baseball cap off the back of the couch, which is strewn with a combination of our clothes. The sight of them mixed together is strange in an exciting way. I've never lived with a guy before or shared space the way Drew and I have been.

"I'm gonna…" Drew comes up blank with an excuse to leave as he pulls on the hat. "I'll see you guys later," he says, then leaves the room.

Once the door shuts behind him, I look back at Amelia.

She's studying me, head tilted. "That was weird."

"Knock a little less aggressively next time, then. Or should we move to one of the cabins?"

"Those are all reserved for guests," Amelia tells me.

I roll my eyes and take a seat on the couch. "Of course. Wouldn't want to mess with the master wedding plan."

"That's not what I meant."

"What were you banging down the door about, Amelia? I'm not mad about anything. We're good."

Her head is still tilted as she studies me, her gaze trailing down and over the mess of clothes I'm sitting on. "You like him."

I silently add to the mental tally of people who have said that to me in the same surprised tone. "What's not to like?"

"You usually find plenty when it comes to guys."

"Nothing wrong with having high standards. And you've never met most of the guys I've dated anyway."

Amelia scoffs, twirling a piece of damp hair as she looks out at the lake. "Exactly. You tell *Olivia* about all of them."

I sigh. "What's your issue with Olivia?"

"I don't have an issue with Olivia. I'm just trying to figure out why you tell your best friend *everything* and me *nothing*, and now, you're offended I'm doing the same."

"I'm not offended. I'm fine. We're *fine*. I thought we established that earlier."

"I never told Lincoln that Simon was our dad. He just …assumed."

My fingers clench, nails digging into the soft flesh of my palm. "He can assume whatever he wants. Is that what Theo's brother thinks too? His parents?"

Amelia's expression answers for her. "It was just…easier."

"Right. Dad's death was just an inconvenience."

"That is *not* what I said. God! You always do this."

"Do what?"

"Twist everything I say!"

"This is the first time I've heard you mention Dad in over a year, Amelia. How could I possibly *twist* that? It's a fact."

She leans against the bookcase, looking down at the ground and then back up at me. "Do you remember going to that mountain with Mom and Dad?"

I blink at her, shocked she's bringing it up. Shocked *she* remembers. "Not really," I finally answer. "But I saw our names written on the post, so I realized we had been."

Amelia nods, expecting that answer. "I remember going. You know what else I remember? You leaving after dinner to sleep over at Indy Wilson's next door. Dad disappeared right after you did. Mom and I sat up half the night, waiting for him. When he got back, he said he lost track of time. Hours! He'd been missing for hours! You were *always* gone when it happened. Off with friends or boys or doing who knows what. And Dad lit up around you. You were his favorite person. I know…I know he loved Mom and me. But you…he hid the darkness from you, Harper. And I know you think Mom and I are heartless monsters for how we acted after he died. You've made that clear. But what were we supposed to do? Climb into bed and hide from the world? What would that have changed? Mom was trying to be strong for us. I was trying to be strong for her."

"I'm weak because I *grieved*? Is that what you're telling me, Amelia?"

"No, I—*dammit*, Harper. This is what I mean about you twisting everything. I'm not calling you weak. I'm just trying to explain…because you've never listened. You wanted to be the one who grieved the most, and you wanted to do it your way— with sullen silences and always wondering what Dad would do or say if he were still here."

Amelia takes a deep breath, sucking in air and letting it out with an audible exhale.

"I didn't want to have my wedding here when Theo first suggested it. And then, the more I thought about it, the more it seemed like a way to *include* Dad. *That's* why I'm getting married here, not because it was convenient or because I didn't care about the history here. Did you ever even consider that?"

To that, I have nothing to say. Because I never *did* consider that. I assumed she chose this venue despite the past, not because of it.

Amelia exhales again as we stare at each other. There's plenty that crackles in the air between us. Petty grievances and ancient resentments and all the things we've left unsaid.

"I'm sick of Dad being this…barrier between us, Harper."

"I am too," I tell her honestly.

"You're my sister, and it feels like we're strangers most of the time. I didn't even know you were seriously dating someone."

I open my mouth to tell her I'm not actually dating Drew. Then, I close it because admitting to lying would only reinforce what she's saying.

"Last night?" Amelia continues. "All that stuff I said about Savannah, those things I told her and the things we've done together? I wanted to tell *you* those things too. I wanted to do those things with *you* too. I thought things would change when we were older. All my friends fought with their older siblings. But then Dad died. You left for college less than a year later. And you never really came back. To be honest, I wasn't sure if you'd come to the wedding if it was *here*. And that's why I didn't ask you to be my maid of honor. Because it would have been too painful and too embarrassing if you had said no."

"I wouldn't have said no, Amelia."

"Okay." She fiddles with the yellow cotton of her dress. "I'm sorry for not asking."

"I'm sorry for making you feel like you couldn't."

Amelia chews on her bottom lip. It's a nervous tic, one I haven't seen her do in years. "Will you give a speech at the wedding?"

"A speech?"

"If I could go back and change things, I would. But the programs have already been printed, and all the plans have been made—"

"It's fine," I assure her. "Savannah is doing a way better job than I would have. I mean, I wouldn't have come up with a hike or a canoe race or any of the other organized stuff we've done this week. We would have just been sitting in floaties on the lake, drinking margaritas."

Amelia's lips twitch. And then a giggle bubbles free.

I smile at my little sister, something in my chest squeezing and then relaxing as we share a moment lighter than we have in a long time.

"So, will you give a speech?"

Fuck. This is an olive branch, one anything but *yes* will burn.

"Are you sure that's a good idea?" I ask. "Me, alcohol, a microphone, and a captive audience?"

Amelia rolls her eyes. "Yes. You're good with words. Way better than I am."

"You're a *lawyer*, Amelia," I remind her. "All you do is talk and write."

"About facts. You're the creative one. Just like Dad was. I want to remember him the way you do."

"You want me to talk about Dad in my speech?"

Amelia nods. "I mean, if you want to."

No pressure.

I can see it in her expression. This is important to Amelia. It will matter to her, my answer. It will affect how our relationship looks going forward. And I'm tired of how it looks now.

So, I find myself saying, "Sure."

A wide smile stretches across Amelia's face. For a second, it feels like I'm looking at a much younger version of my sister instead of the mature adult woman who's about to become a wife. "Thank you, Harper."

I nod. She just said I'm good with words, but I don't feel like I am. There's a lot I want to say in response to everything she just told me, but my thoughts are too disorganized, bouncing around my skull like pinballs. I hope agreeing is enough for now. That it tells Amelia I'm tired of the way everything between us is too.

"I'll see you at dinner."

She spins and leaves the room.

I flop back onto the couch, attempting to process everything that just happened.

CHAPTER ELEVEN

HARPER

F ootsteps interrupt the soundtrack I've been listening to for the past half hour—steady battering of water against wood. I look up to see Drew approaching slowly, hands shoved deep into his pockets as he walks down the long, creaky dock toward me.

I'm sitting in one of the Adirondack chairs at the very end, a pad of paper I found in one of the bedside tables propped on my knee and an empty drink glass by my arm. I came down here after dinner ended, opting out of the game of Monopoly and the spy thriller Austin and Jared started watching, with the intention of writing the speech I'm supposed to deliver on Saturday.

Instead, I've mostly stared out at the lake. The sun set a little while ago, streaks of orange and pink appearing across the horizon and reflecting off the rippling water before gradually fading toward the color of star-sprinkled midnight. I can barely make out anything besides shapes now.

"Hey."

"Hi." I toss the notebook onto the open chair to my right as Drew settles into the one on my left.

He changed into a fleece and a pair of joggers after showering, his blond hair blown ruffled and wayward by the cool night air.

There's a shift of energy in the air between us, something electric and exciting. I avoided looking his way for most of dinner, still processing my conversation with Amelia and also replaying what had taken place right before it. It feels like there's a very different sort of secret between us now than how he came here as a favor, not a boyfriend. Something special and esoteric.

"Amelia asked me to make a speech at the wedding."

He glances at the pad of paper I lobbed. "Is that what you're working on?"

"No. I was planning to…but no."

The few thoughts I jotted down were a continuation of what I had been working on this afternoon and have nothing to do with a wedding.

I hesitate before adding, "You're going to laugh."

His eyebrows fly upward as he studies me, then glances at the notebook again. "No, I won't," Drew replies.

"Yes, you will."

"Try me."

I sigh. "I'm writing a mystery. A thriller. And…I can't decide who the killer is."

Drew stares. Blinks. *Laughs*.

To his credit, he tries to turn it into a cough. But it's not very convincing.

I ball up the lobster-patterned napkin tucked beneath my empty glass and toss it in his direction. "You liar."

"I'm sorry. I'm sorry." He's still chuckling as he rubs a hand across his jaw in some poor attempt to mask his amusement. "It's just…really? How can you write a murder mystery and *not* have a killer?"

"There is *a* killer…I just haven't decided who it is yet. Crime dramas drag the show out for so long because as soon as the identity is exposed, it's all over. I don't want the ending to be predictable. So, I built it up to this massive thing, and now, it's just…stuck."

"Can I read it?"

I stare at Drew, taken totally off guard. It should have occurred to me he might ask. But it didn't, probably because I've never told anyone about the book and I have no basis of comparison when it comes to reactions. "Wha—no. No. Absolutely not."

"Why not?" He gives me a boyish grin that should look completely out of place on a grown man's body. Instead, it looks incredibly endearing. "It sounds like a fresh perspective is exactly what you need. I can tell you who the obvious choice is."

"No one has read it. No one even knows I'm writing it. It's just something I do sometimes."

"You trust me?"

Drew's gaze is intense and searching. And hopeful.

"Maybe," I whisper. But the fact that we're even having this conversation suggests a far more definitive answer.

He nods and looks away, treating me to a glimpse of his strong profile. I trace the curve of his forehead and the angle of his nose, the sharp line of his jaw. His head tilts back to take in the starry sky, his expression peaceful.

Drew is steady. Safe. Qualities I used to think were boring but suddenly consider fascinating.

I wonder what shakes that careful control. If he's this measured and even-tempered on the ice or if that's where he lets loose.

I want to shake his ease, to get a glimpse of everything beneath. To know *him*, not just the famous hockey player or the teenager who lived next door.

And I want *him* to know *me*.

"My dad used to come up with stories," I say, mirroring Drew's posture and looking up at the constellations scattered above us.

You can't see any stars in New York—the city lights are too bright.

"I don't think he wrote the stories down or ever finished any of them. He'd just talk about them at night when he was grading papers or when we were out canoeing on this lake. Whenever I'd ask about the rest of the story, he would say, 'That's life. You'll never know the ending.' And sometimes, I wonder…I wonder if…"

"If he knew the ending?"

"Yeah, exactly."

More than anyone else I've encountered in my life, Drew seems to *get me*. Improbably. On paper, we have little in common. He has two loving parents; I rarely speak to my mother or sister without it devolving into an argument. He's a famous athlete; I take meeting notes and fetch coffee. He's easygoing; I'm grumpy.

But right now, we just feel like Drew and Harper.

We make sense.

"I missed this," I say, shifting my gaze to stare out at the water and snuggling deeper into the soft cotton of my oversize sweatshirt. "The lake. The smell. The sound. Everything about it."

"My parents are talking about selling the Port Haven house," Drew says, his throat bobbing with a hard swallow. "They hardly go up there anymore, and I'm all the way in Washington. It just sits there empty most of the year." He glances at me. "Are you planning to go back? Again?"

"I don't know. I want to…but I also don't, if that makes any sense at all. There are so many places I want to visit, places I've never been and that don't have memories of—that don't have memories yet."

"Like where?"

I shake my head. "Nowhere specific. But I haven't traveled much. I've never left the country. Never even been to the West Coast."

"You should visit."

I meet his gaze for a few seconds before looking back out at the water, not sure if he means visit *him* or just visit one of the states on that side of the country. "Maybe. What about you? Where do you want to go?"

"You'll think I'm a nerd."

I look over, raising one eyebrow. "Trust me, you're cemented in my head as a hot jock."

"You think I'm hot?"

"You knew that." I parrot his line from earlier, and Drew smirks in response.

"There's this bird sanctuary in Germany that's one of the largest in the world. They have thousands of species. I'd love to go there one day."

"You should have been an ornithologist."

He laughs. "Yeah. Maybe in another life. Or after I retire. I just think they're cool. I mean, they *fly*."

"So do planes."

More laughter. "True. Well, I spend plenty of time on those."

"I thought you loved playing." I keep studying him, even after he's looked away, out at the endless expanse of the lake.

"Playing, yeah. Hockey has always been my main priority. It's everything else that gets old. The grind. The travel and the media and the attention and the team drama."

"I have a hard time picturing you not getting along with anyone."

"I'm not Colton's biggest fan. He was flirting with you at dinner."

Flirting is a stretch. But he was definitely *flirty*, and I like knowing Drew noticed. "Technically, I'm single."

Drew leans down and picks up the cocktail napkin I threw at him earlier, tucking it into his pocket before it can blow away into the water. "*Technically*, he doesn't know that."

"You jealous, Halifax?" My tone is teasing.

"Should I be, Williams? It was *my* dick you were grinding on earlier." Drew's voice is deadly serious.

He holds my surprised gaze. This is a new side of Drew; one I've never seen before. He's confident, sure. Assured and prepared. Assertive. But the edge to his expression right now holds something different. Gives me a glimpse of the intensity I was just wondering about.

It's dangerous. Consuming. Overwhelming.

And, *fuck*, does he wear it as well as everything else.

I use the arms of the chair to push myself to standing, taking a couple of steps, closing the short distance between our chairs.

Drew's knees spread, welcoming me between them. His head tilts back further, looking up, up, up until his eyes meet mine.

A slow smile unfurls on his lips, a hint of a challenge evident in the upturn as the smooth fabric of his pants rubs against my bare legs.

Callous palms skate up my calves and settle on the backs of my thighs, pulling me closer until I'm straddling his lap again, settled directly over what I now know is a massive dick.

There's no knock this time. No bed either. The hard wood of the chair digs directly into my shins, but I can't find it in me to care. The rush of excitement and anticipation erases everything else.

Drew's face presses into the curve of my neck as I sink into his lap, his warm breath sending goose bumps skittering across my skin and down my spine. My hips rock into his, a slow grind, chasing more contact. I want him naked. Above me. Inside of me.

"We don't have to do anything," he tells me, like the gentleman I don't want him to be.

"I want to do everything," I reply.

I feel his smile form against my skin. One hand slips under the hem of my sweatshirt, his thumb drawing small, sensual circles right above my hip bone. My heartbeats turn into a wild, erratic rhythm.

"In that case, I've got a room upstairs."

A laugh leaves me in a quiet huff. "Oh, yeah?"

"Mmhmm." His lips ghost across the line of my jaw and back down my neck, the sensual sensation spreading everywhere.

I squirm against him, my breathing embarrassingly heavy. Eager pants that drown out all the other night noises. I can no longer hear the water hitting wood or the occasional loon call.

"You have a whole room, all to yourself?" I manage to ask.

"Nah. I'm sharing it with this girl." Drew's hand moves a little lower, playing with the hem of my underwear, but not slipping beneath. *Yet*, I hope.

"What's she like?"

"Aside from making loud sex sounds while her roommate is trying to fall asleep?" Drew grins. "She's stubborn. Feisty. Determined. The most gorgeous woman I've ever seen."

"I bet you say that to all the girls," I whisper.

Drew shakes his head. "No, I don't."

Then, his lips touch mine, and I'm *lost*. In the sensations. In the anticipation. In the warm glide of his tongue and the slow rub of his fingers right above where I want them.

We kiss and kiss. Desperate, slow, and everything in between. I can't remember the last time I kissed someone like this. There might not have been a last time.

It's languid and unhurried. Searching and focused. Usually, kissing is just a cursory step on the way to more satisfying contact.

But that's all Drew and I do—we kiss.

Tongues tangling.

Hands wandering.

Time slowing.

Until all traces of the day are gone and we're blanketed in total darkness, the buzz of mosquitoes beginning to replace more pleasant sounds. I pull away and stand, grabbing my notebook and my glass before holding a hand out to Drew.

He half-smiles at the gesture, letting me pretend to pull him up while doing all the work to rise out of his chair and tower over me again.

I'm not short. At five-eight, I've been around plenty of guys who were about my height. But Drew is easily over six feet of solid muscle. Beside him, I feel petite.

Rather than take my hand, he wraps an arm around my waist, tugging me back into the delicious heat of his body. It's cool enough to crave now that the sun's warmth is gone—or at least, that's what I tell myself.

The truth is that I just like being close to him. And as someone who is proudly independent and cringes away from most public displays of affection with secondhand embarrassment, that's saying a lot.

We walk together up the dock and across the yard; me nestled into the side of his body, the notebook under my arm and my glass in one hand. We disentangle as we reach the back door, Drew pulling open the screen and me walking in first.

The scene inside is similar to what it was when I walked down to the water an hour ago. Monopoly has been tossed aside in favor of charades, but several of the guys are still watching a film on the television affixed to the wall beside the fireplace. A dramatic action sequence is playing on the screen—what looks like a car chase, peppered by the sound of gunshots.

I head into the kitchen to stick my glass in the dishwasher and then return to the main living area, faking a yawn. "I'm heading to bed."

"No! Play with us! We're losing," Claire says.

"Maybe tomorrow night," I answer, glancing at Drew.

He's leaning over the back of the couch, talking to Jared as he gestures at the television.

"I'm exhausted. After the hike, you know?"

Claire pouts. "Lame. I thought I could rely on you for some fun, Harper! It's barely past nine."

"I might read before bed."

"You can read—"

"She wants to go bang her hot boyfriend, Claire," Savannah announces. *Loudly.* "Let her go do it at a reasonable hour."

There are muffled laughs around the living room. Claire's cheeks turn the same shade as her hair. We obviously weren't the only ones who heard her and Rowan last night.

"On that note…night, everyone," I say, grinning.

I wander toward Drew, trying to act oblivious to the eyes on me. On him. On us.

Aside from the questions from Willa at lunch, there hasn't been much interest in the two of us.

Or at least, that's what I think. Maybe I've been oblivious to it.

These are Amelia's friends. With the exception of Savannah, who practically grew up with us, I barely know most of them. It's starting to feel like that interest was merely hidden, and now, it's obvious. Like I'm overshadowing Amelia's wedding by bringing

Drew when it was only an attempt to make getting through this week a little easier.

I stop next to Drew, my body naturally leaning into his. It's warmer in here than it was outside, but I'm still seeking out his heat. His support. *Him*.

I blame the heavy pour of rum in the mojito I had at dinner. The fizziness in my stomach. The way summer nights flicker with special possibilities, like fireflies in a glass jar.

His arm twines around me the same way it did outside, my side fitting against his, like we're two pieces from the same puzzle. A coziness appears in my chest, burning like a lit match. Drew keeps talking to Jared as I lean against him, acting as if this were a normal occurrence between us.

I focus on the television screen, watching two men race across a rooftop and then swing down a fire escape, until Drew wraps up his conversation with a, "Night, man."

"Yeah. Night, guys," Jared replies.

I shoot Jared a small smile as we start walking toward the stairs, then glance at Drew. "If you want to watch the movie—"

"I don't," he replies immediately.

"Okay."

"Okay," he repeats.

And that unfamiliar, warm glow in my chest burns a little brighter.

CHAPTER TWELVE

DREW

The door shuts behind us with a quiet click, sealing off the sound of activity downstairs.

I've never shared space with a woman before. I'm an only child. Lived with guys on the team in college and got my own place as soon as I was drafted and started playing professionally. And none of my relationships have progressed to the point where we spent more than the occasional night together.

Staying in the same room—sleeping in the same bed—wasn't something I considered when I offered to come here with Harper.

Once I realized, I thought it might be awkward. Strange, at the very least. But this feels like *our* space. It feels empty when she's not in the room with me, even though the entire space is about the size of the entryway to my condo in Seattle.

Harper sets the notebook she's carrying down on the couch. She pulls off the oversize sweatshirt she's wearing, revealing the white tank top underneath. And that she's not wearing a bra beneath, which I'm glad I didn't realize until now.

I didn't allow my hands to travel that far north outside. Or as low as I wanted to explore.

I'm not sure if this will be more than a onetime thing. I don't think Harper is looking for a relationship, and I'm not in a great position to offer her one. Once our season starts, I'll be back to flying all over the country. Back to extra ice time and grueling practices. Late nights and early mornings.

Most people attribute my success in hockey to raw talent or luck. I guess there's an element of both whenever you pursue anything. But I've also worked my ass off to get the career I have. People don't always give enough credit to that third factor, in my opinion. They assume you stumbled into something and made the best of it instead of sacrificing and fighting and digging deep to get there.

Harper cocks a brow as she watches me stare at her, the closest to self-conscious I've ever seen her wear bleeding across her expression. "Whatcha doing, Halifax?"

I feel the smile spread across my face before I register any amusement. It's an involuntary, pleasant reaction. Every time I look at her, I feel like smiling.

"Just enjoying the view," I reply.

Harper rolls her eyes. "I look like a mess."

She does, but in the best way. Windblown hair, freckled cheeks, chapped lips.

"You look hot." I close the distance between us slowly, savoring the way she reacts.

The rapid rise of her chest. The extra flush on her face. The way her pupils dilate despite the lack of less light.

"I can see your tits through your shirt."

The left corner of her mouth hikes up. "Didn't think you'd be a dirty talker, Halifax. Too respectful and restrained."

She smiles wider after taunting me.

It's addictive—this push and pull between us. Harper challenges me in a way no other woman has bothered to do. Few people look beyond politeness. They only search past poor behavior in an attempt to discover redeeming qualities.

"You didn't *think* so?" I step into her, making sure she can feel my cock pressed against her stomach. "Have you spent a lot of time thinking about fucking me, Harper? Imagining what I'd say?" I coast a hand under the thin fabric of her tank top, sliding over the slight bumps of her rib cage until I reach the swell of her breast.

Harper's head tilts back as she sways into me. "I've not, *not* thought about it."

"You sure you're a writer?" I tease. "I'm not sure that was proper English."

Her left hand fists the front of my fleece, twisting the fabric and anchoring me in place, as if she's worried I'm planning to go anywhere but here. "I'm not sure. That I'm a writer, I mean. This..." Her right hand drifts lower, grazing the erection tenting the front of my pants. "This, I'm sure about."

"I'm sure about both," I tell her.

Vulnerability flashes across her face, and I second-guess bringing this topic up again.

In my limited observations of Harper, I've gotten the sense that she shows a lot without revealing anything. Her telling me something she's never shared with anyone else feels like the most precious gift I've ever received. But I know Harper. Or at least, I feel like I'm starting to understand her. Thanking her for sharing or telling her that I won't tell anyone won't go over well.

So, I let the subject drop, right along with the flimsy tank top that finds a new home on the floor. I tilt my head down to kiss her again because I've developed a craving for her lips that kissing seems to feed, not satisfy. I feel her smile even though I'm too close to see the upward curve as she rubs against me impatiently.

I can't explain why everything feels different. I just know that it does. That as desperate as I am to pull the rest of her clothes off and push inside of her, I'm also eager to savor everything about this moment.

The white noise of the air-conditioning hissing through vents. The distant hum of voices downstairs. The way she smells like happy memories—sunshine and lake water and a hint of smoke from the campfire last night, which suggests she's wearing some of the same clothing.

"I've thought about this," I whisper to her, walking us toward the bed. It's a quick trip. A few steps.

Harper's answer is a rapid inhale. She falls back onto the comforter once the backs of her knees hit the side of the bed, her dark hair fanning across the sheets and her breasts bouncing from the movement.

She watches intently as I yank my fleece off and step out of the joggers I pulled on before dinner. I take my time with my boxer briefs, treating her to my best attempt at a strip show.

Based on the red staining her cheeks, I don't do a terrible job. I lean over her, purposefully grazing the soft skin of her stomach before reaching for the rough denim of her jean shorts. I unbutton and unzip, tugging the blue fabric down her long legs before I hover over her, resting my arms on either side of her head and holding most of my weight. Most enjoyable plank I've ever done.

My dick brushes between her legs. Harper gasps, my name spilling out in a desperate tone I've never heard from her before. My head dips so I can kiss her again, one hand sliding down her abdomen and between her legs. I groan when I reach her underwear and realize how wet she is.

Something tightens in my chest as she pulses against my hand, urging me on, and I realize it's for me. That she's reacting like this *for me*. And just like that, my restraint thins to nothing. I'm a little wild. A lot reckless.

I jerk the scrap of lace between her legs, forcing friction against her clit. Her moan is impatient and stunned and a little musical. A song I'd listen to on repeat.

Control is a close friend of mine. But I lose hold of it now, too anxious to hear Harper make that sound again to continue teasing her. I push upright to grab the condom I stuck in my pocket after showering, hoping this moment might happen after we were interrupted earlier.

Harper watches as I tear the condom wrapper open with my teeth and roll the rubber on. Her eyes are wide and heated as she takes me in, a flush creeping down her cheeks and onto her chest. She doesn't make a dick joke or act concerned about my size, which is what women usually do. Sometimes, it's an actual concern. Usually, it's an ego stroke. The absence of either makes this moment feel more real. It feels like we're stripped bare in more ways than one.

I crawl back over her, using my knee to nudge her legs apart. She moans as soon as our skin comes back into contact, the breathy gasp the only sound aside from our heavy breathing in the quiet room.

I tug the fabric of her underwear down as my mouth dips, tongue circling her hardened nipple. I don't know what my obsession with her breasts are—except exactly that. They're hers. And the teenager in me who noticed when they first appeared kind of can't believe that I'm touching them right now.

There's a tug at the base of my scalp as Harper's hand slides into my hair, fisting the strands as I swirl my tongue. Her legs wrap around my waist, trying to guide me where she wants me. My skin sparks every place we're touching, which is almost everywhere, heat and lust spreading like a river in a storm with banks overflowing.

It's not just kissing her that's electric. It's simply her presence, flicking something on inside of me I didn't even realize was dormant.

I'm pretty sure Harper sees herself as a cloud. Drifting and moody and sometimes stormy. But to me, she's sunshine. Bright, golden, and consuming.

"*Please*, Drew," she begs.

She begs without me asking, and it's the sweetest sound I've ever heard.

"You need me to fuck you?"

"*Yes*." It's not really a word. It's desperation.

The head of my cock is already notched against her slit, eagerly waiting. I flex my hips and press into her an inch, the sensation of her pussy gripping me a pleasure so intense it's almost painful. I tease her with a few shallow strokes, barely nudging inside of her before I pull back out, like she's too tight to take me. Which isn't far from the truth.

Harper writhes in an attempt to move closer, her breaths rapid and her pussy fluttering as she tries to take more.

"*Fuck me*, Drew."

I push in another inch, spreading her open and glancing down to watch her take my cock. Harper's breathing shifts from fast to shaky, her thighs trembling as I continue to fill her. She's tight and hot and wet, and I'm worried I'm going to embarrass myself by lasting less than a minute. It takes all of my willpower to press slowly instead of slam inside, letting her adjust to the intrusion gradually.

"Fuck. You feel so good," I murmur, like the words are a secret meant only for her. "So good," I repeat, pressing into her deeper and deeper until I'm bottomed out. Lust saturates the syllables, turning them into a drunken-sounding slur. "You want to come for me, baby?"

The pet name sobers my voice a little. I'm not normally much of a talker during sex. I prefer to focus on the physical. When women mewl or pant over how I'm too big for them, it usually takes me out of the moment. It feels fake almost. Like they're acting.

And I've never called a woman *baby* in my life. But for some reason, I want to use something more intimate than just her name. Harp is an instrument or an insult, not a nickname. Every time I've called her Sunshine, I think Harper has taken it the wrong way. I think she thinks I'm using it ironically rather than how I mean it—like light personified. Hard to ignore or look away from. And *baby* slips out naturally, like my aversion to it up until now has simply been because I wanted to wait and only use it with her.

Harper's hands slide lower, her fingernails digging into my shoulder muscles as we fall into a rhythm of colliding. Moving apart and then crashing right back together.

It feels as if we'd never done this before. Like everything is new and unexplored. Uncertain and exciting.

It also feels effortless. Right, like this was always meant to happen. The way the moon has phases and the ocean tides change.

We seem inevitable.

And it feels *good*.

It shuts off everything else in my head, the small worries that have hung around ever since a woman asked me for an autograph after sex during my rookie season. A wake-up call that my sudden celebrity didn't disappear when I stepped off the ice and pulled off my jersey. That it's all some people saw me as. Hockey has, in one way or another, destroyed every romantic relationship I've attempted.

But with Harper? I was shocked she even knew I played professionally. I'd bet the contents of my bank account that she has no clue what position I play or that the team mascot is a wolf. If *she* ever asks me for an autograph, it will be ironically.

I tell myself this is a normal thing. It feels different with Harper because it's been a long time since I was with a woman who couldn't care less about my job and who knew me before I accumulated any of that fame.

But as I look at her moaning beneath me, feeling more present and more aroused than I can ever remember being, I wonder if that's really all it is.

My hips move faster, too impatient to keep up the slower pace. Too desperate to stay gentle and controlled. Her legs tighten around me as I finally let loose and fuck her the way I've been dying to.

I don't need to ask if she's coming. I can feel it—her inner muscles spasming and clenching around my cock. Heat races up my spine and explodes inside of me, my vision blurring as I fill the condom.

She's loud. And as much as I love hearing her shout my name, I'm also possessive of it. I don't want anyone else hearing it, even if it will just result in some jokes or *nice work* comments from the guys tomorrow.

So, I kiss Harper again, muffling her cries until our bodies still, spent.

"Holy shit." She speaks first, her voice breathless. And a little stunned, which sends a pulse of pride through me.

If I've ruined all other men for her, it will be my proudest accomplishment.

I don't move, enjoying the aftershocks I can feel trembling through her. Appreciating how Harper's legs remain wrapped around my waist and the way her fingers are still digging into my back, like she's as reluctant for me to move away as I am. I memorize the way she looks beneath me, hazy eyes and satisfied expression. Hair even wilder and cheeks even redder.

"Give me a minute, and we can go again."

She laughs. "Don't threaten me with a good time, Halifax. I'll expect you to deliver."

"*Delivering* won't be an issue, Sunshine. I felt how hard you just came around my cock."

Harper rolls her eyes. If I could reach her ass, I'd spank her.

"I told you not to call me that."

"It fits. You look…glowy." I supplant the adjectives I really want to use. Like *beautiful* or *stunning*. *Like mine*.

That last phrase needs to stay buried. Because I'm certain Harper sees this as nothing more but a benefit to this week. A bonus and a way to explore our mutual attraction. I don't want to make things weird between us, especially with the wedding rapidly approaching, where Paul's absence will be felt most keenly.

She snorts. "Glowy? Get up so I can pee."

I pull out of her slowly. Reluctantly.

Then, I roll to the left, onto the comforter that now smells like sex, and grab a tissue from the box by the bed to wrap around the condom.

I wasn't lying about another round. Harper making me feel like a reckless teenager extends to my hormones.

Watching her walk away, all long legs and tangled hair and perky ass, is enough to make my dick twitch like I didn't just come harder than I ever have in my life.

I want to watch Harper ride me. Want to fuck her from behind. Want to see those full lips wrapped around my cock.

More sex isn't all I crave from her, though. I also want *this*. Listening to her hum in the bathroom. Talking to her. Being around her. Soaking up her presence that, no matter what she says, feels like my personal brand of sunshine.

I allow myself to consider the possibility that maybe this isn't a normal thing at all. That this isn't good chemistry or teenage fantasies or an escape from reality.

That maybe it's a *Harper* thing.

That maybe it won't wane after I leave.

That she's going to complicate my life in a way I've never experienced before, and I don't even care.

That pretending around Harper is this easy because I'm falling for her for real.

CHAPTER THIRTEEN

HARPER

I wake up to a delicious soreness between my thighs and an irritating beam of sunlight shining right into my eyes. I groan and roll over, expecting to encounter a warm, muscular body.

I didn't bother staying on my side of the mattress last night. I basically climbed on top of Drew and immediately fell asleep, exhausted after an emotionally and physically draining day. Not to mention feeling thoroughly fucked.

But there's no one else in the bed.

I stare at the white sheets, trying to figure out what time it is. After sunrise, based on the aggravating brightness.

Drew must have gone out on his daily run. But he always leaves the drapes closed so I can sleep in. I'm annoyed he didn't bother today. And that he didn't wake me up before leaving so we could repeat last night.

There's a soft click as the door opens. My eyes squint at the figure entering the room as I sit up, clutching the sheets to my chest. Clothes also seemed unnecessary last night. Now, it adds insult to injury.

Drew left me alone in bed, *naked*. To *exercise*.

Talk about an ego hit.

But he doesn't look like he just came back from a run. He smiles as he approaches the bed, dressed in shorts and the same fleece he was wearing last night, carrying two thermoses.

"Morning, Sunshine."

I don't bother chastising him about the nickname. It's growing on me, honestly. More original than *baby*, although I didn't hate him using that last night either.

"Why did you get up?" I groan. "*And* open the curtains?"

"Because I thought you'd be more agreeable if you woke up slowly."

"If you wanted me agreeable, you should have woken me up with your tongue."

Drew's eyes darken to emerald, but he doesn't move any closer to the bed. "I'll keep that in mind for tomorrow. Come on. Get up."

"What? *Why*? Just go for your run, if you're not going to go down on me."

He grins. "Bossy, huh?"

I fake a yawn, the sheet conveniently dropping when I cover my mouth. Drew seems to have an obsession with my boobs, and I wish I could go back and tell my younger self, who stuffed bras with tissues, that the hottest guy I've ever been with would like them despite their small size.

All the amusement disappears from Drew's face, hunger appearing instead. I'm pretty sure he mumbles a, "Fuck," before walking over to the couch, setting down the thermoses on the bookcase, and sifting through the mess of clothes draped over the cushions.

In the daylight, the room looks even worse than it did last night. The shorts and sweatshirt I wore to dinner are flung around, along with his joggers and two condom wrappers. He wasn't lying about a second round.

Drew tosses a bikini and his hockey hoodie onto the bedspread. "Get dressed."

I lie back against the pillows, not bothering to pull the sheet back over my body.

He's getting quite the view.

I don't have a lot of hang-ups about my body. My small breasts have always been my least favorite feature. But I've also never been this unguarded with a guy before. Never lain out naked and exposed in the daylight, hoping he'll take advantage of the easy access.

"Are you just going to stand there and look?" I ask.

"You didn't seem to mind me *looking* last night," Drew replies, smirking.

"Looking last night came with orgasms," I tell him.

Drew rubs a hand across his face, muffling his words. But I'm pretty sure he says, "Fuck my life," before walking over to me. This time, he drops my bathing suit and his sweatshirt right on the sheets beside me, so I barely have to move to pull both on.

"*Please* get dressed. Because if I get back in bed, we won't be getting out anytime soon, and I…I want to do this with you, okay?"

Curiosity piqued, I sit up. Drew's pained expression and the clear impression of his dick through his shorts make it clear he hasn't lost interest after one night.

I figured sex was no longer a novelty for a hot, young professional athlete. Drew is basically the blueprint for a fantasy. He's the unattainable playboy who holds the same elusive appeal as the most popular guy in school. Knowing he's getting hard from looking at me is a thrill.

I pull on the bikini, then hold up the hoodie with a questioning expression. "You want me to wear this?"

"It's comfortable." He shrugs, running a hand through his hair. There's something so masculine about the motion, the bulge of his bicep and the careless flick of his hand. I find it fascinating, the mundane becoming intriguing whenever he's involved. "You can wear something else if you want."

I slip the sweatshirt on, soft cotton caressing my skin, and stand with a sigh. "Okay, I'm ready. Let's go."

Drew studies me intently, like there might be a quiz later on the color of the bikini I'm wearing underneath his hoodie. It makes me wish I'd been awake to watch while he got dressed. There's a special intimacy about knowing what someone else is wearing beneath their clothes.

And he's looking at me like he wants to tear everything off.

"You told me to get dressed," I remind him.

Drew chuckles, his hand running along his jaw and his eyes trailing my bare legs appreciatively. He hasn't shaved this morning. There's a hint of stubble I'm imagining rasping against the sensitive skin of my inner thighs. My center clenches as heat pools in my belly, snippets of last night filling my mind. An insistent throb starts between my legs, enhanced by the ache as I remember how huge he felt inside of me. How it felt like I might split in half if he kept going and die if he didn't.

"Yeah, I'm an idiot sometimes," is his response, giving me a look like he knows exactly what I'm thinking about before walking over to the bookshelf and retrieving the two thermoses. He holds one out to me. "Here."

I pull my hair back into a ponytail before walking toward him, taking the offered mug and sniffing the contents. "You made me coffee?"

Drew doesn't answer, busy digging in his duffel for what turns out to be another ball cap. He has an endless collection of them stashed in there, it seems.

"Did you bring a suit?" I blurt, suddenly realizing I never asked him.

My eyes snag on the garment bag hanging on the back of the door, which holds my two dresses—one for the rehearsal dinner tonight and one for the wedding tomorrow. In her endless forethought, Amelia coordinated all of our wedding attire to be shipped and stored here so no one had to travel with any finery.

But I'm belatedly realizing Drew didn't have the luxury of planning ahead. He dropped everything and came here as a favor to me—a generous gesture I'm continually appreciating. Because every difficult moment, he's made better. And all my favorite memories here have featured him.

"Yeah," Drew replies, putting his hat on backward. *Fuck me.* I have no idea why it's hotter than having the brim facing ahead, but it is.

"Is it wrinkled?" I cast a quick glance at his duffel bag.

"I travel with suits all the time. Learned how to fold one so it doesn't crease years ago."

"And you brought one to Maine with you?"

"Got one in Portland on my way here."

Dammit. That revelation hits me right in the center of the chest, something warm and wonderful and confusing settling right next to my heart.

Drew is nonchalant as we walk down the hallway and the stairs, not acknowledging the way my eyes keep drifting toward him. I have a basic grasp of Maine geography. I know Portland was not on the way from Port Haven to Lake Paulson. Drew went out of his way, and I can't vocalize how much that means to me. Can barely comprehend it. No one else has ever driven an hour out of their way to buy a suit just to attend a wedding with me.

Hazy, cool air greets us as we step outside. My hands tighten around the warm mug, my lungs filling deeply with the pure oxygen. It's cleansing and refreshing.

"Where are we going?" I glance at Drew, realizing it's a question I should have asked him a while ago.

He's too distracting. His body. His words. His thoughtfulness.

"Fishing."

That *something* in my chest glows brighter and hotter, insisting on acknowledgment. At no point during my mountainside meltdown yesterday did I consider Drew might do something like this. That he might do more than listen.

"We don't have to," he says hurriedly, misreading my expression. "I just thought that—"

"I want to."

"Yeah?" A hesitant hope appears on his face, like he thinks this might be a good thing but isn't positive yet.

"Yeah."

"Okay."

We continue down the path until we reach the rack that houses the canoes. With all the ease of someone blessed with natural athleticism, Drew pulls a dark green one off and drags it across the short stretch of grass to the sandy section that the lake laps against.

I contribute by shamelessly ogling the muscles on display as he does all the hard work.

Drew grabs a tackle box and a fishing pole out of the small shed next to the canoes. He *planned* this, I realize. It wasn't an errant thought or an impulsive decision.

A lump forms in my throat, which I quickly wash down with a sip of coffee. A sip of coffee flavored with oat milk and no sugar. There were multiple mornings this week when I made my coffee in front of Drew, usually right after he returned from his run and I just dragged myself out of bed.

But I didn't think he was paying attention.

And the realization that he *was* is a heady, overwhelming sensation. The same rush when he mentioned noticing how Colton sat next to me at dinner last night.

I never put on shoes. The dewy grass transitions to damp sand as I approach Drew, who's loading up the canoe and pushing it toward the edge of the lake. I follow him like a magnet seeking its opposite pole. It's a compulsion, not a conscious decision.

"You ready?" He glances back at me as he pushes the front of the canoe into the shallows, catching my close inspection of the ass that hockey has sculpted into firm perfection. One corner of his mouth tips up in a small, satisfied smile, which is my favorite of his expressions. Probably because it looks like a secret gesture that I've never seen him give to anyone else.

"Yeah." I swallow and take another step forward, careful not to spill a single drop of coffee as I adjust to a different surface. My bare feet sink into wet sand with each step, the remnants of the coral color I painted my toes popping against the light-gray-brown grains.

"I'll hold it," Drew says, holding out a hand for my thermos.

"I've got it."

"You're going to crawl into the front one-handed?"

I glance at the canoe. The front half is surrounded in water, gently bobbing on the flat surface. "Why don't you ride in the front this time? You rode in the back before."

"Because the back is where the stronger paddler is supposed to sit."

"Who designated *you* the *stronger paddler*?"

"Wanna arm-wrestle me for the title?"

My eyes drift to his impressive biceps. I might be stubborn, but I'm not delusional.

Wordlessly, I hand him my hot coffee, ignoring whatever smug expression he's possibly wearing as I crawl toward the front seat.

The boat rocks with every motion I make, filling me with the rational fear I might tip the whole thing. It matches how I'm feeling internally, a little off-kilter and a lot uncertain.

I expected this week to be an emotional roller coaster.

My dad's absence is most obvious during the big moments, not the ordinary. My high school graduation. Amelia's high school graduation. My college graduation. Amelia's college graduation. Amelia's law school graduation. Amelia's wedding.

Lately, all the big moments have been hers. And that's almost worse than missing him during mine. I'm missing him for her *and* for me. No matter how healed Amelia acts, I know she misses him as much as I do.

Knowing someone is hurting and hiding it is a sharper pain than seeing it expressed.

What I *didn't* expect is Drew. He's the real reason for the dip in my stomach and my sweaty palms. Because things with him were supposed to be simple and uncomplicated, and I'm not sure if I was distracted or delusional when I told myself that.

It seems so obvious now that there was no chance of either. No matter what version of him I encounter—the carefree teenager or the drinking buddy or the understanding friend or the sex god—he's nothing but complicated.

My feelings for him are complicated.

Complicated in a way I've *never* felt about a guy.

In the small ways, like him noticing how I like my coffee, to the burning desire to see him naked again. The way I want to reciprocate and *give* with no signs of selfishness. I want him to confide in me. And I've never been all that enthusiastic about oral sex. But getting on my knees for Drew doesn't sound terrible at all. It sends a rush of heat through me, just imagining it.

I want to please him. I want to affect him. I *care*.

That's what it comes down to, I realize as we push away smoothly from the shore and move out farther into the lake with fishing equipment and a hot drink, just like I did when I was younger.

I care.

I care what Drew thinks about me. I care about how he's feeling. I care that everything between us feels lopsided, like he's given more than me.

Accepting help makes me uncomfortable. But it feels like all I've done is accept things from Drew. His help, his support, his touch.

From Drew, I'll take whatever he's willing to give.

"Tell me more about your book," he says once the Camp Basswood dock is nothing but a distant blur.

I glance over one shoulder at Drew paddling. Then, I spin fully, tucking my knees under me like a little kid as I face him. "Why?"

"'Cause I'm curious."

I look away, out at the mist clinging to the top of the water. "It's not any good."

"Bullshit."

A surprised laugh spills out. "What?"

"You heard me. Bullshit, Harper."

"You haven't read it."

He raises one brow, as if to say, *Whose decision was that?*

Part of me still can't believe he asked. It's above and beyond encouragement. Then again, *everything* Drew seems to do is above and beyond.

I look away, setting some record for cowardly gestures. I didn't think I hid from what scared me. Now, I think I've just never encountered anything that terrifying. Losing my dad just happened. I never had any choice or role in it.

"It's only a hobby," I tell him. "Nothing important."

I hate the words as they leave my mouth. Not because they're a lie. They're true. I sit down and type when I want to escape the chaos in my head. It's like talking with an old friend, someone you know so well because you created them.

I hate the words because they sound like my mom and Amelia. The two of them have always been the logical, reasonable family members.

My dad and I were the reckless dreamers by comparison.

I thought we were the ones living life to the fullest. The ones who saw the beauty in the chaos. And then it got ruined in a way I'll never fully recover from, no matter how much time passes.

Drew switches to paddling on the other side of the canoe, making up for my utter lack of participation.

We should have taken out a kayak instead.

And something in his steady green gaze makes me answer his original question. "It's set on a cruise ship."

"A cruise ship?"

"Yeah. I've never felt the slightest interest in going on one, so I figured it was a safe setting."

"And there's a murder?"

"Yeah. On the second night, after the trivia game. They're all stuck on the boat with a killer."

"Are there obvious suspects?"

"Three. But they all get alibis…eventually."

"Solid alibis?"

"What are you, a cop?" I hook one leg over the side of the canoe, letting my toes drag through the water.

Drew smirks. "Tell me the alibis."

So, I do. I talk through the events that have only existed in my head for months, ever since I started scribbling down random thoughts when I was bored.

Part of me feels ridiculous during the monologue.

Drew is famous. There are people with a poster of him plastered on their walls. Who buy jerseys with his name on the back. And maybe it's a false sense of importance.

But it exists, and here I am, spouting made-up stories to him. More self-conscious than I've ever felt in my life, certain I'm boring him. But Drew looks totally invested as I talk, and that keeps me going despite my uncertainty.

By the time we reach a cove of the lake, the sun has fully risen. It dapples and refracts off the smooth surface, flat and calm from the lack of activity. Drew pulls his paddle in from the water and drops it on the floor of the canoe. Mine never made it into the water to begin with.

"You remember how to do this?" Drew asks me, pulling the tackle box out from beneath his seat.

"Sort of. I wasn't the most attentive student."

"Shocking."

I roll my eyes, watching as he grabs the pole and ties a hook to the end of the line, big hands moving with surprising ease.

"You've been fishing before?"

"My dad and I would go out on Fernwood Lake sometimes. And the two of us went on a salmon fishing trip up in Alaska a few summers ago."

"Your mom didn't go?" I have some fascination with Drew's family. Mainly how they look so functional and happy, compared to mine.

"No. She prefers a pacifist approach when it comes to animals. Gutting fish isn't really her thing."

"Probably a lot of birds in Alaska, though."

Drew laughs lightly, adding a bobber and bait to the end of the pole. "Yeah, there are." He tugs the string tight and glances at me. "You want to cast out?"

I kind of do, only because he made all this effort and I haven't participated much. "You might end up with a hook to the face," I warn.

"I've got good reflexes and a high pain tolerance. It'll be fine."

Drew spins the rod so the handle is closer to me, then extends it until it's close enough to grasp. "Remember how to pinch the line and snap it?"

I nod. Surprisingly, I do.

"Okay. Go for it."

I reel the line out a few inches, pinch it with my thumb and index finger, and then cast out, releasing the line so it sails through the air and lands about twenty feet away with a quiet *plop*.

Drew cheers, and I mock shush him.

"You'll scare all the fish away."

He laughs, leaning back and stretching his legs like he plans to be here for a while. And I don't mind that idea at all.

There's none of the impatience that used to permeate these trips when I was younger, anxious to eat breakfast or go swimming instead. I wish I could go back in time and tell myself to savor those moments. That they'd be limited. But I can't, so I focus on enjoying this instead. Time with Drew is also finite.

He asks me questions about New York as we sit and hope a fish will bite. About Olivia and my apartment and my job. He even asks me about guys I've dated, looking pleased when I admit there's never been anyone I was really serious about.

I'm not brave enough to ask him some of the same questions.

Because despite the comment he made about hockey being his main priority, I can't figure out how he's possibly single.

Midway through listing off some of the artists I've met through working at Empire Records, I feel a tug on the line.

"I got something!" And I sound way more excited about fishing than I thought was possible.

I jerk the rod, setting it before I start reeling it in. Drew's eyes are focused on the water, both of us watching the ripples as the line grows shorter. And then the hook emerges from the water, a small fish flapping and thrashing as droplets fly back into the lake.

"Holy shit. I caught a fish."

Drew leans over, snagging the fish and slipping it off the hook. "It's too small to keep."

I nod, not really interested in watching him kill it even if it was large enough to eat. And *I'm* definitely not going to cut its head off or watch it suffocate.

Instead of throwing it back into the lake like I'm expecting, he holds it out toward me. "Here."

I drop the handle of the pole. "What am I supposed to do with it?"

"Just hold it for a second. I want to take a picture."

"A picture of what?" I make a face as my hand connects with wet scales, the fish still wriggling in a desperate attempt to get back in the water.

"You and the fish," Drew replies in a *duh* tone.

"Hurry up then." My voice gets progressively higher with each word as the fish keeps squirming. I'm increasingly concerned it's going to work its way out of my fist and right into my lap.

"Smile."

I give Drew my best scowl, and he laughs.

My lips turn up in response, glancing at the floundering animal once before I throw it back into the lake. My dad would have been proud. I never managed to catch anything any of the times he took me and Amelia out.

I dip my hand in the lake, rinsing off any residue from the fish. The water feels perfect, refreshing, but not cold. Aside from the day I went waterskiing, I haven't been swimming at all this week. With the wedding tomorrow, I'm rapidly running out of time.

Impulsively, I shimmy Drew's hoodie off. He's rummaging through the tackle box but looks up when he catches my movement, one eyebrow rising as his eyes skim across my body. I can feel everywhere he looks, his gaze brushing across my skin like the whisper of a flame. Not long enough to burn, but enough to tingle.

The air temperature is about the same as the lake water, the sun hidden behind clouds, and the night's chill still lingering.

"Will jumping out of the canoe capsize it?"

"Possibly."

I smirk and stand, then leap overboard.

"And you thought *I* was going to scare away the fish?" Drew calls to me as soon as I emerge from the lake, slicking my hair out of my face and pulling in a deep breath of oxygen.

I wink at him. "Whoops."

I tread water even though it's shallow enough to stand, tilting my head back so my hair fans out in the cool water. I'm hoping Drew will jump in with me, but I'm not sure he will.

Most people give in to me or get exasperated.

Drew does neither. Last night, he made me wait. This morning, he turned me down. But I've never once felt rejected or like I was *too much* around him.

The second splash startles me. My head snaps upright, my

pulse pounding wildly as I watch him swim toward me with quick, efficient strides.

"No point in fishing if there are no fish, right?" Drew stops about a foot away from me, a wry smile on his face.

"It took almost an hour for me to get a single bite. This doesn't seem like much of a hot spot."

He chuckles, the sound reverberating in my chest. "Yeah, I guess not."

I swim closer, one of my hands brushing his beneath the water. The water doesn't dull the sensation. I feel that slight touch everywhere. "Thank you," I tell him. "For getting me to do this. It means a lot, and it's something I wouldn't have done without you. And…I'm sorry for being such a grump this morning."

"I already knew you weren't a morning person, Harper." Drew smiles. "Thank you for telling me. Trusting me. Coming with me."

His words warm me despite the cool water. They also make my skin itch, like it's tightening over my bones. This feels right. But also intense. Unexpected.

"If it were physically possible, I'd give you a blow job right now. And I *hate* giving blow jobs."

Drew lets out a startled laugh. "Christ, Harper."

I have no idea why Amelia thinks I have a way with words. Which reminds me that I still haven't written the speech I'm supposed to deliver tomorrow.

Worry about that prospect dissipates when Drew's hands find me under the water, lifting my feet from the sandy bottom. His palms spread across my ribs possessively, pulling me closer to him and supporting my weight effortlessly.

"What are you doing?" I whisper as he pulls my hair to the side and then tugs on my bikini strap, exposing more of my left breast and then finally my nipple.

"You can't say shit like that and think I won't react."

"Maybe I wanted you to."

"Good."

And then he's kissing me. I moan into it, arousal pulsing through me as his mouth slants over mine. I *love* kissing Drew. Nothing I've ever experienced comes close to this thrill. I would rank it above oxygen or water as an essential to live.

I gasp, unintentionally severing our mouths' connection, when I feel his finger stroke my slit through the flimsy fabric of my bikini bottoms. He tugs the material to the side impatiently, skillfully stroking before slipping a finger inside of me.

Gibberish falls out of my mouth as I ride his hand, a spark of pain mixing with the overwhelming pleasure when he grazes my exposed nipple with his teeth.

"Is this what you wanted, Harper? Is this what you were so desperate for this morning, lying with your legs spread wide open? Trying to get me to fill this perfect pussy with my tongue or my cock?"

If I could manage to form actual words right now, I would say that his fingers are also a fabulous option I'd take at any time. Because they're wreaking havoc on my body and on my thoughts, rubbing a perfect spot that has me barreling toward my third orgasm in twelve hours with a loud cry.

Drew doesn't kiss me when I come, the way he did last night. He watches me moan with a smug smirk, listening to the call of his name as it echoes across the calm surface of the lake. He doesn't stop fingering me until I'm totally spent—my limbs like limp, useless noodles. If he wasn't holding me, there's a chance I'd slip underwater and drown in satisfaction.

My hand trails down the bumps of his abdomen slowly until I reach the top of his swim trunks. I slip my fingers into his trunks, grasping his cock and tugging it out.

Drew's jaw tenses, a low groan filling the silence between us. "You don't have to."

"I know. I want to."

I wish I could see him, not just feel him. Wish I could take him in my mouth. But I settle for tracing the head of his dick and fondling his balls before beginning to jack him off. His head tips back with a louder groan, some of his inhibitions disappearing and a little control slipping.

I can feel each ridge and every vein of his penis as it grows even more erect, pulsing in my hand before his release spills out, washing away into the lake.

"You ever hook up with anyone in Fernwood?" Drew asks suddenly.

"No. Why…did you?" I ask.

Drew shakes his head. "No."

Fernwood Lake is where we spent most of the summers in Port Haven. Horny teenagers still living with their parents would usually spend most of their nights down there. I know Katherine lost her virginity in a cove similar to this.

I never saw the appeal—until now.

Drew tows the canoe to the rocky shore so we can climb back in. I pull his sweatshirt on, and he yanks his shirt on before we set back in the direction of Camp Basswood.

We don't talk much on the return trip. It's a comfortable silence, not an awkward one. Like two people who enjoy being in each other's company and don't feel the need to say something just to avoid it.

I paddle this time, but neither of us is in much of a rush. They're slow, languid strokes that glide us across the quiet lake. In contrast, the dock of Camp Basswood is busy. Preparations are already underway for the rehearsal dinner tonight; hired help setting up tents and tables, while extended family fill the cabins.

Drew steers us right into the sandy inlet, climbing out first and then helping me out. There's another moment where we're basically just holding hands and standing in the shallows until it's interrupted by my sister's voice.

"Morning, guys!"

I turn to see Amelia standing, holding up two strands of lights and critically eyeing the trunk of the massive pine closest to the dock.

"Where have you been?" she asks, flicking her gaze away from the tree and toward us instead.

"Fishing," I reply.

Amelia's eyes narrow suspiciously, probably because she knows how much I used to hate fishing, and I can feel the huge, stupid smile stretching my cheeks right now. "Huh."

Drew drags the canoe out of the water and toward the shed.

I walk over to Amelia, deciding this is as good of a time as any to test our new truce. "I mentioned to Drew we used to go out with Dad sometimes. So…he took me."

Amelia nods slowly. "I'm really glad you brought him, Harper," she tells me. "I haven't seen you this happy since…" She swallows as we both silently fill in the words. "You seem happy."

"My baby sister is getting married. Of course I'm happy."

"I don't mean happy for me. I mean, *happy*, Harper."

I'm a good liar. It's not a trait I'm proud of or embarrassed by.

But I feel guilty all of a sudden for deceiving Amelia when it comes to me and Drew. For making her think I showed up with my soul mate instead of a guy I hadn't seen in over a decade and hardly knew. Because that's the truth, no matter what happened last night. Or this morning.

"Thanks," I say, breaking eye contact and focusing on the lights instead. "What are you doing?"

"Deciding which lights to string up around the yard. Which set do you like?"

Amelia holds up both hands. I glance from one to the other, wondering how offended she'll be if I say I can't see any difference between the two sets. One is more rounded, I guess? Maybe?

"I like them both."

"Not helpful."

"Okay, fine. Left."

She brightens. "Those are the ones I was leaning toward. Can you help me string them up?"

"Yeah. Of course."

Drew emerges from the shed, holding the two thermoses. He glances over at me, winding lights with my sister, and winks before starting up the path toward the house. Giving us this moment together and silently understanding.

And, yeah, we're temporary.

But I really wish we weren't.

CHAPTER FOURTEEN

DREW

After days of relative quiet, it's strange to see Camp Basswood filled with so many people. I'm not really sure when they all appeared. Sometime between Harper and me returning from our early morning fishing trip and me putting on this suit. Amid helping to carry chairs and set up tables.

I tug at the collar around my neck. It's been months since I wore a button-down shirt, and I can't say I missed it. I'm definitely more of a faded T-shirt guy.

I drain the rest of my beer and toss it in a nearby recycling bin. The blue boxes are scattered throughout the yard, next to trash cans that hold the remains of dinner. Traditional Maine fare —lobster shells and corn husks and potato skins. Remnants from the kind of meal you need to experience to appreciate.

Tables fill the lawn that used to be empty, the twinkling lights that took hours to wrap around every trunk reflecting off the surface of the lake. I'm standing with Jared and Luke, playing cornhole, not really registering a word of the good-natured taunts getting tossed around by the guys.

I'm fully focused on Harper, who's dancing with Claire and Willa across the yard on the makeshift dance floor.

And I'm not the only one looking, which pisses me off and is also confusing. Because I can honestly say I've never gotten possessive of a woman in my life.

Until now, I guess.

Harper's dress is strapless. Too much in every way. Too short. Too sexy. Too tempting. The tiny lights strung everywhere reflect off the silky fabric she's wearing, making it shimmer. Her hair bounces around in a riot of dark caramel, as exuberant as her waving arms and bouncing breasts.

I'm not sure when this happened. When a glance of Harper captured me in a way the direct attention of anyone else can't manage.

It becomes obvious when I glance at Theo, who's joined the group and apparently been trying to ask me something more than once. He and Jared exchange an amused glance before he repeats, "You in?"

"In…"

"For the boat ride. Amelia wants us to go out with our families."

I stare at him, not catching how that includes me. As nice as he is, I met Theo a few days ago. *Family* is a stretch.

"You're here with Harper…" Theo says. "So, I thought…"

I'm not sure what he thought, and he doesn't elaborate. Harper and I haven't put any labels on our fake relationship, let alone any reality. But us showing up here together certainly suggests something.

My eyes drift back toward her. Harper is no longer out on the dance floor. She's standing on the periphery, talking with her mother. All the earlier exuberance is missing, sucked away in her tense posture and crossed arms.

"Right." I swallow. "Sure."

"Great!" Theo's response is enthusiastic.

It would be flattering if I wasn't getting the sense he might just want an impartial participant along on the journey. I barely spoke to his parents and haven't spoken to Francesca at all, so I have no gauge of how awkward this outing might be.

I follow Theo through the crowd. Almost every other person we pass stops him to share congratulations. Then, seven times out of ten, they recognize me. Progress is slow, in other words.

By the time we reach the dock, everyone else is already assembled. Alex is on the boat with his and Theo's parents, who I met while appetizers were being passed around. They're just as quiet and smiley now as they were earlier.

Harper is standing next to the Adirondack chair she sat in last night, alongside Amelia and Francesca. A man with a full head of salt-and-pepper hair stands next to them.

Simon Parker, I assume.

My parents were invited to his and Francesca's wedding, which took place about a year after Paul died. Harper has never shared many details about her stepfather with me. I'm struggling to remember if she's mentioned him at all actually, so I feel a strong burst of trepidation as I approach the small group, wondering what I'm stepping into.

Francesca's gaze finds me first, sharp and calculating. She gives no indication of whether or not she finds my presence unexpected as she greets me with a nod. "Drew. Nice to see you again."

"You too," I reply, my eyes automatically seeking out Harper. There's relief in her expression in response to my appearance, and it soothes some of the tightness in my chest.

I walk right up to her, brushing our fingers together. Harper grabs my hand and holds it tight, the contact relaxing us both, before she lifts my arm and drapes it around her shoulders, folding herself into my body until we're flush, her hand still clutching to mine. It's like a warm blanket settling around me, the jealous pinch in my chest from earlier smoothing out.

Shock flashes across Francesca's expression before she regains her composure.

The man beside her smiles as he holds a hand out. "Simon Parker. Nice to meet you."

I meet his gesture, giving him a firm shake. "Drew Halifax. Nice to meet you as well."

A furrow appears between his eyes, bushy gray eyebrows pulling together. "You're...football?"

"Hockey, sir."

"*Hockey*. Of course." Simon chuckles, the sound laced with uncertainty. He radiates the same awkwardness as a fish out of water, his fingers fiddling with the cuff of his suit jacket and his throat bobbing with extra swallows.

"You guys ready?" Theo calls from the boat.

"Yep!" Amelia replies, walking toward the edge of the dock. Her voice is too chipper, projecting the reluctance of someone who's realized they might have made a miscalculation.

Simon and Francesca follow closely behind her.

Harper lets go of my hand and grips my shoulder instead, leaning down as her foot lifts. "My feet are killing me," she murmurs, one heel hitting the wood with a dull thud.

"Theo kind of cornered me. I don't have to come," I whisper back.

"No, you should. Come." Her second shoe falls with a clank. "Unless you don't want to?"

"Well, I was winning at cornhole..."

Harper's teeth sink into her bottom lip, and it's distracting as hell.

"Kidding. Let's go."

It feels like everyone's attention is focused on us as we approach the speedboat. Especially when we climb on board and take seats. I settle down onto the vinyl, still warm from the sun rapidly dropping down the horizon.

Harper sinks into my lap like it's a normal occurrence.

Even if it were one, my body would be reacting this way. Blood rushes south, my slacks too tight and constricting.

The worst part about this dress she's wearing is the way I know exactly what's underneath. How I'm dying to see it all again, unobstructed by lake water.

There's no way Harper is oblivious to my erection digging into her ass. But she carries on a normal conversation with Theo's mother as we skim across the lake while I stare out at the water, enjoying the rush of wind as we fly across the lake.

I resigned myself to living wherever I had the opportunity to play a long time ago. Back when I was an eager kid with a big dream, no lengths seemed too far. Now, I'm a lot closer to thirty than twenty. Most of my college friends have settled down. A few are engaged, a couple married.

There's no void in my life.

But I'm starting to see the downs that contrast the ups. Wishing that I could choose to live on the East Coast for most of the year. Wanting to be close to my parents and to have a place like the properties we're passing, nestled into the shoreline of the lake with this view always one glance away. Wondering what Harper would say if I told her that I wanted more of this—us. Considering if I'm capable of prioritizing a relationship.

Harper's face turns into my neck, her contented sigh filling my chest with affection. "What are you thinking about?" she whispers.

"That I'm really glad I came."

"Me too."

My arms tighten around her, holding her close enough that I can feel the rise and fall of her chest with each breath. We don't separate until Theo parks the boat back alongside the dock.

The party is still going strong, lights and music shining brightly through the darkness. But I want nothing more than to go somewhere alone with the brunette who was just curled up in my lap.

Harper steps off the boat, making a face at her heels as she leans down and picks them up. "I really don't want to put these back on."

"Then, climb on." I turn, offering her my back.

Harper doesn't hesitate, leaping up and winding her legs around my waist. If I wasn't expecting it, I would have stumbled. We walk like that off the dock and back toward the party until we're off the rough wood and into the grass.

"Hey, they're back," Jared calls. "Come on, Drew!"

"I think someone has a crush." Harper giggles in my ear. "If you ghost him once you're gone, he'll be crushed."

The first reference to the rapidly approaching end of this trip, and it offers me no insight into how *she* feels about it. Which, no offense to Jared, I'm far more interested in.

I don't really respond, not sure how to. Harper slides off my back and studies my expression, her head tilted like the angle will help her decipher it.

"Drew!" Luke this time.

I nod toward the game. "Want to play?"

"Uh, yeah. Sure."

I offer a hand, and she grabs it. Side by side, we walk toward the piles of beanbags and two boards set up to the right of the dance floor.

It's another couple of hours until the final guests leave, heading toward the parked line of cars on either side of the dirt driveway.

Harper and I walk inside with the rest of the wedding party, who are all still staying in the main house. Everyone is too tired for conversation or for any of the group activities that have filled past evenings.

We retire quickly, smothering yawns as doors get closed up and down the hallway. Harper walks into our room first, heading straight into the bathroom.

I take a seat on the side of the bed, running a hand through my hair and trying to figure out how to broach this topic.

Want to go on a date with me doesn't sound right, especially considering I have no clue when or where said date would take place.

It's also too minimal.

It doesn't convey the big, sweeping declaration I want to make. Harper needs to get that this is out of the ordinary for me. That, for the first time, I'm not elated about the start of the season rapidly approaching. I'm reliving last year, trying to figure out where flights to New York and FaceTimes could fit in during time that used to be filled with nothing but hockey.

Part of me is also bracing for rejection. Because when I asked Harper about her exes this morning, she was blasé.

It was reassuring, knowing she's not hung up on anyone. But it's also concerning, knowing she doesn't rank a relationship as a priority. It's how I've always been too.

How I don't feel about her.

I've been distracted this week, squeezing in a run most mornings, but not following the stricter routine I've stuck to every other off-season. I should be going to a gym to lift weights.

Avoiding any sugar or alcohol. Instead, I've forgone all that and actually relaxed. Which, while not good for my body, has been great for my head.

I'm not sure if Harper has made any changes this week, though. Not certain I'm enough to rock her routine. I know she feels *something* for me. But it could be fleeting. A fling.

The bathroom door slides open, and Harper steps out, her face scrubbed pink and makeup-free. I sit up straighter as she approaches, still in her dress.

I should say something. I know I should.

Tomorrow will be even more hectic, from start to end, and then we're both leaving on Sunday. The window to discuss anything is quickly closing. And if she touches me or takes off her clothes, rational thoughts are going to disappear very quickly.

But I'm already transfixed, watching her saunter toward me in that fucking dress.

My phone vibrates on the bed with an incoming call.

I glance down at the screen and suppress a groan. *Fuck.*

"Who's Cat?"

I sigh, another swear echoing in my head with more emphasis. *Of course* she saw it. "My ex," I admit.

"Oh." For a single syllable, Harper sure manages to pack a lot into the word. Too much to decipher. "Do you guys talk often?"

"No." I stand and start unbuttoning my button-down, sick of wearing the starched shirt. "We don't."

"If you don't want to talk about it…"

I *don't* want to talk about Cat.

Not at all, and especially not right now. But I also know if I say that, Harper will make assumptions. Inaccurate ones.

She didn't ask *me* about anyone I've dated earlier, and I'm clinging to the hope it's because she was jealous, not that she doesn't care.

"It's fine. It's just..." *Weird*, I silently finish.

Cat—every woman in the past—feels distant when I'm around Harper. Like part of a different lifetime. Like there was a before her, and now, I'm permanently lost in the after.

"She wants to get back together?" Harper's tone is light and airy.

I study her as she pulls pajamas out of her suitcase, trying to discern if her indifference is genuine or fake. The only indication she's more upset than she's letting on is the fact that the pajamas are a silky patterned set. The kind she said she doesn't actually sleep in.

I look away as she changes. Ogling her while we have the closest thing to an argument we've ever had feels wrong.

"I don't know," I answer honestly. "She's best friends with the wife of one of my teammates. I went to their New Year's Eve party a year and a half ago, and Cat was there, visiting. We hit it off right away. But then she left, and I stayed. We kept in touch for the next few months. And we never made the playoffs last season. For the rest of the spring and summer, we were together. But then it...it didn't work out. Probably my fault."

I'm not going to sugarcoat what a relationship with me would be like to Harper. I know she has no clue what my schedule consists of on a day-to-day basis. And if there's any chance of this thing between us going anywhere, she needs to know what she's getting into. I *won't* be able to prioritize her sometimes.

Harper walks over, wearing a pink sleep set, patterned with red flowers. "You couldn't have messed anything up too badly if she's calling you. Tell me why it didn't work out. I can offer a female perspective—if you're looking for one..." She smiles, and again, I can't tell if it's genuine or not. Which bothers me. A lot. "You should get something out of this week too."

"I'm getting *plenty* out of it, Harper." There's a bite to my voice, which she doesn't react to.

Harper ignores me. She doesn't *believe* me, and it has me second-guessing everything. Wondering if I've blown up amazing sex and a romantic atmosphere into something much bigger than it really is. And forget my feelings. I've obviously overestimated hers.

"What happened between you guys?" she asks, giving my confidence another wallop when she takes a seat on the bed, appearing totally unbothered.

I exhale, trying to keep my cool. Something Harper often makes difficult. It's just usually for the better, not worse.

"It just felt like we didn't know how to actually spend time together. Like we could only be around each other for a little while, and then it was just…awkward. I ended it when the season started last fall, and she seemed fine with it. We text now and then, but we haven't *talked* at all, really."

I don't mention that those texts are always initiated by Cat. Or that the latest one mentioned an upcoming trip to Seattle to visit her best friend, which is why she's probably calling. Or that everything that felt off with her before feels wrong now. That the only woman I want to spend time with is the one I'm looking at.

I hope Harper is at least hearing what I'm not explicitly stating. That, with her, it's *not* like that. That there's no awkwardness or boredom.

We're close to the end of this, but I don't want it to be the end of us.

"Maybe you should," Harper suggests after a moment of thought.

My stomach sinks to the floor as I pull off my shirt and drop it on the hardwood.

I wanted to rearrange the face of every guy checking her out earlier. And here she is, suggesting I talk with an ex who wants to get back together.

That's not being on two different pages.

That's two different books entirely.

I step away from the bed, needing to move. "You finished in the bathroom?"

"I—yeah."

"Okay." I stride into the small, attached bathroom, sliding the door shut behind me a little too roughly.

For the first time since I arrived, I wish I had my own room here. Wish I had space.

It's too hard to think with Harper's presence everywhere. The bathroom smells like her, a trace of flowery perfume lingering in the air. The counter next to the sink is littered with lotions and face washes and makeup. The bikini she wore on our fishing trip this morning is hanging off the towel rack.

I clench the counter on either side of the sink, focusing on deep inhales and long exhales. I'm frustrated. Confused. And mostly…disappointed.

Up until right now, I didn't realize how attached I'd gotten to the idea of Harper. To our paths not diverging again.

Not knowing when I'll see her again—*if* I'll see her again—bothers me. Our only remaining connection is the two cottages that sit side by side on Ashland Avenue. One my parents are probably selling soon. The other one filled with painful memories.

I doubt Harper will go back there again. And I don't blame her. If it were me, I'm not sure I would have been able to go back once.

Which leaves me with…nothing.

I'm expecting Harper to be in bed when I step out of the bathroom. She's not. She's lingering by the door in her bright pajamas, clutching the notebook she was writing in down at the water.

"Um, I'm going to go downstairs and work on my speech, okay?"

I feel my brow furrow. "Why are you going downstairs?"

"I need a light on. I don't want to keep you up."

"It's fine, Harper. I don't mind."

I doubt I'll be getting much sleep tonight, regardless. I'll be lying awake, replaying everything that happened today.

Mainly this morning, when we seemed to be headed in a very different direction than the awkwardness currently hovering in the room. I'll have to skip over the scene in the lake since we obviously won't be having sex tonight, and I'm annoyingly turned on by the sight of her in flower-patterned pajamas. I'm turned on by anything she wears, it seems.

Harper shakes her head. "A change of scenery will be good. I'll probably fall asleep in here, and I don't want to go to bed until I finish this." She waves the notebook around like some sort of sparkler. "Good night."

"Night." My response is wooden, and she catches it, posture tensing visibly. I'm hoping she'll walk over here.

Instead, she flashes me a smile and a quick wave, then slips out into the hallway. The door closes after her.

I release a long sigh, leaning down to pick up the white button-down. When I straighten, I ball it up in my fist and then hurl it away as far as I can manage. It lands in a heap on the couch. My aim is as bad as my concentration.

I strip down to my boxers and climb into bed, leaving on one of the lamps for whenever Harper comes to bed. When I check my phone, there's a text from Cat in addition to a missed call.

Cat: *Hey, Drew! Just wanted to let you know I'll be in Seattle September 6–10. Would love to see you!!!*

I shut off my phone, sigh, roll over, and attempt to fall asleep.

CHAPTER FIFTEEN

HARPER

When I wake up in the morning, the first thing I do is roll over to look at the opposite side of the bed.

It's empty. Drew is out running.

Or he left.

But I don't actually believe he would. No matter what happens between us—hot sex or the awkwardness of last night—I don't think Drew would leave unless I asked him to. He wouldn't back out before the wedding is over. And part of me resents that complete confidence.

It would be easier, simpler, and a hell of a lot clearer if I could just write him off as a distraction.

Trust isn't something that I hand out easily. And it's nothing I can blame on my dad. I've always had a lot of people I call friends, but very few I truly consider ones.

I'm not sure when it happened, but Drew is firmly in the latter category.

I basically fled the room after learning about Cat, and I'm not proud of it. Cowardly behavior so different from how I usually act around men that it's almost laughable. One of the security guards for the skyscraper I work in has been asking me out for months. It's almost become a joke between us, but there are uncomfortable encounters too, when I can tell he's serious. I walk past him every weekday anyway—often multiple times—instead of taking the back entrance and avoiding him.

Last night, I tiptoed downstairs to work on the speech I *still* need to finish—like a jealous girlfriend—rather than face how much it bothered me to learn Drew's ex is trying to get back together with him.

Cat.

I wonder what that's short for. Catarina, maybe. She sounds worldly and glamorous and like she's part of his world. Friends with his teammate's wife. She's probably been to a hockey game before. Probably been to Drew's hockey games before.

And that's where the *friend* label gets blurry. Because you want your friends to be happy. You want them to find someone who makes them happy.

But the thought of Drew finding a woman who makes him happy doesn't make me feel *happy*. It makes me feel nauseous.

Learning about Cat's existence has forced me to confront the reality that my crush on Drew might not be ancient history after all. That this week of talking with him and relying on him and sleeping next to him is doing more than just distracting me from what I've been dreading.

That this week *ending* is now what I'm dreading. Waking up tomorrow morning and packing up to leave won't be the relief I expected.

It will be...sad.

I have no idea how to process that. Especially today, of all the days. I can already hear the commotion downstairs, slamming doors and shouts as people prepare for the ceremony and reception set to take place soon. My little sister is getting married today.

With a sigh, I roll out of bed and head into the bathroom. After going through my usual morning routine, I pad back toward the couch that's turned into a temporary closet.

The bridal party is supposed to have hair and makeup done right after breakfast, so I don't bother to do either. I just pull on a pair of athletic shorts and then sift through my suitcase for a shirt that I can pull off over my head without ruining the hairdo, per Amelia's instructions.

My eyes fall to the white button-down Drew wore last night, which lies in a heap on the couch. Without consciously deciding to, I reach for it. The smooth cotton brushes my skin like a caress. It smells like Drew—a smoky, spicy scent I memorized without meaning to.

A recurring pattern. I didn't *mean* to do anything where he's concerned, and yet here I am. Pulling on his shirt because it not only adheres to the dress code laid out in the email Amelia sent out to the bridal party—no shirts that could disturb hair and no changing into our dresses until an hour before the ceremony—but also because wearing it soothes a little of the raging jealousy that's simmered in my chest since I saw that call on his phone.

I tuck the oversize shirt into the hem of my shorts, not caring that I probably look ridiculous, and head downstairs.

Predictably, the chaos I could hear from the room is even more overwhelming downstairs. Strangers rush around with stacks of tablecloths and bouquets of flowers and folding chairs.

I head into the kitchen first, which has become routine. There are blueberry scones on the counter and a few inches of coffee remaining in the pot.

A couple of minutes later, I head outside with my breakfast. It's a perfect day—clear and sunny and warm. The weather this entire week has been sublime. No rain since the storm the night I ran into Drew. If I believed in signs, maybe that's one.

Rather than sitting on the deck, I decide to head down to the water. Tomorrow, I'll be headed back to the city. And while New York has its own special energy, this is what soothes my soul. Natural, not manufactured. The sun-warmed grass and the smooth stretch of the lake just past it. A view I'll miss as much as the man thoughtful enough to leave a light on for me last night.

I want to inhale it. Soak it in. Stamp it in my permanent memory.

And I'm so focused on my destination—on not spilling any coffee or dropping my scone—that I don't see him until he's right in front of me.

I screech to a stop, my eyes shamelessly dropping from Drew's face to take in the mesh shorts and T-shirt he's wearing. Avoiding his gaze and appreciating a different view. Heat spreads across my skin slowly, like a wildfire gathering strength as it finds new kindling.

One of my biggest regrets about my avoidance last night? I *really* wanted to have sex with him.

"Hey."

"Hey," Drew replies, glancing at Jared and Rowan, who are both sweaty and breathing heavily.

Drew looks barely winded.

"Morning, Harper. I need some water," Jared pants before he keeps walking.

After a beat of hesitation, Rowan follows. Leaving us alone. Well, not *alone*. There are about a dozen people milling around the yard, carrying boxes and moving tables as they prepare for the wedding set to take place in a matter of hours.

I focus on my destination—the dock—then glance at Drew. He's looking past me, at the house, and it feels like a metaphor.

Maybe he was really *that* bored in Port Haven. Maybe he's really *that* selfless of a person. Maybe I sounded *that* pathetic on the porch when I told him about this wedding, cheap tequila in hand.

He's here as a favor. As a way to shake up the end of his summer before returning to his routine.

The exact reason he came doesn't really matter. He's leaving tomorrow, same as me. Looking ahead while I'll keep glancing backward.

We'll go back to our lives. Me in New York, treading water. Him in Seattle, listening to thousands of strangers chant his name every night.

Do hockey teams play every night? I don't even know. The chants could only be once a week. Either way, it's very different than my any day of the week. And my total lack of hockey knowledge seems like another sign I don't belong in his world.

"Nice day for a wedding," Drew comments, glancing around at everyone setting up.

I swallow. "Yeah, it is."

His eyes—a shade of green I can't describe but will never forget—meet mine. "Are you okay?"

"Yeah." I nod, then repeat, "Yeah. Today will just be…a lot."

Understanding bleeds across Drew's expression.

Today *will* be a lot. On top of the normal stress and emotions attached to a wedding, there will be a gaping hole where my dad should be. Walking Amelia down the aisle. Sharing the second dance. All next to the lake he loved so much.

After our last conversation, I know it's something Amelia has thought about. Our mom too, probably. But the list might end there.

There's no telling how many of Amelia's friends or Theo's family have no idea there's someone missing. Who might think

Simon is our father, the way Lincoln assumed. There are no obvious physical traits that would suggest differently. We're like a television family, where you can squint and see similarities that aren't biologically accurate.

Drew's gaze lowers. For the first time, he appears to register what I'm wearing. Some mixture of surprise and satisfaction crosses his face. The first one isn't shocking. The second is unexpected.

I open my mouth, waiting for words to magically appear. Chew on the inside of my cheek—hard enough that it hurts. "So, I was—"

"Harper!" Claire calls.

"Har-per!" Savannah sings.

They both appear alongside me, shooting Drew smiles.

"Come on. We've been looking everywhere for you. The photographer showed up early. You're up first for hair and make-up," Savannah tells me.

I glance at my uneaten scone, my stomach grumbling. "I haven't eaten breakfast. Can't someone else go first?"

Claire shakes her head, red hair flying. "You're in all of the family photos. Amelia's almost finished, and then it's you."

"Okay." I exhale, then glance at Drew. "I'll see you later?"

It's a dumb question. I know I will.

But I need confirmation of it somehow. Right now. I need to apologize for my behavior last night. My behavior this whole week, actually. I've been a hot mess for most of it.

Not at all how I'd ordinarily act around a guy I'm interested in. And while people might say to act yourself around someone you like, they don't mean to be the worst version of yourself.

Tipsy, argumentative, insecure Harper has appeared a lot lately. And while I'm incredibly grateful to Drew for sticking by me through those moments, I also really wish I could rewind and do it all over again. For lots of reasons.

"You will," Drew confirms, not looking like he finds my question stupid.

And then, in a move I'm not expecting, he steps forward and kisses my temple. It's a sweet gesture, not a sexual one. But that's right where my mind plummets anyway, stomach flipping as his lips brush my skin. As I inhale the scent clinging to the shirt I'm wearing, mixed with sweat and sunshine.

"Nice shirt."

Butterflies replace hunger in my belly as he pulls away.

I'm barely aware of a distant, "Awww," from Claire or Savannah.

I'm locked in Drew's steady gaze, insanely tempted to forget about having my hair or makeup done and instead wanting to follow him upstairs and telling him to take it off of me if he wants the shirt back.

"Okay, lovebirds."

The plate and mug are taken from me, my hand is grabbed, and I'm towed away, Drew's grin the last thing I see before Savannah hauls me toward the row of cabins. There is a lot of muscle packed in her slender frame. I stumble twice from the force before she slows down. Claire trails behind, carrying my breakfast, as we traverse the dirt path covered with pine needles and approach the closest cabin.

I haven't surveyed the cabins up close. And I don't have a chance to now as Savannah drags me up the steps and inside.

The layout of the cabin is similar to the room I've been staying in but slightly larger. Bedroom, living area, and bathroom. All of the furniture has been shoved against the walls, the couch and the armchairs and the tables, in favor of a vanity that's been set up, complete with a swivel chair and one of those mirrors with all those bulbs outlining the edges.

Amelia is sitting in the chair now. Her makeup has been flawlessly applied, and her hair is half-pinned in an elaborate style. She gives me a small but genuine smile as I appear, the slightest twinge of nerves in her expression. I smile back, then take my breakfast back from Claire and take a seat on the couch.

Daphne, the wedding planner, darts in to ask Amelia something and then darts right back out. I focus on eating my scone and sipping my coffee, making a mental list of all the things I want to say to Drew.

I don't have any claim to him. If some woman realized she made a mistake in letting him go, who am I to stand in the way of that? Parts of our conversation last night are a blur. I was too busy acting unbothered to really listen to everything he was saying. But I'm pretty sure he said they were together for months. That's very different from one week.

It sounds like she never moved to Seattle, which I find interesting. Was she not willing to, or did he never ask?

Savannah plops down on the couch beside me, a blonde girl who looks to be in her late teens next to her. "Do you remember Lorelei, Harper?"

I stare at Savannah's younger sister, suddenly feeling old. Last time I saw her, I think she was in middle school, sporting braces and bangs. "Of course. How are you, Lorelei?"

"I'm good, thanks," she replies, smiling shyly.

"Lor came up with my parents this morning," Savannah tells me.

I nod. "Have you done anything fun this summer, Lorelei?"

Lorelei tucks a piece of hair behind one ear, her fingers twisting in her lap. Savannah and her sister look alike. When it comes to personalities, they are very different.

"I've done a few science camps. And I'm scooping ice cream at Frosty Dream," she adds, referring to the shop where I remember going as a kid. "Besides that, just working on college applications."

"She got all the brains in the family," Savannah mock whispers to me.

I smile, taking the final bite of scone and then finishing my coffee.

"Oh, get this. I mentioned to my dad that Drew is here, and he totally flipped out. I didn't even know he liked hockey. Did you know Dad watches hockey?" Savannah asks Lorelei.

"No," Lorelei responds. "Who's Drew?"

"Harper's boyfriend."

He's not my boyfriend is at the tip of my tongue. But I swallow it because as far as everyone here knows, he is.

"Here, I'll show you a photo," Savannah says, pulling her phone out and opening Instagram.

I watch her fingers fly across the screen as she types in Drew's name and taps on his account.

"How come you don't follow him?" she asks me absently. "You're not listed as a Mutual. Unlike…" She scrolls a little, then laughs. "Everyone else in the wedding party. Even Claire got over her sports aversion."

"Uh, I'm not—I don't—he doesn't follow me. We're not a social media couple." I stammer through an explanation.

Savannah gives me a weird look. "He follows you."

"What?"

She flashes me the phone. And there I am, at the very top of the sixty-eight people Drew follows.

"Huh."

I haven't posted anything in months. The other photos on my

account are mostly snaps from around the city. A couple shots of me and Olivia.

"You should probably change your profile to private," Savannah tells me. "If people find out you're dating Drew Halifax, you'll get tons of random people following you."

"I seriously doubt anyone will care."

Savannah snorts. "Sure." Then, she suddenly grins and clicks out of Drew's profile, navigating to another account. "This is what he looks like," she tells Lorelei, turning the phone toward her.

Lorelei's eyes widen to a comical size.

Has Drew done underwear ads or something?

"What photo are you showing her?" I ask, unable to bury my curiosity.

Savannah smirks and passes me her phone. It's a picture of Drew, posted to the Wolves account. He's at practice, laughing with a dark-haired guy who's half cut out of the frame. The main focus of the photo is Drew's abs, fully visible as he wipes his face with the front of his jersey.

It's...well, it's a lot.

"This got ten *million* likes?" I gape at the number displayed beneath the photo.

"Yep." Savannah pops the *P* as she takes back her phone. "Still think no one will care he's in a relationship?"

"You could have chosen a different photo," I mutter.

Savannah smirks. "This was posted by his team. It could have been from a fan account instead."

"He has a fan account?"

"Fan *accounts* actually." She giggles and nudges my shoulder. "Relax. It's obvious he's totally into you, Harper. We were just having some fun the other night, looking him up."

"Harper! Your turn!"

I stand and walk toward the makeup chair, still in a state of shock.

I knew Drew was famous. But it's never been spelled out in a way so easy and so overwhelming to comprehend.

Do paparazzi follow him around the way they do movie stars? Does he have security? Can he go to the grocery store without getting recognized?

I thought the biggest obstacle between us would be distance, if we pursued anything past today. But now, I'm wondering if I'm capable of being a support system to someone who's under the level of scrutiny Drew apparently is.

My worries last the length of time it takes to get my hair and makeup done. Then, I'm kicked out of the cabin to make room for the rest of the bridal party.

My mom is standing on the front porch when I step outside. She glances over, looking surprised to see me for some reason. It's not as if she didn't know I would be here.

"Interesting outfit."

That's the thing about my mom. She's nearly impossible to read. She can make compliments sound like threats. Stoicism can be sarcasm, coming from her.

"Just trying to abide by the bride's rules." My voice is neutral, just like hers.

She hums, glancing out at the lake. I wonder what she's thinking, being back here.

Memories of trips here have faded over time for me and Amelia. My parents bought the Port Haven house when I was twelve and Amelia was ten.

The years before then have distorted over time. Partly because I saw things differently as a kid and partly because I tried to cling to them too tightly as an almost adult.

If I were braver, I'd ask. But any fearlessness has never

extended to my mother. We've never been close, and time has only increased the gap, never closed it.

"I'm sorry, Harper."

I gape at her for a few seconds before she looks my way and I quickly shut my mouth. I search my memory for another time my mother has uttered those two words and come up entirely blank.

"I shouldn't have spoken to you that way, at the house."

Without her elaborating, I know exactly what way she's referring to and which house she means.

We've shared plenty of arguments at the fancy colonial she and Simon live in, just a few streets over from the house I grew up in. But she's talking about the Port Haven house. About last weekend, when she showed up the morning after Drew and I got drunk on the front porch.

"It's fine," I mutter, because I'm honestly not sure what else to say.

"Your father wanted you girls to inherit that house. You'll never be trespassing there. In fact…" Her throat bobs with a swallow. "We should probably discuss the deed. Now that Amelia is about to get married, you girls can—"

"I don't want it."

There's sadness in my mom's expression, seeping and spreading across her face like dye dropped in water. I'm stunned by its appearance. And also left wondering if I've missed it before. If, like Amelia said, I didn't want to see it before.

"He wanted you to have it."

"He should have thought about that before, then."

"He *wasn't* thinking, Harper." She shakes her head, clearing her throat and smoothing her immaculate updo. Shaking off the most sincerity I've heard from her in a long time. "I just wanted to make sure you weren't upset. This is Amelia's day."

"I'm not upset."

It's true. Tiffs with my mother are like hail hitting a window. Most of what she says bounces off me. It's exactly what the comment about Amelia does.

The implication that patching things up with me is a gift I'm only receiving on Amelia's behalf, as a way to preserve her special day, barely stings.

But instead of walking away the way I normally might, I keep studying my mother. There's a shiftiness in her eyes and an uneasiness to her expression. Something that makes me wonder if maybe I should be paying more attention to what my mother doesn't say than what she does. I'm familiar with how much easier excuses are than the truth.

I guess there's a slim chance my mother and I are more alike than I thought.

"You should go get changed," she tells me. "The photographer will be ready soon."

"Okay." I continue down the steps and up the path.

There's plenty of commotion everywhere, but I'm scanning for one person in particular.

No sign of Drew. Not in the yard and not in the house.

I change out of his shirt and my shorts into the blue dress Amelia selected for the bridesmaids. It's long, dragging on the floor before I slip heels on, with a high slit up one side.

When I get back down to the lakeshore, my mom, Amelia, and Simon are all standing around. I wait for some comment about holding everyone up, but it never comes.

Daphne hands me a bouquet of lavender and blue thistle, then begins giving the photographer instructions.

I head for my family, loosely grouped at the start of the dock.

They don't look like the complete picture I always thought they were without me. A trio of lawyers, driven and successful. Then me, the outsider.

They look *relieved* when I join them. Like I'm less of a divider and more of a missing piece.

"You…you look beautiful, Harper," my mom tells me, taking me off guard for the second time this morning.

My grip tightens around the bouquet I'm holding. "Thanks, Mom."

I wait for the inevitable moment where it falls apart. Where she mentions a son of her friend she'd like me to meet or suggests that I do something slightly different with my hair. I guess showing up with my own date and forty-five minutes with a professional stylist renders both of those typical comments irrelevant. I still wait for *something*.

But my mother just stares at me and smiles.

And I have no idea how to respond. Usually, this is when I'd have a snarky response ready for a passive-aggressive comment. But in answer to silence? To smiling? I have nothing prepared.

So, I just stare back, trying to figure out how many mimosas she's had. Then, I glance at Amelia, resplendent in her ivory wedding dress.

"You look stunning, Ames."

There's a suspicious sheen to Amelia's eyes when I use her childhood nickname. I rarely call her by it. Our dad often did. "Thanks, Harper."

"Okay," the photographer, Liza, calls. "Can I get everyone gathered together? Bride in the middle."

We do as instructed, huddling together as she tells Simon to scooch closer and has Amelia pull her veil to the side.

The shutter flashes over and over again, capturing hundreds of photos in a few minutes. All of us together. Me and Amelia. Amelia and my mom. Amelia and Simon.

Then, "Harper, what about one of you and your dad?"

I stare at the photographer, then glance at my mom. There's a tightness to her expression, like she's waiting for an inevitable explosion.

Me, I realize. I'm the explosion.

She's waiting for me to do the same thing I *always* do. Dodge dinner invitations and sulk during family meals. Make it obvious I won't be shoved into the *happy family* mold.

"That's not neces—" Amelia starts.

"Sure," I say. "That sounds nice."

I walk toward Simon, who appears as shell-shocked as everyone else.

I don't dislike Simon. I wish my mother had waited longer before getting remarried. But I know she was searching for some normalcy, for some comfort.

She and Simon worked together for over a decade in the district attorney's office. There were years of familiarity there. I've never seen them act like an overly loving couple, but they seem happy together. I used to think she married the first man she'd found, but now, I'm considering if maybe they've just always acted differently around me. Walking on the eggshells I spread.

I send Simon a small smile that he returns as I stop beside him.

He's never tried to insert himself into my life in any capacity, which I appreciate. He's always just been there, hovering in the background of my life and respecting the boundaries. And I feel bad for that all of a sudden. Wish I'd made more of an effort with him.

It's awkward, standing next to him, not touching, while Liza snaps photos. But it's also progress, a step forward after a lot of stagnancy.

When my eyes clear from the flashes and I look toward the

house, Drew is standing there in a gray suit. His hands are tucked in his pockets, and there's a proud smile on his face.

A rubber band tightens around my lungs, stealing all of my breath.

I want him to look at me like that forever.

I hold up the hem of my dress and pick my way across the grass toward where Drew is standing, only hesitating when I'm a few feet away. I let out an exaggerated wolf whistle, hoping that will remove any awkwardness lingering from last night. "Damn. You clean up pretty well, Halifax."

"Right back at you, Williams."

We smile at each other like fools. Like giddy teenagers heading to prom.

"Can I get a photo of you two?"

I glance at Liza, then back at Drew. He nods and holds out a hand. I take it, weaving our fingers together before walking toward the same spot on the dock where we've taken all the other photos.

CHAPTER SIXTEEN

DREW

I'm waiting for my drink at the bar when I see Harper stand from her spot at the center table. Her chair knocks into my empty one as she pushes it back into place. I came over here to grab a drink and got caught up in conversation with a college friend of Theo's.

All that's being passed around by servers is champagne. The only alcohol I appreciate the taste of are beer and whiskey. I'll make occasional exceptions—like drinking tequila with Harper. And now, I wish I'd stayed seated at the table, watching her walk toward the microphone set up for speeches.

"Here you go." The bartender sets a tumbler of amber liquid on the counter.

I thank him and drop a ten in the glass tip jar before glancing back at Harper.

One of the thin wisps of fabric holding her dress up has slipped. Harper tugs it back into place before she pulls the microphone from the stand, tapping the top of it once to make sure it's working.

A hush spreads before she's said a word. Harper has that presence about her. That magnetic draw that makes you pay attention.

Her blue eyes scan the crowd, widening slightly as she realizes everyone is already listening raptly.

They keep moving, looking, *searching*.

Until they land on *me*.

And *stop*.

There's a jolt that races through me when our gazes hold. When neither of us chooses to look away. My heart rate quickens as she smiles.

It's a small one. Secretive and knowing. Meant for me, not the rest of the audience.

"Woo," she exhales into the microphone. "Hi, everyone. Like most people, I love public speaking. So, I'm glad Alex took long enough with his speech for me to have a few drinks and fully prepare for this."

Laughter ripples around the room.

"I'm Harper. For those of you who don't know me, Amelia is my little sister. If you don't know Amelia, she's the one wearing white."

Harper glances to her left, where the bride and groom are sitting. Amelia is leaning forward, her chin resting on her hand as she looks at Harper. The hero worship in her gaze is so obvious; it's hard to imagine how Harper doesn't see it.

I don't think she does, though.

I don't think she ever has.

"Amelia is my little sister," she repeats. "But it's never felt like Amelia was younger than me. We're two years apart, and my earliest memory is age four. I don't remember what life was like *without* Amelia. As far back as I can remember, she's always been there. Starting with my earliest memories, playing on the swing set in the backyard or cutting the hair off our dolls and being surprised when it never grew back.

"I'd start kindergarten, or middle school, or high school, and then Amelia would be right behind me. And I was so glad that she was. Because...for those of you who don't know, Amelia is a perfectionist. She always makes it work, no matter how much she is juggling. Whether it was student council meetings or passing the bar while planning a wedding, she made it look effortless. Amelia has always been the one who's had life figured out. She would make honor roll every quarter. I'd forge a parent signature on the forgotten homework slip."

More laughter works its way through the crowd.

"She'd remember each holiday and everyone's birthday. And she'd always put my name on the card, even if I had no idea what the gift was. In high school, she'd cover for me when I snuck out late—as long as I drove her to school in the morning so she didn't have to take the bus.

"When Amelia and I were both home for Christmas, the same year she started law school, she was giddy. Way more excited about torts and contracts and civil procedure than anyone could be. So, I asked her if she had met a guy. She said there was a nice guy in her property law study group, but they were 'just friends.'" Harper smiles and tilts her flute of champagne in Theo's direction. "So, congrats on making it out of the friend zone, brother-in-law."

Alex punches Theo in the shoulder as more laughter echoes round the huge tent that was set up.

"I've always been in awe of you, Amelia," Harper continues. "Of your strength and your determination and your selflessness. I'll never think anyone is good enough for you, but I'm so glad you found Theo. I know you two will have a lifetime of happiness together, and I can't wait to witness it. And I know—"

For the first time, her voice catches, emotions spilling into the words.

"I know that if Dad were here tonight, he'd be smiling the widest of anyone. He would be so proud of you and so happy for you and so thrilled that this new chapter was beginning *here*. I imagine him floating out in that yellow canoe we were always convinced would sink, probably using that white handkerchief he lied to Mom about washing regularly."

Harper's blue eyes drift across the hushed crowd, then return to mine. She lifts her glass.

"To Amelia and Theo!"

Everyone echoes the toast. "To Amelia and Theo!"

Harper smiles and sets down the microphone. The band begins playing again, some poppy tune that sounds vaguely familiar.

My eyes stay locked on Harper. Amelia walks over to her and says something that has Harper smiling again and shrugging. Theo is right behind his new wife, giving Harper a hug.

"Hey. You're Drew Halifax, aren't you?"

I turn to see a tall guy with shaggy brown hair approaching the bar I'm leaning against. "Yeah, I am."

He holds out a hand, which I shake. "I'm John, Cristina's husband."

"Oh. Nice to meet you, man. We missed you this week. Glad you're feeling better."

"Thanks." He grins. "Man, I feel like I missed out. I thought this week was camping in the middle of a forest. Instead, it's this…" He waves toward the giant house and elaborate decorations. "And I missed out on hanging out with you."

I smile back. "You a hockey fan?"

"A *Wolves* fan. My dad grew up right outside of Seattle. My grandparents still live out there. They're going to lose their shit when they hear I've met you. Both huge fans."

My smile grows. "You want an autograph?" I'm half-kidding, but John takes me totally seriously.

"Would you?" He glances around, grabbing a napkin from the stack embossed with *Theo and Amelia* above today's date and flipping it over. "Got a pen?" he asks the bartender.

I chuckle at his eagerness, downing the rest of my drink and taking the Sharpie the bartender hands over. I scribble my signature on the back of one of the napkins. "What's your dad's name?"

"Owen."

"And your grandfather?"

"Jack."

I scrawl *To Owen and Jack* above my signature and slide the napkin over to John. "There you go."

"Wow!" He gapes at it. "Thank you. *Wow*. They're going to flip."

"Hey, John."

Awareness slides across my skin as soon as I hear her voice.

"Hey, Harper. Nice speech."

She stops beside me, and I resist the urge to glance over. "Thanks. I'm glad you made it for the wedding."

"Me too. Just getting to know your guy here."

"Oh, yeah?"

"Yeah. I think you found a keeper."

I look over at Harper, wanting to see her reaction to that comment. There's a mischievous quirk tugging at the lips, painted pink and glossy. "Thank goodness I got your stamp of approval, John. It's how I decide whether to keep or boot all my boyfriends."

John chuckles. "Can always rely on that sense of humor, Harper."

It's a sentence I've heard some iteration of many times this week. Harper is popular among Amelia's friends, and it's a familiar theme from when we were all younger. Harper is a hard act to follow, and Amelia always had to.

John is smiling at Harper, looking at her like he knows her. But I don't know if he does. I don't know if *I* do. Every time I think I'm getting close, she does or says something that makes me second-guess everything.

Harper returns his smile, then meets my wondering gaze, her blue eyes shadowed by the setting sun. Bit by bit, the lights that were strung are becoming more relevant. The closer we creep to the end of the day, the more it feels like the completion of a chapter.

"Came to see if you want to dance?" she says.

"Sure," I answer.

Affirmatives seem to be all I'm capable of responding with where Harper is concerned. *Sure* and *yeah* and *of course*.

Every time I reply with one, it's that feeling of gifting someone a present you picked out that you hope they'll love. Better than anything you could possibly receive yourself.

We both say goodbye to John, and then I follow Harper out onto the dance floor. It's still early in the evening. Only a few couples are already swaying, all of them with decades on us. But I don't care, honestly. The only person here whose opinion matters to me is the girl in my arms.

"What was with the napkin?" she asks as we start to sway.

"His dad and grandfather are Wolves fans."

"He asked you for an autograph? At a wedding?" Harper sounds offended on my behalf.

"I offered," I reply. "Took ten seconds."

"Is it…always like that?"

"Like what?"

"Say you go to the grocery store in Seattle, do people stop you and ask you for autographs?"

"I get all my groceries delivered," I admit, hating that I sound like a rich asshole.

"What about when you go to restaurants? People recognize you?"

"I don't go out much."

Harper heaves a frustrated sigh. "But when you do?"

"Yes."

"Is it weird? Does it bother you?"

"It's strange, yeah. Not something you ever really get used to. But I…I don't know. It's nothing I can control. And it's people who are excited about meeting me. Who are supporting my career and the reason I get paid to do something I love. That's hard to resent, you know?"

"I guess."

I glance down. She's staring off to the right, expression distant.

"Why are you asking, Harper?"

She bites her bottom lip.

"Hey, guys." Jared appears. "Whole wedding party is going out for a joyride. Come on."

Harper smiles. "Sounds great." She appears relieved about the interruption, and I'm not sure what to make of that.

We weave around the tables, following the rest of the wedding party down toward the dock.

Harper stumbles as the path declines, then laughs. "Crap." She grabs my arm to steady herself.

"I think you should stop wearing heels," I tell her, not that I hate her hanging on to me.

"Agreed. I wish I could walk around barefoot all the time," she replies. "But I live in New York, so that's not really an option. The sidewalks there are disgusting."

The reminder of her home address is innocuous. It also twists something in my chest.

I stop walking and lean forward. "Lose the heels and get on."

One of my favorite things about Harper is how she doesn't hesitate. She doesn't waffle or waver. She takes a running start and leaps onto my back.

Her arms clasp around my neck, and her legs wind around my waist. I try to memorize this moment as I walk, so I can forever remember exactly how Harper Williams clinging to me feels.

There's none of the decorum or polite conversation of the night before as everyone piles onto the boat, probably making a mockery of the passenger limit. Austin begins blasting a rap song from a portable speaker, shattering the stillness of the lake.

Amelia and Theo take the seats of honor up front, the white layers of Amelia's dress taking up a large amount of the limited seating. Once we're on board the boat, Harper slides off my back. She immediately gets called into a group bridesmaids photo by Cristina.

I take a seat next to Jared, who hands me a beer and offers up a cheers. We clank bottles and each take a sip, waiting for the photo shoot to end and the boat to start moving.

"Really glad we met this week, man," Jared tells me.

"Yeah. Me too," I reply.

"Gotta say, I'm fucking jealous of Theo, snagging you as a brother-in-law."

I stare at Jared. The math of me and Theo equaling brothers-in-law is missing one essential component.

Theo is married to a Williams sister. I'm not.

"It's not—there's no—I mean, Harper and I aren't…" I stutter like an idiot, thrown by his implication.

Marriage isn't a commitment I've ever considered seriously. It's always been an abstract concept, floating around as a future possibility.

It's never been attached to any woman—and definitely not to one who, up until a week ago, I hadn't seen or spoken to in over a decade. I thought that gap might be obvious to everyone, not that they'd be assuming another wedding would be in the imminent future.

Jared grins. "I'm not there yet either. It just seems in the cards for you guys."

I'm saved from sputtering more half-formed sentences—or asking why the heck he thinks that—by Savannah's appearance.

She plops down in Jared's lap, some of the pink liquid in her glass spilling over the rim and dribbling down her hand. "What are you boys talking about?"

"Guy stuff," Jared responds, giving me a secretive little wink.

I offer a half-smile back before taking a sip of cold beer.

His assumption took me off guard. But I'm also freaked out by how I'm *not* freaked out about it. And not because Harper and I are some combination of pretend and temporary, set to part ways permanently tomorrow.

I'm startled by how clearly I could see us headed in that direction. How the path from here to there could unfold so differently than it did in the past. How sacrifices I resented in the past would look more like opportunities I'd leap at, where Harper is concerned.

"This seat taken?"

Without waiting for a response, Harper takes a seat on top of me. I release a surprised huff that turns into more of a groan when she leans back, soft, satin-encased curves melting against my body.

She curls up in my lap, her face pressing against my neck and her bare feet landing on my thigh. Her body is draped over mine like a favorite, familiar blanket.

When I'm on the ice, it feels like I'm wearing blinders and earplugs. I'm not looking into the crowd or listening to the chirping. I'm focused on one goal—winning—and tune out anything resembling a distraction.

For the first time, I feel that way off the ice. I'm aware of the commotion around me—the laughter and the music and the flashes of phones—but I'm entirely focused on Harper.

And I let myself relax into it. I slip one hand inside the slit that runs up the side of Harper's dress, finding the bare skin of her calf and sliding a palm upward.

I feel her body tense and her breath catch, but I can't see her face. I keep my eyes aimed forward, at the setting sun, acting oblivious to her response. But I'm not, which she knows. She's the only one who can tell—who can feel my erection. Just like I'm the only one who can see the rapid flutter of her pulse just beneath her jaw. Who can feel the heat between her legs as I move my hand even higher, hidden by the fabric of her dress.

It's a secret moment in the midst of chaos. I glance down right as Harper peeks up.

The pink that works its way across her cheeks is more spectacular than the sunset.

We're almost back to the tent when my phone buzzes in my pocket. The list of people who have this number is a short one. The number who would be calling on a Saturday night is even shorter. So, I pull it out of my pocket and glance at the screen, a knot in my stomach pulling taut as soon as I see the name.

"I've got to take this," I tell Jared, who's next to me.

Harper is up ahead with Amelia and the rest of the bridesmaids.

He nods and continues walking with the rest of the guys.

I turn and start back the way we just came before answering the phone. "Mom?"

"My goodness, where are you, Drew? A concert?"

"Just...a thing." If I tell her I'm at Amelia Williams's wedding, a million questions will follow. Including *why* I'm here, to which I have no good answer.

"What kind of thing?"

"Mom. Why are you calling at eleven p.m.? You and Dad are usually in bed by ten."

There's a pause on the other end of the line that makes my pulse race.

"Mom?"

"He's okay, Drew. He just wasn't feeling great after dinner, and so I brought him to Mass West. They're running tests, but everything has come back fine so far. Keeping him for observation is just a precaution."

"You're at the fucking hospital?" I drag a hand through my hair, my heartbeat thudding in my ears.

All I can think of is the last time my mom called with news like this. How she tried to cushion the blow with words like *lucky* and *incredible care* and *recovering well*, but then the truth came out that the stroke had left my father struggling with the most basic of tasks. Ones he's only just regained a mastery of.

"Language, Andrew."

"Sorry." I exhale. "I'm just—I'm just worried. I hate it when you keep things from me."

"I didn't want to tell you until I knew what the doctors said. Nothing you could have done, Drew."

"I could have *been there*, Mom."

"I'm telling you now," she says, a small quiver in her voice.

I blow out a long breath, feeling like absolute shit. The last thing my mom needs is more stress right now. "Okay. I'll be there first thing in the morning."

The helplessness immediately disappears from her voice. "Drew, honey, you only have a little bit of a break left before you have to be back in Seattle. You should—"

"I'll be there first thing in the morning," I repeat.

She sighs but abandons arguing with me. "All right. I love you, Drew."

"I love you, Mom. Tell Dad too, yeah?"

"Of course I will."

"Okay. Bye."

"Bye, sweetie."

She hangs up. I stop walking toward the shore and let the hand holding my phone swing down to my side, staring out at the dark expanse of water, tempted to do something drastic, like fling it into the lake.

This week has been the best I've had in a while. I've dreaded the end of it almost since we first arrived. The lake is incredible, but I know Harper is what has really made the difference.

For the first time ever, I'm not itching to get back to Seattle and start the season. I was banking on having more time with Harper. That we could talk—after the wedding was over—and I could tell her that Cat isn't a factor. That, in a matter of days, she's managed to mean more to me than any other woman *ever* has.

But now, I have no idea what that will look like. My mother's track record of telling me the full truth when it comes to my father's health is spotty at best.

And I know—*I know*—that it comes from a place of love. From the traditional parental role of protecting your child from the uglier parts of the world. But it also freaks me out more, wondering what might be getting withheld.

I thought there was a little more open time before I needed to return to Seattle. And I wasn't assuming that time would be spent with Harper.

But I thought that was a possibility that I could offer her. A gesture of my sincerity before leaving. Now, there's a good chance I'll be in Boston until I have to return home. And no matter how amazing this week has been, my track record with women has made it clear that dating a guy you never see is far from ideal.

Harper seems content with her life as it is—her apartment and living with her best friend and her job and the book she doesn't tell anyone about. Ending things on an awkward note is the last thing I want. And even if Harper is interested in continuing... whatever the hell we are, chances of that conviction lasting through the possible weeks or likely months until we can see each other in person again are incredibly slim.

I've never been good at taking risks when it comes to anything besides hockey.

So, I walk back toward the lights and music with my hands tucked into my pockets, multiple forms of dread tumbling around in my stomach.

I spot Harper almost immediately, my attention drawn to her like the insects buzzing around the lights strung up. Like how a painter narrows in on a muse or a writer searches for a word.

She's talking with a random guy I don't recognize, hands waving animatedly as she emphasizes whatever they're discussing. He grins in response, staring at Harper like she's the most fascinating sight he's ever laid eyes on.

A dark coil of jealousy appears in my chest as I approach them, heavy and foreign. I've dated plenty of women I liked, a couple who I thought I could possibly love. Sometime in the future, like it was a set destination you could arrive at whenever you decided to. Seeing them talk to another man never elicited *this*. Possessiveness pumps through my blood, hot and irritated.

Harper glances over at me, a different, softer smile appearing. "Hey. This is Theo's cousin, Marcus. Marcus, this is my boyfriend, Drew."

I startle at her casual use of the title, one I've never heard Harper use before.

"Nice to meet you, Marcus." I don't manage to muster much fake enthusiasm about making his acquaintance.

Does the fact that he's related to Theo mean he views Harper as family now? I glance at his wide smile and decide not.

I tell myself not to care, but it has absolutely no effect on my annoyance at all.

"Can I talk to you?" I ask Harper.

"Yeah, of course." Confusion creases her forehead, then smooths as she glances at Marcus. "Nice talking with you."

"You too," he replies, his response only for her.

My molars grind as I tell myself to calm the fuck down, turning and heading toward the edge of the tent without another word. Harper follows me.

We end up next to one of the largest pines, its trunk wrapped with thousands of twinkling lights.

"My dad is in the hospital."

Harper's confused expression immediately morphs into a worried one, a furrow appearing between her eyes and some of the color draining from her face. "Oh my God. Is he okay?"

"I don't know. I think so. I mean, my mom said so. But her track record when it comes to this stuff is…not great. She didn't tell me about my dad's stroke right away. She waited to tell me until the doctors were sure he'd be okay, eventually. I get why she did, but I also just…" I let out a long breath. "It makes me always assume the worst, you know?"

Harper nods slowly, still processing.

"I told her I'd be there first thing in the morning. So, I'm going to go pack and try to get some sleep. That way, I can get an early start."

She nods again, the motion a little faster. "Of course. Of course you should. That makes sense."

"I'm sorry if—"

"Don't apologize, Drew. I can't believe after—you came all this way. The suit and the drive and the way you're here at all. I mean, just yeah. Sleep and pack."

She's babbling, and it's cute. If there wasn't this fist squeezing my chest, making it hard to breathe, I'd smile.

But I'm too paralyzed by trepidation. I don't want to discover my dad is worse off than my mom made it sound. I don't want to leave Harper. I don't have a choice about either.

Harper gnaws on her bottom lip. "Do you want…help? Company?"

"It won't take me long to pack, and then I'm just going to go to bed. You should stay. Enjoy the wedding. It's your sister's wedding."

"Okay." She looks disappointed by my response, not relieved.

And I realize there's a chance I just fucked up majorly. Because I want anything Harper Williams is willing to give me, and I just made it sound like I didn't because accepting help isn't reflexive for me. And also because I know the more time I spend with her, the harder it will be to walk away tomorrow.

"Harper!" someone calls. "Amelia is throwing her bouquet."

I don't even look to see who is summoning her. Other people fighting for Harper's attention has been a common theme this week. No longer any sort of surprise.

But Harper doesn't move. "I'll see you in the morning?" she asks, chewing on her lower lip and removing the last bits of gloss.

"Won't you want to sleep in?" I tease, attempting to insert some levity into the moment. "It will probably be a late night."

There's no trace of a smile on her face. No lighter tone. Her voice is serious as she tells me, "Don't leave without waking me up."

I swallow. Because there are hints of everything I'm feeling on her face, and it's messing with my head. Making me wonder if I *should* say some of the thoughts bouncing around. "Okay. I'll wake you up."

"Harper!" someone calls again.

"Coming!" she replies right before grabbing my hand and squeezing it tight. "He'll be fine, Drew."

Another lump works its way into my throat as I nod. Both from the sentiment and the realization that Harper thinks the only reason I'm upset is my dad. That it has nothing to do with her.

She releases my hand, and then she's gone, swept back up into the commotion of the party. I catch a glimpse of the gathering of women around the dance floor before I pass the tent and head inside the main house. It's entirely empty, which feels strange.

I make my way through the living room and upstairs, trailing my hand on the banister in some sad attempt to delay my arrival in the room Harper and I are sharing. It's a complete mess. I'm not a neat freak, and neither is she.

Clothes are strewn everywhere. Bathing suits hang on every available surface to dry. The bed is unmade.

I grab my duffel from the corner where I stashed it, methodically sorting through the clothes I brought. Folding them and stacking them before tucking them in the bag. I fold all of Harper's clothes too, just to keep my hands busy. Once the clothes are dealt with, I move into the bathroom, grabbing my toiletries and leaving hers.

I brush my teeth before storing the toothbrush and toothpaste away. Plug in my phone and check for messages from my mother. None. Search Mass West's visiting hours, which begin at nine.

The drive to downtown Boston is three and a half hours from here. I should leave at five thirty, and I'm exhausted at the thought. I slept poorly last night, spending too long waiting for Harper to come to bed and falling asleep before she ever did.

I turn out all the lights and strip down to my boxers before climbing into bed.

I close my eyes, wishing it were that easy to shut my mind off and fall right asleep. Instead, my mind keeps swirling in answerless circles, the distant sound of the reception barely audible.

The next time I check my phone, it's one forty-five.

I'm confident I haven't slept at all. No sign of Harper or any sound in the house to suggest anyone staying here has headed to bed yet.

I turn all the lights back on and get dressed again. I won't be getting any sleep. It seems pointless to lie here.

After a final sweep of the room, I take a seat on the couch. I don't feel like I can leave without telling Harper goodbye. So, I sit and scroll through social media on my phone until I hear the knob turn. Two thirty.

The door swings open, and Harper steps inside. Blue eyes assess the room. The made bed. The folded stack of her clothes. The duffel at my feet. Me on the couch.

I stand. "Hey."

"Hey." Her heels hit the hardwood with a *smack*. Barefoot

again. "You're already packed."

"I'm not going to be able to sleep. Figured I might as well leave now. I can go straight to my parents' house and then make it to the hospital for the start of visiting hours."

"Right. Of course." One hand runs through her hair, pulling what little hasn't already fallen out of the professional hairstyle free. I prefer it untamed. "Did you hear anything else from your mom?"

"No. Hopefully, that's a good sign."

She nods. "Right. It should be."

We stand and stare at each other, the small stretch of space between us swirling with a lot unsaid. At least, I know there's a lot I'm not saying.

"Well...thanks for letting me tag along this week. Glad I could fulfill your requirements of not ironing my shorts and playing an actual sport."

Harper rolls her eyes, looking less lost and more like her normal self. "We both know you're the one who did me the favor, Halifax. Thank *you*."

"Nah, no favor. You would have been fine without me."

And I mean it. Harper is much stronger than she gives herself credit for.

There's so much else I want to say to her, about her dad and her book and everything else she confided in me this week, but I'm worried I won't do any of it justice. That even mentioning it will destroy the magic of those past moments, pop it like a bubble.

She raises and drops a shoulder. "Maybe."

Then, she's stepping forward to give me a hug, folding around me the same way she did on the boat earlier. Back when I had very different ideas about what us alone in this room tonight might look like.

"Take care of yourself, Drew."

"You too, Harper."

I hug her back, making it last a lot longer than a simple, friendly embrace. She doesn't pull away, and my arms don't drop. We stand there, holding each other until a door slams downstairs, making us both jump.

"Reception wrapping up?"

She steps back, fingers fiddling with the bracelets on her wrist. The metal jangles, the only sound in the room for a minute. "Guess so."

I exhale. "Okay. I should go. Tell everyone I said goodbye?"

"Yeah, I will."

I don't ask what else she'll tell them. We never discussed the logistics of what our "relationship" ending would look like. It's a burden that will fall solely on her since these are her friends and family, not mine. People she'll encounter again, not me. Another reason she shouldn't be thanking me. It feels like I got a lot more out of this than she did.

I pick up my duffel and swing it over one shoulder. "Look me up if you're ever in Seattle, okay?"

Harper half-smiles. "Yeah. Let me know your dad is okay."

"I will." My fist clenches around the nylon straps I'm holding. At the reminder of what's driving the sudden urgency concerning my departure and the imminence of it all of a sudden.

I force myself to start walking, past her and toward the door. It opens and closes easily, and then I'm in the empty hallway, Harper out of sight.

If I try hard enough, I think I can still hear her in the room on the other side of the door, but I keep moving instead of continuing to stand here. Until I'm far enough away that I can't even pretend anymore.

CHAPTER SEVENTEEN

DREW

All the lights are on in the lower level of my parents' house when I pull into the driveway just after six. I didn't hit any traffic, unsurprisingly. But I drove slower than usual, especially along the winding roads of Maine's wilderness. I knew it would be a while before I was back in the state.

My original plan was to return to the Port Haven house after the wedding. But I didn't leave anything there, so it didn't make any sense to make it a stop along the way of this trip. I'd rather keep my last visit there as the last one—for now anyway.

As soon as I step out of the car, I know it will be a hot day. I miss Maine's cooler temperatures immediately—the shade of the pines and the breeze off the water. The air here feels stagnant and sticky, never losing the heat from the day before.

I grab my bag from the back and start up the brick walkway toward my childhood home. It looks the same as always—proud facade and meticulous landscaping.

My dad mows the lawn religiously along with spreading new seed and fertilizer. The green stalks are a source of pride. And my mom loves flowers. She picks ones to attract her favorite birds, cultivating fragrant blossoms and turning the beds surrounding the house into an explosion of color.

When I came home earlier in the summer, they were both outside, tending to their respective plants. The normalcy of that scene is one I'd give anything for right now.

I ring the doorbell, not bothering with the key stored under the planter to the left of the door. Knowing my mom, she was already on edge about spending the night in the house alone. I don't want to freak her out even more by letting myself in and suddenly appearing.

She opens the front door a few seconds later, the mask of worry cracking when she sees me.

"Drew!"

I muster a smile. "Hey, Mom."

She steps forward and squeezes me, the top of her head barely reaching my shoulder. I'm taller than my dad, too, by some bizarre twist of genetics.

"How early did you leave?" is her first question when she pulls away, looking me up and down in that way moms do.

"Early. I couldn't sleep. Figured I'd come straight here and we could head to the hospital together."

As soon as I mention the H-word, worry clouds her expression once again.

"Have you heard anything else?"

She shakes her head. "They'll only call if anything changes, so it's good that they haven't."

Not hearing anything isn't exactly reassuring either. But I keep a smile on my face as I walk into the entryway, knowing that's not what she needs to hear.

"Visiting hours start at nine?"

"Yes."

"Okay. I'm going to go take a shower."

My mom nods. "You hungry?"

"Not really."

She smiles. "Yeah. I'll make something, just in case."

"All right," I say before heading for the stairs.

"Drew?"

"Yeah?" I glance back at my mom, who hasn't moved.

"Thank you for coming."

"*Of course*, Mom. Of course."

She smiles. Nods once. And then turns and starts toward the kitchen.

I remain standing in place for a moment longer.

I don't have much of a say in where I play. Originally, I was drafted to Florida, then traded to Seattle a couple of years later. I'm lucky to have stayed there ever since. And I *like* Seattle. I like the city, and I like the team. But it's far away from the people I *love*.

After another few seconds standing frozen, I head upstairs. I've offered to get my parents a place closer to me. They always insist it would be a waste of money, that they'd rather rent something or stay with me when they visit. Their whole lives are here —friends and familiarity.

Being back in my childhood bedroom is always strange. It's a time capsule to my past. Labeled folders of essays I wrote in high school. My college jersey, framed on the wall. Lego sets I assembled as a kid.

I dump my duffel bag on the bed, unzipping it and rapidly realizing almost everything inside is dirty. I step out of my room and walk over to the railing that runs along the top of the stairs.

"Mom?"

"Yeah?" she calls back.

"Okay if I put a load of laundry in?"

Even all the way down in the kitchen, I can hear the surprise in her voice when she responds, "Of course."

The place where I was supposed to be staying for the past week—the Port Haven house—has its own washer and dryer. The place where I was actually staying—Camp Basswood—did not. Or if it did, I didn't use it.

I haul my bag down the hall and open the doors that enclose the washer and dryer, pulling out T-shirts and swim trunks and shoving them into the machine unceremoniously.

Something falls out of the pocket of my joggers as I grab them. I bend down to pick it up, my movements stalling when I see the lobster pattern printed on the napkin.

I remember shoving it into my pocket. Remember everything that followed.

I should toss the napkin. Instead, I tuck it into the pocket on the outside of the duffel bag before finishing filling the load and starting the washing machine.

After I've showered and changed into clean clothes, I head downstairs. The scent of eggs and bacon emanates from the kitchen. Despite my anxiety, my stomach rumbles as I walk inside and find my mom standing at the stove.

"You find the detergent and everything okay?" she asks.

I snag a strip of bacon from the plate. "I'm capable of washing my own clothes, Mom."

"Doesn't seem that way if you came home with a load of laundry the same way you did in college. I'm worried what the Ashland house looks like now."

I roll my eyes. "I cleaned before I left...last weekend."

"Last weekend?"

"Uh-huh."

"Where were you this week?"

"I was at Lake Paulson."

"Lake Paulson? What were you doing there?"

"I went to Amelia Williams's wedding. It was last night. That was the 'concert' I was at."

"Amelia Williams…Paul and Francesca's daughter?"

"Yeah."

"How on earth did you end up there?"

"I ran into Harper Williams in Port Haven. They still own the house next door, you know."

My mom nods. "I know."

"Well, I caught up with Harper, and she mentioned the wedding and that she wasn't bringing a date, and so I just… offered to go with her."

"Really?" An amused smile touches my mother's lips. Much better than the worry that was pinching her face earlier, but also an expression I can't help but feel like is at my expense. "You had the biggest crush on that girl."

"No, I didn't." The dispute is automatic. And a lie. Because, yeah, I did. *Do*.

"Okay, sweetie." Her smile is indulgent now.

"*Anyway*, that's why I didn't do any laundry. I guess there must have been a washer and dryer at the camp, but I brought enough not to worry about it until now."

"How was the wedding?"

"It was nice. The guy she married—Theo—is a cool dude. Everything was right on the lake, which was beautiful."

"What about Harper?"

I grab another piece of bacon. "What about her?"

"Would you call *her* beautiful?"

"Mom."

"I haven't seen her since she was seventeen. I'm just wondering."

I chew and swallow, as if delaying my answer will make any difference in the outcome. "Yeah. She's beautiful."

"Are you going to see her again?"

"Probably not." The truth tastes bitter, ruining the crispy meat I just consumed.

"Why not?"

"*Why not*? Mom, I live in Seattle. She lives in New York. It's…complicated. It was just a week. Just some fun."

"Hmm," she hums. "You don't usually mention your *fun* to me."

"Jesus," I groan. "Forget I said anything."

Her eyes are twinkling as she turns off the stove and adds some scrambled eggs to the plate of bacon I'm already working on. "Fine. I won't say anything else about it. But just for the record, convenience isn't a requirement when it comes to love."

The mood is light as we eat breakfast. My mom catches me up on the past few weeks since I saw them. The gallery opening they went to and the golf tournament my father participated in.

Once we're in the car, headed to the hospital, we both sober a little. As I drive, I keep catching my mom's twisting hands out of the corner of my eye, her anxiety spilling out and saturating the air in the car.

I let her take the lead once we're at the hospital, following her through the maze of hallways until we reach the room where my father is staying. I didn't ask my mom if she told him I was coming, and it's obvious she didn't as soon as we step into the room. His face lights up as soon as he sees me, first with excitement and then turning sheepish.

"I told you not to bother him," he grumbles to my mom. "Doctors say I'm fine. All clear to discharge."

I look him over, the knot that's been in my chest since my mom called last night finally loosening when I register that he does look fine. He's not even wearing a hospital gown, already dressed in his usual summer uniform of slacks and a polo shirt.

"You'd better bother me, Dad," I say, stepping closer to the bed to give him a hug.

He hugs me back tightly. "You're supposed to be training and relaxing, not hanging around hospitals."

I pull back and look him over again, closer. "You sure you're okay?"

He nods. "Got the all clear about an hour ago. Was just about to call your mother."

A nurse enters the room then, clutching a clipboard. "Just a few more forms for you to sign, Mr. Halifax. Then, you're all set to leave."

My father nods, taking the clipboard and pulling the pen from the top to scribble his signature. The nurse's eyes flicker to me as he flips to the second page.

I know the second she recognizes me.

"Wow. You're Drew Halifax."

The scratch of pen against paper isn't loud enough to cover my dad's chuckle. He's always chuffed when people recognize me. Finds it funny or something of a novelty. His hand moves slower until he's no longer signing anything. "You a hockey fan, Abigail?"

Of course he's already learned the nurse's name. My father could become best friends with a brick wall.

"I am, yes," the nurse responds.

She's eyeing me with interest, not just excitement. She's young and blonde. Pretty and peppy. And yet the amount of interest I can summon is zero. All I offer her is a polite smile.

My dad continues signing the forms, chatting away with Abigail the entire time. Thankfully, the conversation doesn't include hockey—or me.

I retreat to one corner of the room and pull my phone out of my pocket. I pull up Harper's name and stare at the blinking cursor, chewing on the inside of my cheek as I deliberate on what to send her.

Drew: *He's fine. Getting discharged now.*

I'm not expecting an immediate response. It's only just past nine, and Harper wasn't out of bed before ten a single day aside from the one morning we went fishing together.

But she likes it right away. Three dots appear at the bottom of the screen and then disappear. Appear and then disappear. Anticipation churns in my stomach.

"Drew?"

I glance up. Both my parents are studying me curiously. Abigail is nowhere in sight.

"You ready to go?" my mom asks.

"Oh, yeah. Yep. Let's go." I shut off my phone and stuff it into my pocket, waiting for a buzz that never comes as we leave the antiseptic scent and fluorescent lights behind.

The air outside is hot and humid, but at least it's fresh.

My dad takes the passenger seat while my mom slides into the back. There was a time when my dad would have insisted on driving, but he happily settles into the seat next to me instead.

I'm glad he knows his limits. Or is learning them at least. But it's also a reminder that the next time, the news might be different. That life is short and sacred.

Traffic is terrible on the drive home. By the time we pull back in the driveway, a full hour has passed. And my phone never vibrates with a new notification.

I could have—should have—asked her a question, I guess. About how the rest of the reception was. Or about when she's returning to New York. I'm out of practice with pursuing a woman, as ridiculous as that sounds.

My mom fusses over my dad as we head inside. The house feels fuller with him here, not as empty as it was when I arrived this morning.

My dad follows me into the kitchen as my mom heads upstairs.

"Ready for the first game against Los Angeles?" he asks as I pour myself some water. "Getting close now."

I glance at the fridge, where the Wolves' schedule is proudly affixed with two magnets. "Yeah, I'm ready."

My dad leans against the counter. "You're not excited for the start of the season."

"Of course I am."

"Tell that to your face, son."

I roll my eyes. "I just…I met someone."

It doesn't feel like enough. Just a meeting or just someone. I more than met her, and Harper isn't just someone.

But my dad and I have never discussed girls, not really. Not more than a teasing comment when I was younger. There's never been a girl I *wanted* to talk about.

Until now. And he doesn't appear nearly as surprised as I was expecting.

"Mom told you?"

"Just that she thought there was someone. No details."

"When?" I wonder. "I've been with them both the whole time."

My dad grins. "You've been distracted this morning."

My mind flashes to the message she never responded to. Just acknowledged. "I don't think it's going to work out."

"She doesn't live near Seattle, I'm assuming?"

I shake my head. "No. She lives in New York."

"New York? Invite her over so your mother and I can meet her!"

"You've already met her. Harper Williams."

"Harper Williams." Surprise, then sadness crosses my dad's face. "Paul's daughter?"

I swallow and nod. "Yeah."

"Always wondered what happened with that family."

"They're...okay."

My phone buzzes in my pocket. I whip it out, only to deflate when I see the name on the screen isn't the one I'm hoping for.

"I've got to take this, Dad."

"Sure," he agrees.

I step out the sliding door that leads to the back deck, staring at the swing set my parents had installed when I was a toddler and never got taken down. They're saving it for my kids, I guess. Maybe. It's never a possibility that's occurred to me before.

"Hey, Cat."

"Drew!" Her voice is high and excited. "How are you?"

Sad. Exhausted. Confused. "Fine. You?"

"I'm great. Did you see my text, that I'll be in Seattle soon?"

"Yeah, I did. I'm sorry I didn't respond yet. I just—"

"Don't worry about it. I know you're super busy. I just wanted to let you know. So, hopefully, we can meet up?"

I pinch the bridge of my nose and exhale. "Look, Cat. Nothing has changed in my life, okay? I'm still—"

"I'm coming to Seattle to look at apartments, Drew. A spot finally opened up in the Seattle office. I'm starting at the end of September!"

"That's great, Cat," I say.

"You looked at a place by the waterfront, right? I'm thinking that's where I'd like to end up. No water views in Phoenix! I'm so sick of the desert."

"No water in the desert," I agree, sounding like a total idiot. "Look, Cat—"

"We can start slow, Drew. Just hang out a few times and see

where it goes. I know your schedule is hectic. I'll try to be more understanding this time."

"I met someone else," I blurt.

There's a long stretch of silence before she asks, "Is it serious?"

It shouldn't be. Who falls in love in a week? Fools.

But I think of Harper's laugh. Her eyes. Her teasing.

And there's a good chance I'm a fool.

"Yeah, it's serious."

"Oh."

"I'm sorry," I apologize, not knowing exactly what I'm apologizing for.

We broke up almost a year ago, and in that time, I've never given Cat any indication I was interested in getting back together. But I feel bad anyway. Only sociopaths savor someone's pain.

"It's fine," Cat replies. "I'm happy for you."

"Thanks." The sentiment is as empty as hers was. "I'm sure I'll see you around, yeah?"

"Yeah, probably."

"Bye, Cat."

"Bye, Drew."

I hang up and stare out at the yard for a while before heading back inside.

CHAPTER EIGHTEEN

HARPER

I'm sitting on the cold tiles of the bathroom floor, staring out the window at the fading sunshine, when Amelia calls. I strongly consider not answering. I'm not in the mood to talk to anyone. Not in the mood to do *anything*, honestly.

And that's the realization that forces me to answer. Because it scares me a little, how my life has felt sucked free of color ever since I left the lake. It looks white and bland, just like this bathroom.

"Hey!" I answer. "How was the honeymoon?"

Amelia sets off at a mile a minute, talking about samples of champagne and striped umbrellas and sun-drenched villas.

I, "Mmhmm," and, "Yeah," my way through the honeymoon recap, focusing more on the sharp scent of bleach and rhythmic rub of the sponge as I resume scrubbing during the lengthy descriptions.

Hearing Drew's name is what regains my full attention.

"Sorry, what did you say?" I ask. "My cell service is a little spotty."

There's a pause, where I can practically hear Amelia rolling her eyes on the other end of the line. In addition to apathy, I seem to have lost my ability to tell a convincing lie.

"I *said*, I made dinner reservations for me, Theo, you, and Drew tonight. I need to kick this jet lag and get out, so I'm back on a better schedule."

You and Drew.

Those three words hit me like a hard object. Air leaves my chest in a huff.

"Why don't you and Theo just go out together?" I suggest. "Aren't you still supposed to be in that *can't get enough of each other* newlywed phase?"

"We had dinner, just the two of us together for the past two weeks. And we're both exhausted. We need a couple to eat with!"

"Doesn't Savannah live in the same building? I'm sure she and Jared would love to go out with you guys."

"I'm not asking Savannah, Harper. I'm asking *you*."

I bite back a barb about how she didn't prioritize me over Savannah when it came to choosing her maid of honor. But I'm trying to move past that. It feels like we *have* moved past it. Amelia sent photos from their honeymoon in Saint-Tropez. She's calling and inviting me to get dinner now that we live in the same city for the first time since I left for college. Vastly different interactions than any we've had in the past years.

For once, my reluctance has nothing to do with Amelia.

I drop the sponge and lean back against the cabinet beneath the sink with a sigh. "Sure, I'll meet you for dinner. But..." I swallow, absorbing how much it hurts to think the next words, much less speak them. "Drew won't be there. He—uh..." I'm so, so tempted to simply say he's not in New York. Amelia knows his team is based in Seattle. But I'm on a new quest to be honest with my sister, so I admit, "Well, we broke up."

"You *did*?"

I expected Amelia to sound smug—as shitty as that sounds. To be unsurprised to learn another relationship of mine imploded, at least. There have been plenty of comments over the years about how short my relationships are.

But all I hear is surprise in her voice. Real shock, like it's nothing she saw coming.

Unexpectedly, that hurts worse.

"Yep." I tilt my head back to study the cracked plaster of the bathroom ceiling. It's better than picturing the expression Amelia is probably wearing right now.

"What happened?"

I flip the sponge over and start on a fresh patch of grout. Wondering what my sister is really thinking. Probably some version of *Harper can't keep a guy*.

"It just didn't work out. It was a summer fling, and summer is over, so…" I clear my throat. "Anyway, like I said, you should go out with Savannah and Jared. Or Claire and—"

"They're all busy tonight."

"Right." I laugh humorlessly. So much for a new chapter. "I was your third choice. Probably lower. Did you check with Willa too? What about—"

"Stop it, Harper. We're all on a group text together. I mentioned dinner when they were asking about the honeymoon. It had nothing to do with not wanting to see you."

"Fine." I exhale, too exhausted to argue. "Let's do dinner. Text me the time and the address, okay?"

There's a pause where Amelia doesn't speak. Doesn't hang up either. "Are you okay, Harper?"

I drop the sponge and swipe some hair out of my face. "I'm fine."

"You promise?"

"I promise. Professional athletes are notoriously terrible at relationships. I dodged a bullet probably." I huff a quick breath. "Just text me the dinner details, yeah? I've got to go."

We hang up, and seconds later, my phone vibrates with the address for a restaurant in Greenwich Village.

I'm still on my hands and knees, scrubbing tiles, when Olivia gets home.

I hear the front door slam, followed by, "Harper?"

"Bathroom," I call back.

Olivia appears in the doorway a few seconds later, her nose scrunched as she pulls her long hair up in a messy ponytail. "What the hell are you doing on the floor?"

"I'm cleaning." I resist adding a *duh* at the end, but it resonates through my tone.

"Huh." She props a hip on the doorframe, crossing her arms. "Is this related to Hockey Hottie?"

"Nope."

Olivia makes a disbelieving sound. I gave her the rosy version of my week with Drew when I got back to New York. Ran into a guy I barely knew when I was younger, went to a wedding with him, he left a little early because a friend needed him.

None of the deeper conversations or heavier moments.

No mention of Drew's father's health because I'd rather everyone think I rank below a friend than betray Drew's confidence. Claire asked me if it was a female friend on Sunday morning, and I told her yes because I'm dramatic or a masochist. Or both.

I thought it would make the eventual announcement that Drew and I were over easier. I'm not sure anything has that power.

"You should call him."

I continue scrubbing. Olivia has told me that multiple times, and it makes me wish I'd led with the whole story. Wish I'd explained how I was a mess most of the week. How I relied on him too much and how he was dealing with his dad's health.

There's an unanswered text sitting on my phone that's proof of my cowardice. I liked Drew's message about his dad being okay as soon as I saw it, immensely relieved.

And then I sat and stared at my phone for twenty minutes. Typed and deleted.

I had no idea what to say. We'd said goodbye just hours earlier, and it had an air of permanence. I'd asked him to let me know his dad was okay, and he had—because Drew is reliable.

So, I debated on what else to say until Savannah was banging on my door about brunch, and then I was swept up in goodbyes until the drive back home. Busy doing the laundry I'd never gotten around to doing at the lake and going back to work. And now, it feels like too much time has passed to text Drew, let alone call him.

I don't want to *bother* him.

And I can honestly say that's never been a concern of mine before. Usually, I'm happy to let silence stretch and move ahead with my life.

"Are you going to clean the kitchen too?" Olivia asks, still hovering in the doorway, watching me. "Because there's—" She yelps when I grab a towel from the rack and toss it at her, laughing.

"Why don't *you* clean it?"

"Because I have a life, dear friend."

She's teasing, but she's right. Ever since I returned to New York, I've gone to work and come home. Eaten ramen in my pajamas and secretly worked on my book.

"Does your busy social life have room for dinner tonight? Amelia just called."

"The two of you are getting dinner?"

"Plus Theo. They're fighting jet lag, apparently. She wanted me to bring Drew, but…"

"You broke the news about Hockey Hottie?"

"I told her we broke up, yeah. And stop calling him that."

"It's not my most original nickname, true. But he's hot, and he plays hockey, so I'm sticking with it."

"You're just assuming he's hot."

"We have internet access here, you know. I did some research."

My eyebrows rise. "*Why?*"

"Because I was curious. It seemed like you actually liked this guy, which is practically worthy of a national holiday."

I sigh.

"You almost finished in here? Because I need to shower…"

"Yeah. Five minutes, okay?"

"Okay." Olivia disappears from the doorway.

I finish scrubbing, stand, and stretch before washing my hands. After Olivia is finished in the bathroom, I take a shower as well. She calls a goodbye through the bathroom door before leaving to get drinks with some nurses from the hospital.

I put on a dress and slick on some mascara and lip gloss, double-checking my clutch for my phone and money before heading for the stairwell. The air outside is warm, but not unbearable now that the sun has set. I decide to walk, checking the address again on my phone before I set off.

The city streets reverberate with light and activity as I walk, passing giggling groups and strolling couples. Most of the stores I pass are closed at this hour, interior lights glowing dimly. The occasional restaurant has noise or activity spilling out from it.

When I reach the entrance to the restaurant, there's a line out the door. Unsurprisingly, Amelia picked a popular place. I spot her and Theo as soon as I'm inside, pointing to their table when the maître d' asks if I have a reservation and then weaving my way through the crowded restaurant. There are two chairs across from Theo and Amelia, but only one is unoccupied.

My steps stutter for a second until I realize the man sitting across from Theo has light-brown hair, not blond.

I don't know why Drew is where my mind jumped, anyway. I doubt Amelia or Theo asked for his number. They would have no way of inviting him for dinner. And he's in Boston—or Seattle—now.

But my pulse is still pattering from something that feels a lot like disappointment when I reach the table.

Amelia glances up and smiles. "Harper!"

She looks bronzed and relaxed. Happy. Of the two of us, I probably look like the one battling jet lag. Sleep has been evasive lately.

"Hey!" I inject enthusiasm into my voice as I hug first her, then Theo.

The stranger stands, holding out a hand for me to shake. "Nice to meet you, Harper. I'm Christian."

"Hi, Christian." I give his hand a solid shake, looking him over as I do.

He's got the investment-banker vibe going for him. Tailored suit, neatly trimmed beard, expensive haircut. Confident, but not pompous. There are laugh lines crinkling the corners of his brown eyes as he smiles at me.

"Christian and I went to college together," Theo supplies. "He's been in Tokyo for the past year, handling some major deal. Just moved back to New York, when? Four days ago, man?"

"That's right," Christian confirms, taking the seat next to me. "Been a bit of a whirlwind. And I was so bummed to miss the wedding. Sounds like it was a great time."

"It was perfect," Amelia gushes, exchanging a look with Theo that makes me feel very, very single.

And very, very grateful I didn't show up solo to their wedding because I'm only just noticing how lovey-dovey they look, and I think I have Drew to thank for that.

Christian and Theo reminisce about a camping trip they took in college while I peruse the menu. Based on how close Christian and Theo are acting, I'm surprised his name didn't come up during the wedding. But I was distracted by Amelia's friends, mostly. And Drew.

I take a sip of the wine Theo ordered for the table as soon as I think his name again. It feels weird—wrong—to be out with another guy. And I don't know how to process that when I ordinarily couldn't care less. There were a few weeks last winter when I was dating two guys at once.

"So, what do you do, Harper?" Christian asks after we've all ordered entrées.

I already pieced together he's some sort of big-deal venture capitalist, so I'm expecting a lackluster response when I tell him I work as an executive assistant at Empire Records.

Instead, he lights up. "That's so cool."

"Christian was in a grunge band in college," Theo says, chuckling.

"It was *not* a grunge band," Christian disputes, but he's laughing too. "We had promise."

"Right, right. I forgot about the manager who wanted to sign you. The same one who thought all the Rolling Stones were still alive, right?"

"She thought that about The Beatles," Christian corrects.

"Much better," Theo responds.

"It all worked out how it was meant to." Christian glances at me. "You like working at Empire?"

I shrug. "It's a paycheck."

Amelia tilts her head across the table, her hand half-extended toward her wineglass. "I thought you loved your job?"

"Not sure *love* is the word I would use. It's fine. Nothing to complain about."

"How long have you worked there?" Christian asks.

"Since college. So, five years. I moved here with my best friend right after graduation. Worked as a barista for a few months while I was interviewing around and then applied for the job at Empire along with a bunch of others. It pays well, and I like the people I work with, so I've stayed."

I also have no idea what else I would do, but I keep that thought to myself at this table since everyone else has fancy, important jobs.

Our waiter appears, balancing plates of food. The cacio e pepe I ordered gets set in front of me, steam rising from the cheesy pasta.

"Hey, did you see the email from Colton?" Christian asks Theo as we all begin eating.

"No. What email?"

"About fantasy hockey. What is he thinking? We always do football. I didn't even think Colton could *name* a single hockey player."

There's a pause before Theo responds, during which I keep my gaze firmly fixed on my pasta. "Guess he just wants to do something different."

"Huh. You a sports fan, Harper?" Christian asks.

Is this karmic payback for something or just terrible timing?

"Uh, no," I answer, stabbing at more pasta. "Not really."

"Me neither. But it's great for networking with clients. We mainly go to basketball games. Maybe I should try a hockey game sometime."

I say nothing in response, just twirl some more pasta.

Amelia jumps in, asking Christian a question about his job.

I pretend to pay attention while finishing my dinner, then excuse myself to use the restroom. It's as nice as the rest of the restaurant, decorated with black marble and gold accents. The stalls are wide and spacious. I move like molasses, stopping to peer at the framed articles on the wall, in no hurry to return to the table. Finally, I lock myself inside one to use the toilet.

When I open the stall door, Amelia is leaning against the long counter that runs beneath the mirror, arms crossed. My steps stutter, surprised by her sudden appearance, before continuing to walk toward the sinks.

I glance in the mirror behind me. "All the stalls are open, you know."

"What happened with Drew?"

My stomach swoops unpleasantly as I turn on the water and squirt soap on my hands. "I told you, it just didn't work out."

"Why not?"

"I don't know. It doesn't matter. Why do you care?"

"You brought him to my *wedding*, Harper. He's in the photos. I was just hoping he would stick."

"You were *hoping he would stick*? Jesus, Amelia. I wish you'd clarified that wedding dates had to come with a no-return policy."

She huffs a sigh. "I'm sorry. That came out wrong. That's not what I meant. You just seemed really happy together. I'm surprised it…changed."

I rinse my hands and grab a paper towel. "It wasn't real, okay?"

"What?"

"Me and Drew? It wasn't real. I ran into him in Port Haven on my way to the lake. Told him about your wedding and that I was…that it would be a lot because of Dad." Surprisingly, neither of us flinches. "He offered to come with me, and I said yes because I'm an idiot sometimes. We were never together, and so we never broke up. He did me a favor by faking being together, and now, he's probably back with his ex."

"Bullshit."

I blink, stunned. Amelia isn't a swearer. "That's what really happened. I don't—"

"He was obviously into you, Harper. Everyone could see it. Savannah has texted me twice, asking if I think she and Jared will get invited to your wedding. It's a little insulting, actually. She's more excited about your hypothetical wedding than she was about my actual one."

I roll my eyes. "There's no wedding, hypothetical or otherwise, so Savannah doesn't need to worry."

"It wasn't fake for you, right?"

I play with the bracelets on my wrist. "Just a silly crush I never got over. Let's go. Unless you actually came to use the bathroom, not interrogate me?"

Amelia just stares at me. "You had a crush on Drew when we spent summers in Port Haven?"

Everything about this moment is bizarre. Standing in the restroom of a fancy restaurant, discussing my childhood crush on the guy I brought to her wedding as a buffer because we used to be unable to get through a full conversation without one or both of us walking off.

"Yeah. Can we go now?"

"I didn't know."

"I know. We never told each other that stuff."

"He asked about you."

"What?"

"That last summer. Drew invited both of us out on his dad's boat. I showed up alone and told him you weren't feeling well because I wanted to be something other than Harper Williams's little sister for once. But he kept asking about you, and I realized he had really invited *you*, not the both of us. I was embarrassed—and jealous. I think Drew felt bad afterward, so he invited me to get ice cream. I embellished everything else. I didn't think you'd notice or care."

That explains Drew's confusion when I asked about his relationship with Amelia, I guess.

"That was all forever ago now."

"You never answered my question. Was it fake for you, or do you actually have feelings for him?"

"I basically knew him a week. That's not long enough to develop actual feelings for someone."

Amelia arches a brow. "No?"

"No!" I insist, surprised my rational, levelheaded sister is acting like it's a possibility. "It's not."

"I knew I wanted to marry Theo the first time I met him."

I blink at her. "No, you didn't. You said you were just friends and that—"

"I *lied*, Harper. Because it's terrifying to admit you like someone, let alone love them."

I exhale. "Amelia, it's just not—"

"No excuses, Harper. You *lit up* around him. I noticed. Theo noticed. Mom noticed. Simon noticed. Everyone noticed. That's rare. And special. And *real*."

"He's *Drew Halifax*, Ames. There's a post of him that got *ten million likes*. His ex sounds like a supermodel. He lives in Seattle. I'm not—we would never work out."

Amelia smiles instead of nodding in agreement. "You're *Harper Williams*. He'd be lucky for a shot with you. And I think he knows that, which is why you should fight for him."

Then, she spins and leaves the restroom, making it clear the only reason she came in here was to tell me that.

CHAPTER NINETEEN

DREW

I'm standing around in the living room, talking with Daryl Henderson, the backup goalie, when I hear my name being called from the kitchen. I turn and look at Lewis Cameron, who's waving the phone I left charging in the air.

"Some chick named Harper is calling you."

"Ooh, she's hot," Carter Evans contributes, leaning over to look at the screen.

I know exactly what he's seeing—the photo of Harper in my hoodie, laughing at the fish doing its damnedest to escape her. An inclination I have no understanding of.

I practically jog into the kitchen, but I'm too late.

Lewis is already answering, a shit-eating grin splitting his freckled face. "Drew Halifax's phone. What's your emergency?"

"You dick." I grab the phone from Lewis, body-checking him against the counter of the kitchen island for good measure. "Don't answer other people's phones."

"Don't leave your phone lying around then," Lewis retorts.

I flip him off over one shoulder as I walk out of the kitchen, heading toward the front entryway and away from most of the commotion.

"Hello?"

"Hi."

Hearing Harper's voice is like soothing a chronic ache. I didn't realize how much I wanted to hear it—how much going without it affected me—until I'm listening to it again and the dull ache of its absence finally eases.

She clears her throat, and then there's a rustling sound on her end that makes me think she might be in bed. My body responds to that thought, reminding me that my ridiculous notion of fucking Harper Williams out of my system was exactly that.

It's been three weeks since Amelia's wedding. Aside from the single text about my father, we haven't spoken once. And it's bothered me. But I'm not sure if she wants anything from me, and so I've allowed my busy schedule to act as an excuse for not finding out. For not reaching out.

I step out onto the front porch.

Lewis lives in a ritzy neighborhood just outside the city. It's where most of the guys with wives and kids settle. Lewis's family is gone for the week, visiting his in-laws, while he's stuck here for practice. He's played it off like it's no big deal, using the empty house as an excuse to have us all over tonight.

But I have a new understanding of the downsides of a commitment this massive. I was incredibly lucky my dad's stroke happened over the summer. If it hadn't, I wouldn't have been able to spend two weeks with him after it happened. Same with the more recent scare.

Air with the slightest hint of chill seeps through my cotton shirt as I walk along the porch.

"Is this a bad time?" Harper asks as I realize we've both been sitting in silence since we exchanged greetings.

"No, it's a good time. Great time. I'm glad you called." I take a seat in one of the rocking chairs, wincing at my too-chipper tone. "How have you been?"

"I've been okay. You?"

"Yeah. Not bad. I'm back in Seattle. Preseason officially starts Tuesday."

"Was that one of your teammates who answered?"

"Uh-huh. Sorry about that. I left my phone out charging, and he took it as an open invitation."

There's a pause.

"Your dad is still doing okay?"

"Yeah." I exhale. "Doctors are keeping a close eye on him, but nothing has come up. I'm glad it happened while I was still on the East Coast. It's a long trip otherwise."

"It is."

Mentally, I cuss myself out. The last thing I want to do is remind Harper of the geographical distance between us, and it was one of the first things out of my mouth.

"How's the book coming?" I ask, opting for a total conversation shift.

"It's not. I'm giving up on it for a little while…or maybe just *a while*."

"Oh." There's more I want to say in response, but I'm not sure it's my place to. I don't want to be one more person in Harper's life who tells her what she should be doing.

"Amelia and Theo got back today."

"How was the honeymoon?"

"It sounded amazing."

"That's great," I say sincerely.

"Yeah. We got dinner together tonight, which was nice. Felt like…steps forward. Maybe. I don't know." Harper laughs, and there's more rustling. I'm eighty-nine percent sure she's in bed. "Parts were awkward."

"You don't have the solidest foundation to build on. Give it some time."

"Things with Amelia were fine, actually. It was weirder with Christian."

My stomach sinks, dread dropping like a lead weight.

I'm too late. She's moved on. And knowing there was a chance that could happen was nowhere near as painful as the reality.

I grasp on to the word *weird* like a life raft, using it to keep my voice even. "Who's Christian?"

"He's a college buddy of Theo's. When I told Amelia about us —I mean, that there isn't an us..." Harper sighs, and it turns into a quiet laugh. "Anyway, you don't want to hear about my awkward double date."

I don't.

But I also do, especially if she keeps using adjectives like *awkward* to describe it. It summons back a spark of hope that was just snuffed out.

Silence stretches between us. And I decide, *fuck it*.

"We're playing New York in two weeks."

Eternities pass as I wait for Harper to respond.

"In New York," I add when she still says nothing. As if that wasn't obvious. "Will you come? I can get you a ticket. Or tickets, if you want."

If she shows up with *Christian*, at least I'll know where I stand. Nowhere.

"You want me to come to your game?" She sounds surprised, and that surprises *me*.

"Yes. I—*yes*."

"Okay."

"Okay?" Relief suffocates the two syllables, thick enough that I'm sure she can hear it.

"Yeah. Sounds fun. Can I bring my roommate, Olivia?"

"Of course." Another burst of relief, knowing that's the first person she thought of. "You can bring whoever you want. I'll have tickets left at the front desk for you."

Harper laughs. "Okay, hotshot."

"You haven't seen me play before. I could suck."

"You won't suck. You're good at everything."

"Everything, huh?" My voice lowers, deepens. "Do you have any specific examples?"

"Nope. It's just a general observation."

I chuckle. "Okay. How about this? You think it over and then call me back tomorrow night to tell me what you came up with?"

There's a long stretch of silence, where I'm sure I overstepped.

"Are you getting back together with Cat?" The question comes out in a rushed exhale, so it sounds more like *are-you-getting-back-together-with-Cat.*

It takes me a few seconds to decode what she's wondering. To reconcile the inference that she might actually care with the realization that I never conveyed my true feelings on the topic the way I should have. I got distracted by the wedding and my dad and the fact that Cat was already a nonfactor for me, and I never considered she might be a factor for Harper.

"No."

"No?"

"*No*," I repeat with more conviction. "I was never—fuck, Harper. I thought I'd made it clear. There's nothing there. When I talked to her, I told her that I was interested in someone else."

Another beat of silence that doesn't sound nearly as long.

"I'll call you tomorrow."

I smile. "Okay."

"Okay," she repeats.

We both linger on the line.

"Hey, Harper?"

"Yeah?"

"Don't take this the wrong way, but I'm glad your date sucked."

"Good. It was your fault."

Then, she hangs up, leaving me sitting on Lewis's porch with a wide, stupid smile on my face.

CHAPTER TWENTY

HARPER

I survey the pile of clothing covering most of my bed, hands on hips.

I'm nervous. And I'm nervous that I'm nervous.

For the past two weeks, I've replayed my conversation with Drew over and over again. The rowdy background noise when one of his teammates answered. The disappointment in his voice when I said I'd stopped writing. The excitement when I agreed to go to the game tonight.

We've talked and texted a few times since. But those conversations have all been lighthearted and playful. Flirty.

And now...I'm nervous. Torn between wishing I were already at the game and that much closer to seeing him and hoping I got the date wrong and actually have another week to mentally prepare.

"You rea—hot damn."

Olivia strolls into my bedroom with the confidence I'm trying to channel, wearing leather leggings, heels, and a sweater that hangs off one shoulder. Meanwhile, I'm standing in the middle of my room in a lacy bra and matching underwear and nothing else, amid nearly every item of clothing I own.

My best friend looks me up and down. "Well, that's one way to get his attention. You do know it's *cold* in hockey rinks, though, right?"

I throw a slipper at her before flopping onto my bed. "I have nothing to wear."

"You're lying on a literal pile of clothes."

I sit up. "You know what I mean."

"I know that you've had two weeks to plan for this. How did you not decide what to wear two weeks ago?"

"Not helpful."

Truthfully, I've avoided thinking about tonight. Planning for tonight. Because I have this horrible habit of thinking that looking forward to something might ruin it. And I also thought assuming I wouldn't be nervous and panicky about tonight—therefore deciding not to plan ahead—might mean I *wouldn't* be nervous and panicky when tonight arrived.

But the game didn't get canceled.

And I *am* nervous and panicky.

So, now, I'm stuck, outfit-less.

Olivia smiles, finding my conundrum funny. She's a terrible best friend. "You're lucky I've dated too many athletes. Hang on."

She darts out of the room, moving effortlessly in her high heels. I'd break my neck, attempting a similar maneuver.

"Put on a pair of jeans," she calls from the hallway.

I roll off the bed and do as she said, pulling on my favorite pair.

Olivia reappears a few seconds later, tossing me a plastic shopping bag. I catch it and pull out a ball of blue-and-white material that unfurls as I hold it up.

I stare at the logo on the front for a minute, then turn it around to look at the back. *Halifax* and the number twenty-three are written in bold block letters on the back, the white writing standing in stark contrast to the navy background.

"You want me to wear his *jersey*? Doesn't that seem…I don't know…*desperate*?"

Olivia laughs. "You *like him*, Harper. Let him *know* you like him. Plus, I dated jocks in high school. Trust me, he'll like this." She winks as I consider how Drew looked at me the two times I wore his clothing. A jersey is similar, right? She might be right. "Come on. Put it on, or we'll be late."

"Why do you even *have* this?"

"I ordered it after you told me about him. Was planning to give it to you for Christmas, as a joke. Hurry up, put it on."

I pull the jersey on, then slip my phone, apartment key, ID, and credit card in the back pocket of my jeans. Glance around my room to make sure I'm not forgetting anything else. It feels like I might be, but I hope that's just the nerves.

Tonight feels monumental.

I'm not sure if that's dramatic or just my insecurities talking. Nothing about me and Drew feels like something I'm familiar with. Not the fact that he saw me in the awkward stages of adolescence. Not the way he saw me cry over my dad or snipe with my sister. Even the sex felt different. Exposing in a way I've never experienced.

And I'm terrified by how it feels like I'm still fumbling around for the switch in a dark room. Worried it will all fall apart between us once I admit to myself that I'm invested in Drew Halifax.

I'm a polished version of myself this time. In my city with my makeup applied and my hair curled. Not fresh out of a rainstorm or sunburned from a day on the lake. But it still doesn't feel like enough armor. It feels like he'll see all my vulnerabilities, anyway.

It's nice to be seen.

It's also scary.

"Harper!"

"Coming!" I call back.

One final deep breath, and I leave my room, flipping off the light. Plunging the room into darkness.

Olivia is waiting next to the front door, practically vibrating with excitement. I push away my worries. At the very least, this will be a fun night out with my best friend. Our schedules didn't line up well for most of the summer.

It's only two stops on the subway from our apartment to the arena. I've been here once before for a concert, but never for a sporting event. I'm shocked—stunned—by how many people are here.

Everywhere I look, it's packed. Everyone is shoved together like sardines, fighting for space as they stream through the entry points. A sea of color and anticipation.

Olivia and I fight through the crowd to the ticket counter. There's no line here, only one window open.

"Hi. I'm here to pick up tickets?" The second sentence comes out like a question, betraying just how out of my element I am.

"We're sold out, sweetheart," the ticket attendant tells me, a condescending smirk growing as he takes in the jersey I'm wearing. "Especially to Seattle fans."

Olivia huffs beside me.

"They're reserved tickets," I tell him. "Should be under Harper Williams."

The man rolls his eyes. "Fine." He heaves a sigh, like doing his job is some massive inconvenience to his evening. "I'll look."

He disappears, and for a split second, I panic, sifting through worst-case scenarios.

Maybe Drew forgot to get the tickets. Maybe they gave them to someone else by accident. Maybe...

"Here you go."

A white envelope appears on the counter, my name neatly typed on the outside. I open it and peer inside. There are two tickets and two passes attached to lanyards.

"What's this?" I ask, pulling one lanyard out to show him.

The attendant's eyes widen. "That's, uh, that's an all-access pass, miss. Should get you into any restricted area."

"Like the locker room?" Olivia asks, grinning. "Because I've always wondered what—"

"Thanks for your help," I say, even though he was a jerk up until he realized I might be someone important.

Then, I grab Olivia's hand and pull her in the same direction everyone else is heading. Olivia laughs as she follows me toward the escalators that are packed with fans entering the stadium.

Most of the jerseys are the same white and red as the banners decorating the walls, but there's an occasional flash of navy to match what I'm wearing.

Literally match.

Every Seattle fan I see appears to be wearing a Drew Halifax jersey. It's...weird. Objectively, I knew Drew was famous. I saw Jared and the other guys fawning over him at the wedding. And the infamous Instagram post. But it's not anything I've seen firsthand, in person, until now.

We get through the metal detectors. I automatically start toward the next set of escalators that everyone is streaming toward.

"Wait." Olivia tugs at my sleeve. "What section are we in?"

I glance at the tickets that just got scanned, squinting at the tiny numbers. "One ten."

"We don't need to go up to the balcony then. Come on."

I follow her through the crowd. The scent of fried food and popcorn fills the air, swirled around by all the activity. My stomach grumbles. I picked at a salad earlier, but that's all I've had since lunch.

Ten minutes later, I spot the sign for section 110. We walk through the concrete tunnel, and all of a sudden, the ice appears.

The aroma of popcorn and hot dogs is replaced with the smell of *ice*, I guess. Something cold, spiked with adrenaline. My heart rate picks up as I look out at the stretch of frozen water, pure white with stark red and blue lines. Red goals sit at either end, light gray netting enclosing the back. Tall boards separate the ice from the seats.

"What row?"

I glance away from the ice at Olivia. "Um…" I pull out the tickets again. "Three?"

Olivia nods and starts down the stairs. I follow her. Down, down, down until we're only three rows back from the vertical boards that surround the ice.

I glance down at the tickets. "This can't be right."

Olivia shrugs and sits. "He *is* on the team. I'd hope he could get good seats."

"But this is…"

I look over one shoulder, back toward the tunnel we walked through. The crowd streaming in was nothing in comparison to the number of people packed in here. There are hundreds. Thousands. Row after row after row, stretching way back and up toward the rafters that boast brightly colored banners.

"Wow." I turn back around, focusing on the ice that looks close enough to touch.

The lights dim a few minutes later. Colored spotlights flash across the surface of the ice, and music begins blasting. A montage of highlights is played on the Jumbotron, players scoring and colliding and flying up the ice.

I know nothing about hockey. My father preferred books and fishing to mainstream sports. Simon will watch a football game on Thanksgiving but prefers discussing antitrust law. As far as I know, the only sport he has any real interest in is tennis. I've never dated a guy with more than a passing interest in any sport.

So, I was expecting to be bored. To sit through however long a hockey game lasts, distracted by the anticipation of seeing Drew again.

I was *not* expecting to be unable to look away as players start stepping onto the ice. The red jerseys I don't care about are closer to this end, partially blocking my view of the blue end. I only catch glimpses of Seattle players circling the opposite goal.

They all look *massive*, towering giants balancing on two blades. Flying by with speed and power—it's like standing next to an interstate. Graceful and ginormous. It's breathtaking. Arresting in a way that's difficult to look away from.

"What number is he?" Olivia asks, also squinting at the far end of the ice.

I glance at my shoulder to check. "Twenty-three."

"That's him, by the goal."

I follow Olivia's gaze, focusing on one of the navy jerseys standing by the goal. Sure enough, *Halifax* and *23* are written on the back. We match.

The warm-up ends, players filing off the ice and the national anthem being sung. The starting lineup for both teams is announced over the loudspeaker. New York's is greeted by cheers. Seattle's with boos.

Drew leans over and says something to the guy next to him

when his name is announced. His teammate punches him in the shoulder, saying something in response and then laughing. This is a side of Drew I've never seen before. A part of his life I've never been privy to.

And it's *massive*, in comparison to the little details I know about him. This huge thing that's a lot larger than him, but that he's a big part of.

He's important. Adored. But Drew has never made me feel small. He lifts me up instead.

The game progresses in a blur of loud collisions with the boards that surround the ice and announcements over the loudspeaker that make little sense. Olivia researches hockey penalties on her phone, whispering rules about hooking and boarding to me.

Halfway through the second period, Drew scores. It's a *blink and you'll miss it* moment, where one of his teammates passed him the puck and a quick flick of his wrist sent the puck flying. I thought it was lost in the goalie's bulk until I saw the red buzzer behind the goal light up.

I jump out of my seat, ignoring the surrounding grumble from New York fans.

Olivia leaps up, too, and we bounce around, watching the blue jerseys mob Drew and listening to the announcer drone, "Washington goal scored by number twenty-three, Drew Halifax, twelve minutes and fifty-three seconds into the second period. Assisted by number thirty-three, Troy Crawley…"

The buzz of excitement remains in my blood for the rest of the game, even as the clock ticks down without another goal despite New York's desperate attempts. The final score is one to zero.

Drew won the game.

Olivia tugs on my arm as we follow the heavy stream of

people exiting the seating area. Most of the fans are downcast and disappointed, many of them grumbling about the home team's lackluster performance.

"You should go see him by yourself," she tells me. "I'll take the subway back and see you at home."

"But you said you wanted to meet him."

"I do. But this should be your moment. Go show off how good you look in blue."

I nod, giving her a hug. "Okay."

"And if things go well"—she wags her eyebrows—"text me so I know you didn't get trampled in here, okay?"

I laugh. "I will. Thanks for coming, Liv."

"Always. Have fun!" She waves and then disappears into the crowd.

I step off to the side, pulling out the lanyard that came with my ticket and squinting at it, hoping it has some indication of where to go. Nothing. I start walking, stopping when I spot a security guard wearing the stadium logo.

"Excuse me. I'm trying to get down to where the players are."

I half-expect him to look at me like I'm crazy. He doesn't.

He glances at my pass and nods toward a door a little farther down the hall. "Head in there. Show that to the guy at the bottom of the stairs, and he'll tell you where to go."

"Thank you."

I follow his instructions, stepping into a concrete hallway and then heading downstairs.

There's another guard at the bottom, who glances at my pass. "You're good. End of the hall."

I nod and thank him, continuing to walk. Voices sound up ahead. Gray concrete has been replaced by glossy photos and the New York logo. Shiny hardwood floor.

Nerves fizz in my stomach as I approach the doorway at the end of the hall and glance around. Nothing but unfamiliar faces look back at me. It's a large, rectangular room with about a dozen small groupings standing around. I step inside, intent on heading toward the far wall. There are no signs of any of the players, so I assume they haven't come in here yet. Maybe they're showering? Celebrating?

"Harper?"

I glance to the left, my eyes widening when I recognize the middle-aged woman smiling at me. "Mrs. Halifax. Hi. It's nice to see you."

"It's *wonderful* to see you." Drew's mother engulfs me in a warm hug, squeezing me tightly. "And please call me Becca. You remember Aiden?"

"I—yes, of course. Hi, Mr. Ha—Aiden."

Why didn't Drew mention his parents *were coming?*

I've met them before, so it's slightly less awkward than it would otherwise be. And they're both as friendly as I remember. But still, it's weird. They know my messy family history. Know about my dad and why we stopped coming to Port Haven. And I have no idea what they know about me and their son.

Becca beams at me. "Drew was right. You're gorgeous."

"Oh. I, uh—thanks."

"Stop smothering," Aiden chastises his wife. "It's bad enough we showed up unexpected."

That makes more sense—that Drew wasn't aware his parents were coming. But it still adds an uncomfortable dynamic to an interaction I was already apprehensive about.

"Drew should be out shortly," Becca tells me. "It usually takes about twenty minutes."

"Oh. Okay."

"You work in the music industry, Drew said?"

"I'm just an assistant."

"No such thing as *just* an assistant."

I smile at that, appreciative of her attitude. Becca continues peppering me with questions, many of which suggest Drew mentioned me to his parents, while we wait for him to appear.

CHAPTER TWENTY-ONE

DREW

My eyes search the room as soon as I step inside. There aren't many people waiting in here since tonight was an away game. Not many families made the trip, especially for a preseason game. Most of the guys headed straight for the bus to go back to the hotel instead of coming in here.

I tell myself it's fine if she didn't stay. If she didn't use the pass. But I know it will mean something if she didn't.

And then I spot her. It feels like it's been a lot longer than five weeks since I last saw her. Harper's hair is loose and curled in a way I've never seen before, and I appreciate it for no other reason than it suggests that she made an effort, and I hope that means something.

But then I realize what she's wearing, and I'm almost certain it does.

She's wearing my jersey. I can't see the back, but I can see the Wolves logo on the front and the twenty-three on the shoulder.

At this point in my career, I've seen hundreds of people wear my jersey. Maybe thousands. But this feels very different. This is the person I could see *taking* my last name, not just wearing it.

The shock and satisfaction dull my reflexes. It's not until I'm a few feet away that I realize I know who Harper is talking to.

My dad chuckles when he spots my shocked expression first. "Three hours on the train, and he barely even noticed we're here, Rebecca."

My mom and Harper glance over as well.

"I'm just…surprised," I say, finally tearing my eyes away from Harper. "I had no idea you guys were coming."

"That was the goal. Thought it would be a nice surprise since you don't play in Boston until December."

"Of course, it's a nice surprise," I respond, sneaking another glance at Harper.

She looks nervous, a little uncertain.

"Well, we'll head to the hotel," my mom announces. "Great game, sweetheart." She steps forward and gives me a hug.

I release her and glance at Harper. "You hungry?"

Hesitantly, she nods.

"Why don't we all get dinner before you guys go to the hotel?" I ask, reaching down and grabbing Harper's hand.

I squeeze it. After a second, she squeezes back.

"Oh, no, we don't want to impose. We just wanted to see you, Drew," my mom says.

My dad hides a grin. She absolutely wants to impose. Before I came out here, I'm sure she was asking Harper a million questions. I can see the eagerness in her expression. They haven't met a girl I had any interest in for years.

"You won't be imposing at all," Harper says.

I give her hand another squeeze.

"I…" my mom says, and my parents exchange a glance. "All right then."

"That way." I nod toward the door marked with an Exit sign.

My parents head for the hallway, Harper and me right behind

them. There's a lot I want to say to her, but nothing that I really want my mom and dad overhearing. So, I settle for wrapping an arm around her shoulders, pulling her against me until our sides are melded.

"I missed you," I whisper.

She glances up at me and smiles. "Nice goal."

"Nice jersey." There's a lot more I'd like to say about it—do to her while she's wearing it—but my parents are still in earshot.

Harper shrugs. "I liked the color."

I chuckle. "Uh-huh."

We end up at a Mediterranean restaurant close to the arena, which Harper suggested. It's half-empty, the few patrons barely paying us any attention.

I down two chicken shawarma wraps while Harper nibbles at falafel. Predictably, my mom pelts her with questions while we eat.

"Drew mentioned your sister just got married?"

"Yes, she did," Harper replies. "On Lake Paulson."

"Oh, that's such a beautiful area."

"It is," she agrees.

My dad and I talk hockey. Ever since I started playing, it's been our tradition. We recap every game together.

I know a lot of guys whose parents put pressure on them. Who dread discussing games with their dad. I feel very lucky I'm not one of them. That my dad has supported me and been the one to tell me he's proud of me, even after games where I played like shit. That he never second-guessed my chances of making it to the professional level and cried when I got drafted.

I discreetly hand the waitress my credit card when my parents head to the restrooms together, my mom rationalizing she might as well go while my dad isn't blocking her in the booth.

"I wasn't expecting there to be that many people there

tonight," Harper says, dropping the fork in her empty dish and then taking a sip of water.

I feel the corner of my mouth tug up. "No?"

"I didn't know *what* to expect, really."

I thank the waitress as she brings the receipt for me to sign, scanning it before signing. If I haven't paid before my parents get back, they'll argue with me about taking care of the bill.

"Does it ever bother you?" she asks.

"What?"

"The expectations. The pressure. It looks like a lot."

I tuck my card away and fold up the receipt. "I'm usually focused on the game, not who's watching. It doesn't bother me most of the time. Tonight was different."

"Because your parents were there?"

This girl. "No. Because *you* were there, Harper."

My mom chooses this moment to reappear, closely followed by my dad. Predictably, they argue when I tell them I already paid for dinner. It lasts until we're out on the sidewalk, saying our goodbyes. My mom is already yawning by the time they catch a cab toward their hotel. The last time either of them was up past ten was the night my dad ended up in the hospital. Usually, they're asleep by now.

Once the taillights of the yellow car disappear, I turn and kiss Harper.

She gasps into my mouth, clearly not expecting it.

No matter how old I am, it still feels weird to kiss a woman in front of my parents. Even if I made it incredibly obvious to them both how much I liked her. Now that they're gone, it feels like every second I wait is a wasted one.

So, I just…don't.

I kiss her the same way I did at the lake because this feels the same as it did at the lake. It's *her*, not our surroundings.

Her surprise disappears quickly. Then, she's kissing me back, arms winding around my neck and fingers pushing into my hair as she matches my urgency.

When we finally separate, we're both breathing heavily.

"I've been dying to do that."

"Yeah?" Her tone is dazed. A little unsteady. "Since when?"

"Since the last time I did."

I grin at her startled expression. This is the last time I'll see her in person for…I have no idea how long. My schedule for the next few weeks is grueling.

It will be at least a month until I'm able to come back to New York. If she *wants* me to come back.

But I want her to know *I* want to come back.

A car horn honks, drawing my attention to the busy traffic and bright lights.

"I like New York."

"We do have a lot of pigeons here," Harper replies. "And I know how you feel about birds."

I chuckle, but I don't say what I'm thinking. That if there was a reason to love New York City, it's *her*.

But that confession feels like too much, too soon. As much as I want her to know how I feel, I'm terrified of scaring her off. To admit that I won't be able to spend much time here until April at the earliest. June, if we go as far in the playoffs as everyone on the team is hoping.

I wish we'd met at the start of the summer. If this moment had happened in May, I could have relocated to the city for months.

"Wanna get a drink?" she asks me suddenly.

I nod. "Sure."

CHAPTER TWENTY-TWO

HARPER

Drew and I walk to a popular club I've been to a couple of times before with Olivia or friends from work. It's the first place that popped into my head and only a couple of blocks from the restaurant where we ate with his parents.

"Wow." Drew glances around as we walk across the crowded, sticky floor. "You know all the little-known local spots, huh?"

I punch his shoulder—and possibly sprain a knuckle—as we approach the long bar top that runs across one wall of the club. Strobe lights dance around, music pulsing through speakers loudly enough that it vibrates off everything.

"You sure you're up for this?" I basically have to shout in the noisy room.

"What do you mean?"

"I don't know…are you tired after the game?"

Drew laughs. "Don't insult me."

"I was *complimenting* you, Halifax. You hustled out there."

Another laugh.

We reach the counter.

"What can I get you?" the bartender asks.

Drew looks to me. "Shot of tequila."

I glance at Drew, raising an eyebrow. "Make it two."

The bartender nods before shuffling off to retrieve our drinks. He returns less than a minute later, the colorful ink on his arms shifting as he sets the shots down.

I look around the club as Drew pays, tapping my fingers on the metal counter while I watch people talk in booths and gyrate on the dance floor.

When I look back at Drew, he's salting a lime. I don't realize I'm smiling until I feel the pinch in my cheeks as my facial muscles start to protest.

"Cheers."

"Cheers."

We clink glasses and then down the shots, followed by salty sourness.

Drew makes a face. "I forgot how much I hate tequila."

"You didn't complain this much last time."

"Well, you were obviously intent on getting hammered. I wasn't going to let you drink alone. Or walk in the rain to get whiskey or beer."

"So, you brought salt instead?"

He flashes me the lopsided smile that never fails to make my heart race, both dimples appearing. "Yeah, I brought salt instead."

I glance down at the discarded green wedges for a few seconds before glancing up at Drew. "So…hockey."

He leans closer, lips leaning upward as he fights a smile. "Yeah?"

"I don't know enough about it to ask you any questions," I admit. "We've never really talked about it, though, and it's obviously this huge part of your life. I'm just curious."

"Curious about what?"

"When did you start playing?"

"I was four."

"Did you play other sports too?"

"Yeah." He rests both forearms on the edge of the counter. "I tried it all. Baseball, football, lacrosse. But...I don't know. Hockey was always different. I just felt comfortable. Like it's what I was meant to be doing."

"That sounds like a nice feeling."

He studies me. "What did you think of the game?"

"Honestly?"

"Nah. Lie to me if you hated it."

He grabs my hand, flipping it over and tracing a line across the center of my palm. My heart takes off at the speed of a gallop. As fast as the glide of skates carving ice.

"I loved it."

"Really?" There's a new spark in his green eyes, satisfaction and surprise swirling.

"I thought I *would* hate it—no offense. But it was exciting. Not like football, where it takes twenty minutes to move the ball two feet."

A low laugh rumbles in Drew's chest. "I think you mean yards."

I roll my eyes. "This isn't going to work if you're all about the sports lingo."

"Will it work otherwise?" he asks.

I hold his gaze. "You tell me."

Drew exhales. "Regular season starts in ten days. We'll play eighty-two games. Travel thousands of miles. It's exhausting. But I love it. I live for it. I'm insanely lucky, getting paid to play." He glances down at our tangled fingers. "That week at the lake? Felt like the start of something. And I—"

"Excuse me?"

Drew and I both glance to the left, toward a group of girls

who are gathered alongside the bar right next to us. The woman closest—a curvy blonde—is eyeing Drew in a way I really don't appreciate.

"Oh. My. God. You're Drew Halifax, aren't you?"

I suck my bottom lip into my mouth, tasting the remnants of smoky alcohol, lime, and salt. Resigning myself to the inevitable flirting and fawning.

"Nope."

My head jerks toward Drew in shock. He's smiling apologetically at the group of girls, who are now exchanging confused looks.

"I get that a lot. Guess I look like a quarterback."

His hand tightens around mine, and then we're moving. Away from the bar and into the press of bodies dancing in the center of the room.

I hear a distant, "Wait!" before we're surrounded by the crowd.

Drew pulls me behind him until he suddenly stops toward the center of the dancefloor. One tug of his hand, and I'm positioned in front of him. This is nothing like the last—and only—time we've danced together. No one I know is staring. The song playing has a percussive beat that rattles my bones. Air leaves my lungs in a huff as his hands grab my hips. We're surrounded on all sides, pressed together by the pulse of the music and the vape smoke that lingers in the air.

He's controlled.

On the ice earlier, he body-checked a guy into the boards hard enough to make my teeth rattle. But for the rest of the game, he was focused. He made hurtling down the ice look leisurely. Scoring a goal appear effortless. His grip on my hips is relaxed, not tight.

So I challenge him a little, stepping back so the slim distance between our bodies shrinks to nothing.

Drew's hands tighten reflexively just above my waist, absorbing the small step. The jersey I'm wearing slips, his fingers brushing bare skin instead of polyester.

I can't hear his inhale over the pounding music. But I can feel the rapid movement shift his chest.

Need pools in my stomach, hot and insistent, as his hands explore. They slip under the loose fabric and splay across my stomach. I arch back against him, hoping his hands will move up or down. It's dark and crowded out here, everyone wrapped up in their own little worlds.

I grind back against him in silent desperation. Annoyingly, his hands return to my hips, holding me still.

"Drew," I whimper, his name a mixture of arousal and irritation.

I'm not sure if he hears me or if my annoyance is obvious.

"Not here." His lips graze my ear as he whispers the words to me.

I turn around in his arms so I can see his expression. He's already looking down, the strobe lights only exposing flashes of his expression.

"Why won't you touch me?"

His grip tightens. "I'm touching you right now."

"If you're not into this anymore, you can just tell me."

Drew surprises—and irritates—me by laughing. "You think I'm not *into this*? That I what—got my fill of fucking you?"

I nod, a little hesitantly, because his expression is making it obvious that isn't the right answer. But that is what I thought. I know why I took so long to reach out to him after Amelia's wedding. But Drew *never* did. And he's a nice guy. Nice to everyone. Nice to Cat. I don't know what this night means. If it means anything.

"Troy left his gym bag in my car last summer, and I didn't drive for three days. Worst thing I've ever smelled in my life. *That's* what I've been thinking about ever since we started dancing, so I don't embarrass myself." His hands tug me closer, so the bulge in his pants is pressed firmly against me. "Trust me, that's nothing you ever need to worry about. I'm so fucking attracted to you, I have to think about sweaty socks baking in the sun."

My nose wrinkles. "How romantic."

"I missed you." There's humor in his voice. But also sincerity. Before I can decide how to respond, he adds, "We had to be quiet at the lake. I can hardly hear anything in here." His lips move lower, ghosting along my jawline. "When you scream my name, I want to *hear* it, Harper."

"Let's go."

A laugh rumbles in his chest. "You wanted to come here."

I shrug. "Inviting myself straight to your hotel seemed desperate."

The amusement disappears. "I want more than sex with you."

Suddenly, I wish we weren't facing each other.

It's too intense, looking straight at each other while having this conversation. It's a different sort of isolation, standing in the middle of a sea of strangers and a center of commotion, but only focusing on one other person.

"Would you have called me if I hadn't called you?"

Drew prods the inside of his cheek, shaking his head very slightly. "I don't know. I wanted to call you as soon as I left. Every day since I left, I've wanted to call you."

"But you didn't."

He sighs. "I fell for you more in a week than I've ever cared for anyone else. Truthfully? That scared the shit out of me. And you acted like we were a fling that had run its course."

"You were leaving. Your dad was in the hospital. It hardly seemed like the right time to invite you on a date!"

I try to pull away, but he won't let me.

"You asked me earlier if we'll work out, and I copped out. What I should have said is, 'I sure fucking hope so.'"

He spins me so my back is to his front again, slipping one hand under the jersey—*his* jersey—that I'm wearing. Lust surges through me as his palm spreads across my stomach, hot skin and possessiveness.

I'm sweating. Swimming. *Drowning*.

There's a hum inside of me that makes it impossible to think or focus. I just relax against Drew, letting him support most of my weight. Relying on him.

I thought I was fine without him.

It was easier to separate everything when there was literal distance between us. When I didn't know what it was like to have him here, in New York, with me. It's startlingly easy, imagining this as my normal. Everywhere I've been before is more exciting with him by my side.

My head tilts to the side and up, and I meet the eyes already watching me. "I like dancing with you."

What's meant to be a whispered confession comes out more like a shout, thanks to the loud music.

Drew's mouth brushes my ear. "I like doing everything with you."

So simple. So earnest. So scary.

I'm teetering on the edge of the cliff, so close to falling.

It feels like this—right here with him—is exactly where I'm meant to be. It's a foreign, giddy sensation.

I'm usually looking ahead. Or behind.

This stillness is strange. No pull to another place.

It's peaceful in a way nothing else has ever been.

"I think it's going to work out," I whisper to him.

I'm not sure if he heard me…until I feel his arms tighten around my waist.

CHAPTER TWENTY-THREE

HARPER

My fingertips tingle, and my stomach twists as Drew's palm lands on my lower back, guiding me through the ornate lobby of the hotel.

A few people give us second glances. Maybe because he's in a smart suit, and I'm still wearing jeans and a hockey jersey. Maybe they recognize Drew as the player it belongs to. Maybe they're just nosy.

The elevator is filled with the same heavy tension that permeated the cab we took back here from the club. Rife with anticipation and expectations. The nerves that dominated my stomach earlier make a reappearance, fluttering around. It feels like I'm filled with shaken champagne.

Only our fingers brush as we step out of the elevator and head down the hall.

"Does the whole team stay here?"

"Yeah." Drew's voice is low, husky, as he swipes the room key against the electronic pad. It flashes green, and the door swings open.

I walk inside first. The furnishings are nice but generic. Bed, armchairs, television. Stock photos of the New York skyline in frames on the walls. The curtains are open, city lights twinkling against the midnight sky. I keep walking toward the windows, listening to the rustle of movement as Drew closes the door and switches on a lamp.

I pull the curtains closed before I turn around, watching Drew watch me. He's hovering beside the bed, gaze intense as he pulls off his suit jacket and tosses it on one of the armchairs.

My approach is slow. Methodical steps that do nothing to betray the way blood is whooshing in my ears and my heart is racing like I just finished running a marathon.

"I like you in my jersey," he tells me, rolling up the sleeves of his button-down.

"Olivia told me to wear it."

"Remind me to thank her whenever we meet."

"Will that be happening?"

He steps closer, so I have to tilt my head back to maintain eye contact. "You tell me."

I reach forward, running a hand down the soft cotton of his shirt until I reach his belt.

Drew holds my gaze as I undo the buckle, the clank of metal and the rasp of leather against fabric the only sounds in the room for a few seconds. Drew groans when I pull his dick free, fisting his erection. I want him to do something about the throbbing between my legs. But I want this more. Giving him pleasure feels like a privilege instead of a chore.

Impulsively, I sink to my knees, only stopping to lick a path along the V of muscle that points straight to his cock. Blow jobs often bother me. Oftentimes, they feel more intimate than sex. There's a shift in the power dynamic. One person receiving while the other gets nothing. Or at least, that's what I thought.

Right now? I don't feel inferior to Drew or annoyed he's

about to get off while I won't. I feel *powerful*, watching his eyes flare and his Adam's apple bob and his abs clench. He's doing nothing to hide the effect I'm having on him, and it makes this a thousand times hotter.

He's ruining me, is what he's doing. With the way he's looking at me—possessive and consuming. With the way he looks—like a masterpiece of male perfection. The bulky pads he was wearing earlier are all gone. I'm the only one who gets to see him like this.

Everywhere I look is corded muscle.

Everywhere I touch is firm skin.

I want to affect him the same way it feels like he's consuming me. I take him in my mouth, the hum of desire amplifying to a new degree.

"*Harper.*" Spilling out of his mouth, my name sounds deranged. Desperate. Desired. The intensity in his gaze sears away everything else.

I withdraw with a wet suck. "Tell me what you like."

"Your mouth on my dick," he immediately answers.

I half-laugh, half-snort as I grip the base of his shaft, spreading my saliva and using it as lubricant as I continue to jack him off. I circle the base and then cup his balls. "I'm serious."

"So am I." His hand rises, thumb brushing against my bottom lip. "These lips spread around my cock? That's the biggest fucking turn-on. You look perfect like this."

Desire burns brighter. Hotter.

I breathe through my nose, suctioning him even deeper down my throat. Reveling in the power I'm experiencing as Drew fucks my mouth with the same confident determination he displayed on the ice earlier. The same way Drew does *everything*.

I feel him jerk against my throat, growing impossibly harder.

And before I can decide if I'm willing to swallow, he's pulling away. Lifting me and dropping me on the bed.

"When I come, I want it to be in the tight pussy I can't stop thinking about."

Oxygen is suddenly hard to come by. Breathing feels like an inconvenience, something I don't really have the time for or the mental capacity to accommodate.

I think I manage an, "Okay then," but I'm not entirely sure. Syllables sound more realistic than entire words at this point.

Drew tugs my jeans off roughly, yanking off my underwear just as impatiently. And then his mouth is where the lace was wedged, soft suction replacing coarse fabric. Sounds I don't recognize spill out of me, mixed with his name.

I should feel self-conscious. I should be overthinking this. That's what has happened every other time a guy has gone down on me.

But I can't process anything besides how *good* it feels. Grinding against his mouth. Feeling the insistent stroke of his tongue as he licks and sucks and bites. My hands find their way into his hair, tugging at the blond strands in a way I hope conveys *don't you dare stop*.

Heat builds quickly, rising to a higher and higher climb. Until it feels inevitable—a fall I want to fight like hell to delay, but also can't wait for. Watching his head between my legs feels like the aftermath of too many tequila shots. Everything is hazy and warm. A respite from reality.

His tongue is a tease. Running circles and licking lines and pushing me closer and closer to the edge. Stoking flames and letting them simmer.

I moan and thrash and *beg*, and I can feel his satisfaction as I *shatter*. Release races through me, erasing everything else. I float on a cloud of bliss, the pleasure so intense that it practically burns.

Everything is still sensitive and shaking when he flips me over, adjusting my body like he's the one in control of my movements, not me. Which is accurate right now.

All I'm wearing is a bra and his jersey. Drew's hand slips inside the baggy polyester, just like he did before. Unlike earlier, he slides all the way up, palming and kneading my breast through the lace before he flicks the clasp open to allow full access. I arch into his touch, electricity racing through me when he twists a nipple and adds a bolt of pain to the remnants of pleasure.

I can feel him behind me, hot and hard and so big that I can't extinguish the spark of nerves, even knowing I've taken him before. I tug at the arms of the jersey, intent on taking it off so I can feel him skin to skin.

"Don't." He grabs both of my hands, pinning them above my head.

"I put this jersey on so you could take it off."

I'm proud of that line. Drew is definitely better at dirty talk than I am. But that sounds sexy.

Drew runs the thick head of his cock against my slit, then uses it to tap my clit, causing my hips to lurch. "I want to fuck you while you're wearing my jersey."

"Is that some athlete kink?" I ask, figuring he'll just respond with a yes or a laugh.

Instead, he exhales. "You want to know some truths, Harper Williams? I've never fucked a woman wearing my jersey—never even cared if she wore it. Do you know what else I've never done? Never taken a girl to dinner with my parents. Never spent two hours agonizing over a single text. Never slept in the same bed for a week. I'm *in* this, Harper."

His hips press closer to mine as his cock slides through the wetness, delicious friction mixing with anticipation.

"You look incredible in anything you wear, Harper. But in this?" One hand slips back under the polyester shirt, cupping my breast and pulling another moan out of me. "In this, you look like *mine*."

I whimper, the mixture of his words and touch too much.

"Say you're mine, Harper."

"I'm yours," I gasp. "I'm yours."

"Fuck. One second."

I know what he's getting. And I'm not great at conveying feelings with words. But I want to give Drew something I've never given anyone else.

"You don't need one. Not unless *you*...need one."

I'm glad he can't see my face. Relieved I can't see his. Of course my romantic implication would be sullied by the suggestion he's sleeping around.

"Why would I *need one*, Harper?"

I squeeze my eyes closed. I'm so *bad* at this. Even when I try to be open, I look half-shut. "Never mind."

It's silent behind me. All I can hear is the thud of my heart.

I'm working up the courage to sit up and look at him when Drew speaks again. "I haven't been with anyone else since February."

Relief floods me, relaxing everything that tensed. "I'm clean. And on birth control. If you...want to."

There's no pause. I'm not ready, not expecting it. He slams inside of me, big and thick and borderline painful, the thrust no longer teasing or reserved. It's not the gentle rolling grind of last time. It's harsh and messy and thrilling. His grip of my hips is tight, holding me exactly where he wants me as his huge cock wrecks me.

I feel unhinged. Unsteady. The way he fills me is so satisfying, but I also feel like I'll never get enough. He plays my body like an instrument custom-designed for him, teasing me with his dick the same way he did with his tongue, sensing when I'm close and slowing.

My hands grip the sheets so tightly that it hurts, holding on for dear life as I push back against him, meeting each thrust.

It builds to a point I know I won't recover from. The pressure explodes, coating my body in pleasure. My thighs shake and my toes curl. And just when I think it can't get any better, his fingers find my clit, and his cock swells inside of me. Foreign warmth pulses—a partial reminder of why this feels so different. The rest is all Drew.

He flips me over and kisses me, the wet slide of his tongue skilled and satisfied. Obviously not caring where either of our mouths have been. I can taste myself on his lips, and it's surprisingly erotic.

When he pulls away, I know what he's looking at. I can feel the liquid seeping out of me. Drew looks me over with a primal possession that makes it hard for me to think. Difficult to breathe.

Mine, I know he's thinking.

I look it, lying here in his jersey with his cum dripping out of me. Usually, I find possessiveness presumptuous.

But I might be screwed because nothing in me wants to deny it.

The buzzing ends, then picks up again. With a groan, I toss a searching arm out, reaching for where I vaguely recall leaving my phone.

Without bothering to check the screen, I raise it to my ear. "Hello?" I croak.

I feel Drew stir in bed beside me, which wakes me up more than the buzzing. I never got used to waking up in bed with him. It was a novelty every time. Still is.

"You're alive. Great."

"Olivia?"

"Yes, it's me. The best friend you were supposed to text if you weren't coming home tonight?"

"Crap." I rub my eyes with my palm. "I totally forgot."

"Yeah, that's what I figured. I just knew I'd feel guilty if you'd actually been kidnapped or trampled or something."

I huff a laugh. "So considerate."

"You still with him?"

"Um..." I glance at Drew, who's smiling up at the ceiling, eyes open and one arm propped behind his head. Shamelessly, I let my gaze explore. "Yes."

"Good." I can hear the smile in her voice. "See you later."

"Bye, Liv."

I set my phone down and turn toward Drew. Wordlessly, he holds his arm out. I roll over, snuggling up against his chest.

"Sorry I woke you up."

Callous fingertips raise goose bumps on my skin as Drew traces absent circles on my arm.

"Don't be. I'm glad you have friends who look out for you."

I hum an agreement, then correct him. "Friend."

"Hmm?"

"I have a friend who looks out for me. And I mean, I like the people I work with—mostly. Amelia lives here now. But aside from Olivia, I'm really bad at letting people in. Things with my mom aren't great, and I barely *know* Simon. I just...seeing you with your parents tonight...you have all these family and friends, and I just…" I swallow. "I want you to know what you're getting into. Not that we're getting into anything, but—"

"We are." He sounds so confident, so sure, that a little of the chaos in my head immediately quiets.

"When do you play New York again?"

"December."

"Will I see you before then?"

Drew's chest falls with an exhale. "Before then, yes. Soon? Probably not. This is the year we're gunning for the Cup. Coach has got us running extra practices and—"

"It's fine, Drew. I get it. I mean, maybe I don't. I know nothing about what it's like to be a professional athlete. But I get…I was so *proud* of you tonight. It was weird, being there and seeing all those strangers wearing your jersey and booing when you scored. But it was also one of the coolest things I've ever experienced, seeing you play. I want you to do whatever it takes to win and to do what you love."

Drew says nothing for a few seconds. Long enough that I wonder if he took that the wrong way, like I don't want him around.

But then his fingers tug my hair, forcing my head back enough that I can see his expression. See the fierce emotion there. "I only called you Sunshine ironically once," he tells me. "Every other time, it's been because that's how I feel around you. Bright and happy. Being around you makes me so fucking happy, Harper."

"I'm falling in love with you," I whisper.

His fingers continue playing with my hair, my favorite smile appearing. "Good. I've been falling for a while, baby."

CHAPTER TWENTY-FOUR

DREW

I wake up slowly, confusion blanketing my mind as I blink at dark, unfamiliar surroundings. There's one thin strip of light sneaking through the heavy curtains, sending a stream of sunshine across the patterned carpet.

My eyes snag on the crumpled navy-and-white jersey lying on the rug, and it all comes rushing back. Dinner with my parents, dancing with Harper, the words she whispered in the middle of the night.

She's still asleep, lips slightly parted and hair spread in a wild halo on the white pillow. I stare at her, taking full advantage of the opportunity to catalog every detail without coming off like a creep or a sap.

After last night, I think we're on the same page. I *pray* we're on the same page because last night also illuminated I'm in way deeper with Harper than I realized.

It felt right, having her at dinner with my parents last night. And it felt fucking incredible, being inside of her bare. I'd never *not* worn a condom with a woman.

Ever since I got drafted, I've heard crazy stories about the lengths some girls will go to in order to trap a professional athlete. Lewis had a woman contact his wife last season, claiming he'd knocked her up on one of our road trips. I hate thinking the worst of people, but I'm not oblivious to what eighteen years of child support on my salary equals.

But I didn't hesitate with Harper. I took what she was offering without second-guessing or regret. Just the memory of it—what her pussy looked like, dripping with my cum—is enough to make my morning wood thicken into a sizable erection.

I'm debating on sneaking into the bathroom to take care of it when she stirs beside me. A minor miracle, considering we were up most of the night and it's only just past seven.

Harper stretches languidly, the sheet sliding and pulling until it's barely covering her chest. Immediately, my gaze falls to her tits. The carnal instinct to fuck her in my jersey prevented me from looking my fill last night. Her sleepy eyes blink up at me, a pink flush spreading across her chest as she registers where I'm looking. It's cute how shy she appears after I've already explored every inch of her.

"Morning." There's a husky quality to her voice, almost a rasp.

"Morning."

"What time is it?"

"Just past seven."

Harper groans and tosses an arm across her eyes. "Crap. I have to go home and get ready for work."

"I'll go back with you."

Her arm slips, surprised blue eyes meeting mine. "You don't have to do that."

"I know I don't, but I'm doing it, anyway. The team bus doesn't leave for the airport until ten. I'll stop for some coffee while I'm out. Just let me shower and change."

She grabs my arm as I start to move away. "Fuck me first."

Like that's a request I'll refuse.

I smirk, rolling so I'm hovering above her. Harper's breaths quicken. I can see the rapid thrum of her pulse just below her jawline. I lean down to kiss it, then suck the skin.

"You're insatiable," I tease.

"You're hard," she shoots back. "And if you won't be back until December…"

"I won't be back for *hockey* until December." I slip one hand between her legs, groaning when I discover she's already soaked. "For you? For the chance to fuck you? I'd fly back here every morning, just to wake up like this."

My hips lower, grinding my dick against the wetness that's gathered. We both moan at the friction. Her pelvis lifts, searching, but I don't push inside her yet. Not when I know it *will* be a while before we wake up in bed together again.

We're playing in DC tonight, then Anaheim in two days. Squeezing in a flight that takes eleven hours round trip isn't going to happen soon—or frequently.

I want to savor this. And despite the fact that we had sex about six hours ago, I know it's going to be a struggle not to come as soon as I'm inside of her.

Harper isn't interested in slow though. Her hands run down the bunched muscles of my back before digging her fingers into my waist and rubbing up against me. "*Fuck* me, Halifax. Or I'll take care of things myself."

A growl works its way out of my throat. Because now that she said that, it's all I can picture. Her rubbing herself and me getting to watch. It's a fantasy I didn't even realize I had until right now.

But I'm working with a tight time frame and a weeping dick, so it will have to become a reality another day.

I dip my head into the crook of her neck, inhaling deeply. She smells like sex. Smells like me. "Do you want me to wear a condom?"

"No." Her fingernails bite into my skin, spurring me into movement.

I reach down and fist the base of my cock, sliding it up and down her slit a few times before I push into her. Tight heat clenches around me, zings of arousal racing down my spine. Her legs fall open, and she takes me deeper and deeper until I'm fully seated inside her pussy. It feels so good, although *good* isn't really the right word. Transcendent. Life-altering.

My balls are already tingling *before* she whispers, "Roll over so I can ride you."

I comply with a groan, watching her hair fall and her breasts sway as she settles over me. Entranced by the sight of her thighs spreading as she sinks back down onto my cock. By the way her teeth bite her bottom lip as she circles her hips. I rub her clit, and then she's convulsing around me, setting off my own release as I fill her with streams of cum.

Harper collapses against my chest, her breathing heavy and her heart racing fast enough that I can feel it. I reach up and brush her hair away from her face, tugging the strands gently so I can see her satisfied expression. Her fingers trail along my rib cage and down my arm, tangling our fingers together.

It's simple. Chaste contact, compared to how thoroughly we explored each other's bodies last night and this morning.

It's nothing I've ever done before though. A different kind of intimacy that I never craved or sought out. A sort I can't imagine sharing with anyone but Harper.

We lie like that until she whispers that she has to leave to get ready for work. And so, reluctantly, I roll out of bed to shower.

CHAPTER TWENTY-FIVE

HARPER

Most mornings, I dread my commute into the office. This morning, I abhor it. All I want is to travel back in time. To relive the past twelve hours over and over again. Now that I'm surrounded by familiarity and normalcy—walking through the crowded subway station and up the stairs of the same stop I get off at every weekday—it feels like it was all a dream. A glimpse of someone else's life.

I reach the top of the stairs and turn left, headed toward the skyscraper that houses Empire Records' New York offices, stealing sips of the coffee we stopped for on the way to my apartment. One reminder that everything was real.

He walked me up to my front door and kissed me goodbye before rushing back to the hotel to pack and meet the bus that's taking the team to the airport. And, based on the upcoming schedule Drew described on the walk from the coffee shop to my apartment, it's normal for him.

Part of an ongoing cycle of games and travel and practices. And when there's a pause in the cycle, he'll be in Seattle, hundreds of miles away. Going from *never* being in a serious relationship to an intense, extremely long-distance one is likely a recipe for disaster. It's also a more appealing option than not trying at all.

It's an overcast gray day, which matches my mood. A slight chill permeates the October air, announcing fall's impending arrival. My hair is still damp from the shower I took before getting dressed for work, swinging around in the subtle breeze.

I pass the massive fountain located right outside the main entrance. A few feet from the glass doors, my steps slow. I recognize the woman standing out front, holding two coffees.

"Hey." Amelia waves at me with one pinkie, the rest of her fingers clutching the paper cup.

"Hi." I stop walking, studying her curiously.

Amelia has never come to my office before. To be perfectly honest, I had no idea she even knew where I worked. The exact building at least. I know the name of the law firm where she just started as a first-year associate, but I certainly couldn't point to it on a map.

And she obviously wasn't just walking by. She's here, waiting for me.

"A little chilly this morning, huh?" I fall back on the least original topic of all time to counteract the awkwardness hovering between us. I used to know what to expect from Amelia. Now…I don't.

"I have a deposition at Smith and Lawrence this morning," she states, disregarding my weather comment entirely. "Just down the street. And I also realized when you were talking about your job at dinner that I've never been here before. So, I thought I'd just stop by…with coffee."

She holds out one of the cups. I take it.

"Thanks."

Amelia is eyeing the cup I'm holding. "You already stopped."

"No such thing as too much coffee," I say. "I didn't get much sleep last night."

Amelia and I have never had the type of relationship where we discuss boys or crushes or sex. We're not discussing it now—or at least, *she* doesn't know that's what I'm referring to—but I still shift uncomfortably, wishing I hadn't added that last bit.

Her brow furrows. "Everything okay?"

"Yeah—yes."

We lapse into silence.

"Uh, well, I should…" I tilt my head toward the building entrance. I'm already running late, mostly thanks to the addiction to Drew's body I've developed.

"Right. Yeah. I just—look, I know you said it was nothing with Drew. But he's here. Theo watched the game last night with some buddies of his. Anyway, if you reach out, maybe—"

"I went to the game last night, Amelia."

"You did?"

"Uh-huh."

"Did you talk to him?" Her eyes are alight now, brimming with excitement. With interest.

I don't know if it's always been there. For a long time, it felt like Amelia went out of her way to act indifferent toward everything happening in my life. Maybe that was my resentments and insecurities talking. Maybe she's changed, the same way it feels like I have. Either way, there's an unfamiliar tug in my chest, absorbing her investment.

"Yeah, I did. We went out to dinner with Aiden and Rebecca afterward. And then back to his hotel room."

Realization washes over her expression. "So, the not sleeping…"

"I didn't mind," I respond, winking.

Amelia giggles. And I get a glimpse of the woman who looks like my *little* sister.

"I really need to head up. We have a nine a.m. staff meeting, and I'm already running late. But…maybe we could get drinks this weekend?"

"Drinks sound good," she replies. Her expression is shy. A little uncertain. But also excited.

"Great."

We share a smile, and then I turn and head toward the doors. I drain the dregs of the first coffee and toss it into the trash can that sits to the right of the entrance before walking into the building lobby.

"Morning, Harper."

I smile at the security guard sitting at the desk beside the elevators. "Hey, Jasper."

"You free Friday night?"

I'm often running late to work. Snuggling in warm sheets is just always preferable to getting dressed and going to work. But I'm even later than usual today, which makes it one of the worst possible days to pause. Usually, I toss a, "Not this week," or, "I'll check my calendar," Jasper's way and then keep walking.

Instead, I stop, setting my second coffee down on the ledge that runs across the front of the security desk. "Why are you asking?"

Jasper is frozen, his olive skin suddenly paler than normal. This—me stopping—isn't part of our usual routine. He runs a hand through his cropped black hair, chuckling awkwardly. "Uh, you're hot?"

I laugh softly. This is part of why I've never stopped before, I guess. He's good for my ego.

"I'm also insecure and emotional and a poor communicator. Do I still sound hot?"

"Uh…" Jasper spins the pen he's holding, looking wholly unsure about how to answer.

I exhale. "My answer isn't going to change, Jasper. You don't need to keep asking. Okay?"

"Okay," he repeats.

I nod and keep walking.

"There was a longer list, just so you know," he calls after me.

My head shakes as I step onto the elevator, jabbing the button. A smile spreads across my face, anyway.

When the doors open on the main floor of Empire Records, Piper is waiting, tapping a heeled boot impatiently. She glances up from her phone, surprise registering as she takes in my damp hair and untucked shirt. I'm usually a little more put together when I show up at the office.

I ask, "What are you doing?" at the same time she says, "I thought you were in the conference room."

Realization slams into me. "Shit. That's today!"

Artists don't come into this office very regularly. Most of them have meetings in the main Los Angeles office. But they occasionally take place, and today happens to be one of those rare days. A meeting I've been helping plan for weeks and entirely forgot about until this exact second.

Piper gives me a *duh* look. A year younger than me, she was a summer intern who overlapped the start of my time here by a few weeks. After graduating, she was hired full time. Unlike me, she's here for the music, not the paycheck. All of the times we've hung out together outside of the office, she's taken me to see "undiscovered talent." Admittedly, they've all been really good.

"Is Carl already in there?"

"Not last I saw. He's running late."

I hide a smile at the derision *he* drips with. Today's meeting is with Kyle Spencer, indisputably the king of country music. Which happens to be the one musical genre Piper holds no appreciation for.

"Okay. I'll be waiting in there."

I catch Piper's nod before I hurry to my small office. I quickly wind my damp hair into a bun and tuck in my shirt before heading down the hall to the conference room.

Carl arrives a few seconds after I've taken a seat. We exchange pleasantries and small talk until the door opens again. Kyle Spencer strolls in, followed by a man I recognize from our last meeting as his manager. Piper trails behind.

I take careful notes throughout the meeting, hiding yawns behind my coffee cup. Sleep sounds so good. And so far away.

Kyle is one of the label's top-performing artists. Which means he gets the gold-star treatment when it comes to everything, including Carl's attention. Most of the meeting is ass-kissing, partly by executives in the Los Angeles office calling in. For some reason, Kyle always insists on having his meetings in New York.

By the time everything wraps up, it's nearly noon.

Carl and Kyle's manager step out into the hallway, leaving me and Piper alone with Kyle.

He leans back in his chair and stretches, fixing a pair of hazel eyes on me. "You were here last meeting, right?"

I nod, resisting the urge to add, *And the meeting before that and the meeting before that.*

In Kyle's defense, those meetings were more heavily attended. Some of the LA executives flew in, plus more assistants from this office. There's a stomach bug going around that has half the office out sick at the moment.

"Hard to forget that face."

I resist the urge to roll my eyes.

He's flirting with me. It would bother me more if he was actually acting interested in me. But his attention isn't on *me*. It's directed at Piper. And she's oblivious, glancing through papers at the other end of the table.

"Want to get lunch? Or dinner?"

I cough. "I appreciate the offer, but that won't work with my schedule. I can get you some restaurant recommendations, if you'd like?"

Kyle cocks his head, studying me with more intensity than I'd have expected. "Boyfriend?"

I want to say, *None of your business*. But he's a big deal, and as much as I don't love my job, I don't want to lose it either. "I have one, yes."

That gets Piper's attention. Her head whips toward me, auburn curls bouncing. Last she knew, I was as single as she is. She doesn't call me out on what she obviously thinks is a lie, though.

"He the possessive type?" Kyle asks, a western twang smoothing the question into the drawl. He seems more interested than offended.

"I want to fuck you while you're wearing my jersey."

I chew the inside of my cheek to keep my expression neutral, then nod. "Very."

Kyle looks past me, at Piper. Focusing his attention where it's been this whole time. I don't think he realizes I've noticed that. I definitely don't think Piper has noticed that.

"What about you, Pippa?"

"It's *Piper*, Kyle," she snaps. Entirely oblivious to the gleam in Kyle's eye that tells me he's well aware of her correct name.

"Sincerest apologies, ma'am."

I have to bite my bottom lip to keep from smiling. His teasing flies right over Piper's head, though.

"You certainly have a way with words," she snips.

"The Recording Academy seems to think so."

Piper's spine stiffens further at the unabashed reminder of Kyle's successes. He and Sutton Everett are the two most popular artists Empire has ever signed. And Sutton is stepping back from music after announcing she's expecting her first child early next year. Kyle is the singular star for the time being.

"Of course they do. Who *doesn't* love a song about beer, a rusty pickup, and a broken heart?"

Kyle's smirk widens. "Are *you* free for lunch?"

"Excuse us for one moment," Piper says, standing. "I just need to have a quick chat with my colleague."

Piper stands and walks into the attached studio, tossing me a look that makes it clear I'm supposed to follow her. After flashing Kyle a polite smile, I follow her inside and shut the door.

As soon as it clicks shut, Piper spins, throwing her hands up in the air. "Why did you lie, Harper? Take one for the team! You're way better at the socializing stuff. And you know I can't stand country singers! Now, I'll have to go to lunch with him!"

"The only country singer I've seen you unable to stand is Kyle Spencer."

"He's annoying."

"He's *gorgeous*, Piper."

She sniffs. "Would your possessive, *imaginary* boyfriend appreciate that comment?"

"He's not imaginary."

"Oh, yeah?" Piper crosses her arms. "Who is he then?"

"Don't freak out, okay?"

"Why would I freak out? You already stuck me at a meal with my nemesis."

I roll my eyes. "He's not your nemesis. And…because you freaked out when I told you I knew him when we were younger."

Piper's forehead wrinkles as she studies me. "What are you—wait." She pulls in a sharp breath. "No way. No *fucking* way."

"I ran into him when I was back in Maine for my sister's wedding. Things…progressed from there."

"You're *dating Drew Halifax*?" She runs through a whole octave with that question.

My mouth opens to deny it.

It's what I always do. I say, "It's casual," or, "Not really." I make it obvious I'm not attached.

But what comes out is, "Yes."

I wasn't the only one expecting a different answer.

Piper's mouth gapes open. "Holy shit."

She drops into the chair next to the microphone, studying me like I'm a science experiment.

"I told you we knew each other."

"No, you told me you swam in the same body of water as him. *Once*. That's very different from *I'm fucking him*."

I laugh. If Piper ever leaves here before I do, I'll be very bored at work.

"Okay, well…"

"Does he have brothers? Single teammates?"

"He's an only child. I don't know about teammates." I study her. "I thought musicians were more your type."

"Too egotistical."

"That makes me think you haven't met many professional athletes."

Piper's nose wrinkles. "Cowboys aren't my type."

I didn't bring Kyle up, but don't mention that. "He sings for a living. He's not out roping cattle."

"Whatever. Just tell me how big his dick is."

I choke on a laugh. "What?"

"It's huge, right?"

There's a burst of static, and then a bored drawl fills the studio. "Howdy. As entertaining as this conversation has been, ladies, I thought you might like to know I can hear every word you're saying in there."

Piper's eyes close. "Shit."

I'm staring off into space when the door opens. I glance over at Olivia, who drops her backpack on the floor with a sigh and then kicks off her clogs.

"Hey."

"Hey." She walks over toward the couch where I'm sprawled, still in her scrubs.

"How was work?"

"I lost a patient." She takes one look at me, the bottle of wine, and the blanket, and she plops down on the couch next to me.

"Shit, Liv. I'm sorry."

She settles into the cushions, tipping her head back to stare at the ceiling. "Then, I hooked up with Dr. Olsen in the on-call room, so the day didn't entirely suck."

I couldn't do Olivia's job. She's an ER nurse, caring for people teetering the line between life and death. But if I were in that position, I would want Olivia to be the one caring for me. She brushes some of the most challenging aspects of her job away like they're inconsequential, but she also loves harder and cares deeper than anyone I've ever met.

"Who's Dr. Olsen?"

"He's the guy I told you about. Chief of surgery. Basically runs the hospital. Also thinks he's God's gift to women."

I snort. "So, exactly your type?"

Olivia sighs. "Basically."

I shake my head before grabbing the bottle of wine, taking a swig, and passing it over to her. She studies me before taking it.

"How was *your* day?"

"It was fine," I reply dully.

Following the morning excitement regarding Kyle Spencer, I spent the rest of the day looking over spreadsheets of quarterly earnings and obsessively checking my phone for texts from Drew. So far, nothing.

I know he's busy. Know he's playing tonight.

But I hate this uncomfortable itch of uncertainty. Not knowing if I should text him. Expect to hear from him.

I have no idea what a relationship between me and Drew looks like. Neither of us used that word even.

"You sure?" Olivia asks.

Pointedly, she glances at the half-empty wine bottle. I didn't even bother with a glass.

I exhale, studying the opposite wall and narrowing in on the crooked frame above the television. We've talked about straightening it ever since we moved in.

"I can't stop thinking about him. I checked my phone a hundred times today. Is that normal, or am I going insane?"

Olivia laughs.

"It's not funny!"

"It's a *little* funny," she counters. "I'm not used to seeing you like this."

"I wish people would stop saying that," I mutter. "I'm not some robot with no emotions."

"I know you're not. But I know that because you let me know you *care*. Because you brought me a coffee when we had that nine a.m. seminar. And you went to that awful bar with the uneven floors with me for three weekends straight just because I thought the guitarist in that band was cute." She nudges my arm with her elbow. "Let him know you *care*, Harper."

"I'm so worried I'll mess it up. I've never…I've never felt

this way with a guy." I glance at Olivia. "Do you think I'll mess it up?"

"I think you went through a hell no one should ever have to experience. I think even anyone who's never been hurt is scared of loving and losing. I think that you can be strong and independent and also rely on someone else. And…I think that you've picked guys you knew you wouldn't fall for—until Drew Halifax showed up like a knight in hockey pads. Maybe it won't work out. But if you don't try, it *definitely* won't work out."

She pats my knee and then stands, walking down the hall toward her bedroom.

CHAPTER TWENTY-SIX

DREW

A sharp whistle cuts through the cold air, signaling the end of practice. I inhale deeply, savoring the scent of carved ice before pulling off my helmet and gloves.

I run a hand through my sweaty hair, my breaths uneven from the last drill, before skating to the center line and filing off the ice after Troy. He's busy complaining about a cramp in his right leg. I'm barely listening. My mind is distracted now that practice is over, already leaping ahead to my plans once I leave the rink.

The atmosphere in the locker room is playful and relaxed. Not only did practice go well, we're about to have two days off after an exhausting start to the season.

I shower quickly, say goodbye to the guys, and then head toward the parking lot. I'm almost to my Chevy—undoubtedly the oldest car in the lot—when I hear Lewis calling my name. I stop and turn, shading my eyes from the sun and watching him jog toward me.

"Hey, man. So glad I caught you."

"Yeah. What's up?"

"Look, I hate asking you this since you already do a ton of PR stuff. But everyone else I've asked is either already going or busy, so…can you go to the wildlife fundraiser on Saturday night? They want ten guys from the team there, but Mary's mom is offering to watch Suzie, and Mary wants to do a weekend trip to Vancouver. I missed the last trip I promised I'd take her on, and I'm trying to not end up in the fifty percent of marriages that don't work out, you know?"

"Right. Yeah. Of course I'll go."

Lewis's face lights up, relief emanating off him. It's not enough to counteract the disappointment I'm experiencing. It's not his fault I'm incapable of drawing boundaries when it comes to hockey.

I was hoping to visit Harper this weekend. We played last night and don't have practice until Monday. As of twenty minutes ago, I thought I had about sixty hours free.

I didn't want to jinx anything, so I didn't tell Harper or book a ticket. And now, I'm wishing I had done both last night, so I would have had a good reason to tell Lewis no.

I don't know what I'm trying to prove. I made it. I got drafted. Won a gold medal. And still, I seem incapable of easing back.

Being a professional athlete isn't a typical job in many regards. But the time commitment is the part I struggle with the most. It's too easy to blur the line between work and life, to the point that it doesn't exist at all. There's always more I could be doing. More training, more ice time, more mental preparation.

The drive back to my condo is a depressing one. My truck makes a concerning sputtering noise that reminds me I still need to make arrangements for the Mercedes that's sitting in my parents' driveway to get shipped here.

Once I'm home, I pick up around the condo since the cleaning lady comes tomorrow and then pull a frozen meal out of the freezer, popping it into the microwave.

Troy texts right as it beeps, asking if I'm going out tonight.

I text him back, telling him I'm busy.

I wouldn't mind hanging out with the guys tonight. Some distraction. But I know they'll be headed to the bars downtown, and that's something I'm much less interested in. It's usually a standard blur of drinks and fans and girls.

At one point, I ate that attention up. Found it flattering and exciting. Work hard, play hard. Now, it seems empty. It feels more like a distraction I was using to avoid the truth—I don't have much in my life besides hockey.

I toss my phone down, grab the food, and turn on the television. The game film I fell asleep to last night is paused—because I have no idea how to spend my free time if it's unrelated to hockey.

My phone buzzes with a new notification. I glance at it reflexively, then sit up when I see her name on the screen.

Harper: *How was your day? A pigeon shit on me while I was walking home.*

I laugh, the sound echoing off the empty walls.

Drew: *Call me when you can. I need details.*

Thirty seconds later, my phone vibrates with a video call. I answer it and sink back into the cushions, smiling at an annoyed Harper. The irritation melts away when she looks at me, flashing me a shy smile as she flops down on her bed with wet hair and pink cheeks.

"Hey."

"Hey." I tuck an arm behind my head, not missing the way Harper's eyes track the movement.

We talk and text regularly. But we haven't seen each other in person in weeks, not since I was in New York as part of preseason. It's been agonizing for multiple reasons.

Based on the way Harper is looking at me, I'm not the only

one aware of every mile between us. It pisses me off even more, knowing this weekend was my chance to erase all the distance.

"What's wrong?"

"Nothing." I paste a smile on my face.

"Don't say nothing. Say you don't want to talk about it if you don't."

I exhale. "I thought I'd be able to come to New York this weekend. Then…something came up."

There's a beat of silence that feels like it lasts a lot longer than seconds.

"It's okay. I understand."

"Will it always be *okay*?" I ask.

Some of the color fades from Harper's cheeks. And I hate—absolutely *hate*—that I'm the one who dimmed it.

"What do you mean?"

I sigh and sit up, running a free hand through my hair. "I mean, this will keep happening, Harper. I don't work a normal nine-to-five. And if I'm lucky, I still have some years left."

"Don't plenty of the players have girlfriends? Families even?"

"Yeah, and it's a strain. Two of my teammates just had divorces finalized. It's not…I'm just trying to be honest with you about what this will look like."

There's a long pause, during which I rethink every word I just said.

"Are you having second thoughts?" Harper asks quietly.

"*No*! No, of course not. I'm worried you might, and I—Harper, I—"

There's a flurry of commotion on her end of the line.

"What about this?" is called out in a voice I recognize as belonging to Harper's best friend, Olivia.

Harper looks to the left. "Last one was better." She glances back at me. "Liv has a date tonight."

"It's not a date!" Olivia shouts.

Harper rolls her eyes. "The *chief of surgery* asked her to go to a fundraiser with him. Olivia is the talk of the hospital."

"It's a *work event*," Olivia hisses.

Harper and I laugh.

"Are you still doing my hair?" I hear Olivia yell.

Harper glances at me, regret covering her face. "I can call you back in a little while? I've got to pack for my mom's this weekend, but…"

Fuck, I realize. "I'm sorry, Harper. I totally forgot."

It should make me feel better—that this weekend wasn't a possibility, anyway. She'll be home in Connecticut, celebrating her mom's fiftieth birthday.

But I feel worse. It feels like we're both getting pulled in opposite directions, not just me.

"It *is* okay," she tells me softly. "It'll keep being okay. I promise."

I exhale, holding on to those words like a lifeline. "Yeah, okay. I lo—" Mid-word, I stop speaking.

I haven't said it before, and neither has she. Those three words have hovered in subtext, but I want the first time to be spoken in person.

Harper's blue eyes are wide—she's well aware of what I almost just said. She looks startled, but not freaked out, which is a relief.

"Harper!" Olivia calls.

I smile. "I'll talk to you later, okay?"

She nods. "Bye, Drew."

The call ends. I toss my phone on the couch with a sigh and go back to watching hockey.

CHAPTER TWENTY-SEVEN

HARPER

Fall foliage blurs by in a stream of yellow, orange, and red. I shift against the buttery leather of the backseat. Usually, I make this trip in my Jeep. This year, Amelia asked if I wanted to ride with her and Theo.

So, here I am, smooshed in the backseat with the bags, listening to Amelia and Theo discuss a rock-climbing documentary. Aside from that, the trip hasn't been terrible.

My relationship with my sister is very different than it looked last year when I showed up for my mom's birthday. It's a time we all gather together because it's less painful than coming together for the occasion that's just over a week later—the anniversary of my dad's death.

I'm not sure if this year will be any less uncomfortable than it's been in the past, but I'm hopeful it will be. Amelia and I have gotten drinks a couple of times. I showed up at her office once with coffee, to return the favor. There's no ease to our relationship. We're both trying, obviously so. But it's definite progress.

My mom is another story. We haven't spoken since Amelia's

wedding, and that's the main cause of the knot in my stomach as we pull into the driveway of my mom and Simon's house.

Theo grabs the bulk of the bags, leaving me and Amelia with one each as we walk up the front path toward the brick Colonial.

The door opens before we reach it, Simon standing in the doorway. "Hello! Welcome!" He hugs Amelia and Theo, then hesitates when he reaches me.

When I visit, I usually make it a point to have my arms full when I walk in, avoiding this moment. This time, I drop my suitcase and give him a hug. It's brief and slightly awkward. But again, it's something.

"You guys made good time," Simon comments. "Your mom is still out, running a few errands."

I glance around the open first floor. Everything is as immaculate as usual, dark floors and white walls decorated with framed watercolors.

"Can I get you guys anything to eat? Drink?" Simon asks.

"I'm all set," Amelia responds.

"Me too," I add.

"I'm going to put these upstairs and then I'll take some water," Theo says.

"Water coming right up," Simon says, then heads toward the back of the house, in the direction of the kitchen.

Amelia pulls off her jacket and hangs it up in one of the cubbies. I set my suitcase in the one next to it, but don't take my coat off.

"I'm just going to go for a quick walk. Stretch a little after the drive."

Amelia eyes me, but doesn't comment as she nods and then walks deeper into the house. She probably knows exactly where I'm headed. It's a trip I take every time I'm back here, and I've never hidden it.

The cemetery where my father is buried is a five-minute walk from the house. Down two blocks and across the street. Sometimes, I wonder why my mother moved so close. If it was a conscious decision or a nonfactor.

I reach the entrance and start along the path. The grass has turned from green to patches of brown, but there are no dead leaves around. Everything is well-maintained.

I turn left at the fork in the path. I slow my steps, surprised to see someone is already standing at my father's grave. Shocked to realize I *recognize* her.

"Mom?"

She rises from her crouched position and turns around. "Hi, Harper."

"I—you—" I clear my throat. "I wasn't expecting to see you."

Her smile is tight. "I could say the same to you. Amelia said you weren't arriving until late afternoon."

"We left earlier," is all I can think to say as I walk forward to stand beside her. "Do you come here often?"

"Once or twice a month."

"I didn't know."

"I know."

We stand side by side, silently paying our respects before turning and heading down the slope. I can see my mother's Volvo parked in the small lot.

"Do you want a ride back to the house?"

"Uh, sure." I follow her over to the SUV, climbing into the passenger seat.

"How are you?" my mother asks as she buckles her seat belt.

The words sound stiff. They also sound like trying.

"I'm okay. I haven't seen Drew in a while. That's been…hard."

Rather than turn on the car, she just sits. "I remember the day

Amelia came to my office and asked if she could go out on the Halifaxes' boat. I thought nothing of it, really. I was relieved Amelia looked excited. Happy I wouldn't have to feel guilty for working on the Falcone murder instead of spending time with you girls. But…"

She looks away, off at the rows of gray stones.

"I still remember mentioning it to Paul. I said something about how Drew seemed like a sensible boy, how I was happy he was who Amelia was choosing to spend time with. I even joked he'd make a good son-in-law. And your father…he said, 'Not unless Harper figures a few things out.' I didn't think about it again. Not until I saw you two together and realized…"

She shakes her head, still not looking at me.

"He's been gone eleven years, and he still knew you better than I do."

A large lump appears in my throat. There's a suspicious burn in my eyes. "You *stayed*, Mom. I know it wasn't Dad making the decision. That it was the struggles talking. and that he didn't *want* to miss the rest of our lives. But still, he left us. You stayed. And you held everything together so that I could fall apart. I never thanked you for that, and I should have."

It's not until I hear a quiet sniffle that I realize she's crying. And then I'm crying too, tears streaking down my cheeks. We lean into each other in a way that's unfamiliar yet reflexive.

"I love you, Harper," she whispers.

"I love you too, Mom."

I'm not sure how long we sit like that until she presses a quick kiss to my head and then starts the car.

And I'm not sure why I choose this moment to tell her, "I'm writing a book."

She glances over at me, obvious surprise on her face. "Really?"

"Yeah. It's a thriller. A mystery, kind of. I could have written a fantasy or a romance. But I wrote a story about seeking truth. About right and wrong. And…it made me realize that I'm not all Dad. I'm half you."

There's a long pause before she responds, punctuated with a couple more sniffles. I don't look over, giving her a chance to school her emotions.

"I'd like to read it."

"It's not finished yet." I don't add that there's someone else I want to read it first, worried it might offend her.

"When it is then."

"Okay."

The short drive back to the house is silent, both of us absorbing the shift in our relationship that just took place.

"You know"—she glances over at me once we're parked in the driveway—"I saw a billboard advertising flights between New Haven and Seattle not too long ago."

"That's kind of a random leap from my book, but sure."

My mom laughs, and the sound of it makes me smile. "Go grab your stuff, and I'll drive you to the airport."

I blink at her. "What? It's your birthday."

Years of feeling guilt-tripped into coming here, and the first time there's minimal awkwardness, I'm basically being shoved out the door.

"The best gift you could give me is being happy, Harper. You should go spend this weekend with Drew."

"But—"

"Do you want to go?"

"I mean, yes, of course. But—"

My mom is already out of the car and barreling toward the house with the trademark tenacity that's more familiar than tender moments. When she bursts inside, Theo, Amelia, and Simon are all sitting in the living room, glancing up with identical startled expressions.

"What's—" Amelia starts.

Our mom is already in motion, heading toward the back of the house. "Where's the travel credit card, Simon?"

"The travel credit card?" He stands from the armchair he was sitting in. "I'm not sure. Maybe the hutch? Or my office? I can go look—"

"I need it! Now!"

Simon casts a confused expression my way. "Is everything okay?"

I shrug. "She wants to ship me to Washington."

"Isn't that where the Wolves play?" Theo teases.

"You're going to see him?" Amelia squeals.

That's all it takes for the house to descend into total chaos. It's so opposite from the way every gathering in recent memory has looked—awkward, stiff dinners and forced conversation—that I basically just stand and stare, feeling like I've fallen into some parallel universe.

"One flight with tickets available!" Theo calls. He's on Simon's laptop, looking up plane tickets. "Maple Leaf Airlines, leaving in…fifty-three minutes."

It's twenty minutes to the nearest airport.

"There's no way I'd make—"

"Book it!" my mom shouts. "I found the travel credit card!" She rushes into the living room and hands Theo a blue card.

I gape at her. "Mom. You can't seriously—"

Once again, I'm cut off.

"Simon, pull the car out of the garage. Amelia, get her bag. I told Simon to put her in the Sailboat Room."

Sure enough, my suitcase is no longer in the cubby where I left it.

My mother named all the guest rooms. Usually, I laugh about it. Right now, I'm too busy gaping at everyone racing around, slamming doors and grabbing keys.

"This is cra—"

My arm is grabbed, and I'm getting pulled toward the front door. Less than a minute after my ticket was purchased, we're all in Simon's SUV, careening down the quiet street.

"Jesus," I huff from my spot wedged between my mother and Amelia. "Way to make me feel like a fifth wheel you guys can't wait to get rid of."

Amelia rolls her eyes.

My mom forwards me the email with the plane ticket attached. My eyes bug out when I see the price for the flight.

"I'll pay you back for this," I tell her.

"Don't be ridiculous, Harper," is her response.

I did not expect fast driving from Simon. He's always struck me as the type who's never gotten a speeding ticket in his life. But he gets us to New Haven in fifteen minutes, meaning I might actually have a chance of making this flight.

Goodbyes are rushed. I hug the members of my family one by one, each of them urging me to hurry so I don't miss my flight. I rush through security and sprint through the terminal toward the gate. It's not until I'm huffing and puffing, waiting for the one other person who hasn't boarded the plane to Seattle yet to have their ticket scanned, that I realize I don't know Drew's address.

I pull out my phone and text Becca. She gave me her number at Drew's game in New York, but I never thought I would actually use it.

I'm immensely relieved when my phone vibrates with a message from her right before the safety demonstration starts. I could just text Drew, obviously. But I want to surprise him.

The plane taxis off the runway, and then we're airborne, the lights of New England fading to pinpricks on the ground.

CHAPTER TWENTY-EIGHT

DREW

"You look miserable," Troy comments, dropping down in the chair next to mine.

I don't deny it, just grunt in response before taking a sip of water.

"I would be, too, if I was avoiding all the women eye-fucking me and completely sober." He claps my shoulder. "Come on. Let me buy you a drink."

"How many women have you used that line on tonight? At an *open bar*?"

Troy grins and leans back, spreading his long legs. "You're supposed to be my winger off the ice too, Halifax. Not sulking in a corner."

"I'm not sulking. Just ready to leave."

For the past three hours, I've schmoozed and socialized. Signed autographs and made small talk.

It's exhausting being known as the friendly, accommodating guy. Powers, one of the rookie defensemen, has been sulking in a corner all night, tugging at his tie and glowering at anyone who passes by. All he was expected to do was attend.

But me? People expect more from me.

"Let's go then."

"It's not supposed to end for another half hour."

Troy scoffs. "Davies won't care. He's having the time of his life."

We both glance at the Wolves' general manager, who's smiling widely and waving his arms around.

"Okay, yeah. Let's go."

Like the oversize child he is, Troy fist-pumps the air. "Afterparty at your place?"

"Sure."

"Sweet!" Troy's off in the blink of an eye to round up the rest of the guys.

Powers predictably declines. And Bouchard, the center who rounds out the first line with me and Troy, left with a blonde about an hour after we arrived. Seven of us pile into two cars and head toward the downtown high-rise I bought when I was traded to the Wolves.

On the drive, I pull out my phone and text Harper.

Drew: *I'm almost home, if you can talk tonight?*

Dots appear and then disappear twice before a response finally comes through.

Harper: *How about tomorrow instead? Long day.*

Drew: *Yeah, of course.*

I stare at the exchange until the phone screen dims and then shuts off, wishing she'd send me another reply. But nothing comes through. With a sigh, I shut off my phone and climb out after Troy.

It's chilly tonight, feeling more like winter than fall. I'm relieved when we step into the warm lobby and start toward the elevators. Mentally, I review the contents of my fridge. I'm probably going to need to order food. The meals served at events like the fundraiser tonight are almost always terrible. Fancy with unintelligible names and weird aftertastes.

"Halifax." Troy nudges my arm.

I follow his line of sight to a figure sitting on the lobby couch.

I blink. Once. Twice. Three times.

Harper is still sitting there.

She glances up, taking in the commotion as we walk across the lobby. I don't really think. I just react, rushing toward her and wrapping my arms around her middle. My arms tighten until all the space between our bodies has disappeared, the realization she's actually here sinking in slowly.

She's *here*. In Seattle. In the lobby of my building.

"Surprise!" Harper smiles up at me, her blue eyes bright and captivating.

"You're here," I state, like an idiot.

"Yep."

"What about your mom's birthday?"

Harper's lips twitch, like something about my question amuses her. "Believe it or not, she basically shoved me on the plane. It was quite the afternoon."

"You going to introduce us to your girl, Halifax?" Troy cuts in, his usual obnoxious self.

I glance over at the guys huddled, waiting. "This is Harper. Harper, these are some of my teammates. The interrupter is Troy. And Dean, Banks, Logan, Julian, and Isaac."

"Nice to meet you guys," Harper says.

"Guessing your place is out?" Troy smirks.

"Yep." I grab Harper's hand and her bag, dragging her toward the private elevator for the penthouse.

"Condo nine twelve, Harper," Troy calls after us. "Come down when you get bored."

Harper laughs before I pull her into the elevator. As soon as the doors are closed, I kiss her.

I've never been more grateful to have a private elevator in my life. Most of the time, I don't even bother using it, riding up or down with Troy instead.

Harper moans into my mouth, her hands tugging at my shirt and tie.

"You're always dressed up while I'm not," she grumbles.

I chuckle. "Both of us naked sounds like a good way to fix that."

"I agree." She kisses a line down my neck. "But you look really hot."

The elevator doors open, revealing my condo. Harper lets go of my shirt and steps out, her mouth forming a comical O-shape as she takes in the huge windows that reveal a breathtaking view of the city with the dark water of the Puget Sound visible just past it.

The furnishings are minimal. Most of them came with the place. The couch is a plush sectional that could comfortably sleep three. The only decoration on the walls is the flat screen television. The living space opens right into the kitchen, which is mostly marble counters and shiny appliances I hardly use.

Harper tugs off her sneakers and leaves them on the plush rug, already making a mess. I trail after her as she looks around.

"This place is *really* nice," she declares, moving toward the windows and staring out at the view.

It is nice. It also feels like a home for the first time, having her here. I've never trusted anyone enough to let them into my personal space like this. Even with Cat, I'd always sneak into whatever hotel she was staying at. It seemed sexy and exciting at the time. Now, I think it was an early sign we wouldn't work out.

I pass her, heading into the kitchen. "You hungry?"

"Starving. I skipped both lunch and dinner by accident."

I open the fridge, surveying the contents. "Okay. I have—"

"Come here."

When I glance back toward the living room, Harper has pulled her jacket off and sprawled on the couch, her dark hair a wild halo.

I shut the fridge door and walk over, looking down and smiling at the sight of her lying like a snow angel. "I thought you were hungry."

She sits up, grabbing my tie and pulling me down on top of her. "Can anyone see in these windows?"

"I don't think so. This is the tallest residential building in the whole city."

"Have you ever fucked anyone here?"

"On this couch or in this condo?" I ask, knowing full well it's the same answer.

"I was talking about the couch," she replies, nose scrunching in a way that makes me think she might be jealous. After torturing myself with thoughts of all the single guys who live in New York City and can offer her more than occasional phone sex, it's nice to see her annoyance.

"Never brought a woman here, Harper." I smile, lowering my mouth so our lips are *almost* brushing. "You're cute when you're jealous."

Her hand rises, fingers trailing along the length of my jaw. "I missed you so much."

An inhale gets stuck in my throat. "I've never hated living here more," I confess.

I'm worried about how the distance will affect us—affect her. But I also hate it for myself. Every night, I wish I were coming home to Harper, not an empty condo.

Her hand drifts to my hair, fingernails lightly scraping my scalp. "It will always be okay," she tells me.

Suddenly those three words are right there, waiting. Words I've never said before but am completely certain of.

I'm distracted from saying them when her hand reaches for my belt, deftly undoing my pants and fisting my erection. I groan at the contact, weeks of fantasies paling in comparison to the real thing. She strokes me gently, teasing tugs that are like gasoline thrown on a fire of desire.

I whisper her name as I push her sweater up as far as it will go, warring between the urgent need to thrust inside of her and the desperate desire to see her naked on my couch.

Harper decides for me, shimmying out of the leggings and underwear she's wearing but not bothering to remove her sweater. Then she's back beneath me, the wet heat between her legs open and waiting.

I sit up, watching pink paint her cheeks as she absorbs the way I'm looking at her.

"Touch yourself," I rasp.

Her teeth sink into her lower lip as she listens, trailing her fingers up her thigh slowly. Seeing it on a screen is very different from experiencing it in person. I can smell her arousal. See the trust in her eyes as she spreads herself wider, fingers glistening as she pleasures herself.

My dick throbs as I watch her hand move, lips parted and eyes fluttering. Her breathing quickens into pants, her motions turning erratic instead of even. Need, desperate and carnal, burns through me. There aren't hundreds of miles between us right now.

I don't bother taking my pants all the way off or getting rid of my shirt before I pull her hand away and replace it with my tongue. I settle between her legs, licking her pussy with languid swirls of my tongue and sucks on her clit.

Harper writhes beneath me, pulling my hair and rocking her hips until she reaches release.

She's still trembling when I start to ease inside of her.

She gasps my name as her body stretches around me, adjusting to the intrusion. "Fuck. You feel so good."

I hook her knee around my hip, opening her up wider and savoring the way her pussy pulses around me. I dip my head, kissing her mouth before moving my lips along her jaw and down her neck. Harper's breathing turns heavy and uneven as her head turns to the side, allowing me better access.

I almost lose it, surrounded by tight, wet warmth. Her nails dig into my back as I fuck her with rapid, deep strokes. And then she's coming again, and I finally let myself follow, a euphoric rush of possessiveness coursing through me as I fill her.

She turns and snuggles into me, both of us enjoying another form of intimacy that distance doesn't allow for.

Neither of us move until her stomach grumbles. I laugh, standing before pulling my shirt and tie off and adjusting my pants. Harper grabs the button-down and swaps it for her sweater, flashing me a devilish smile that makes me think she's realized how much seeing her in my clothes affects me. Her dark hair is a mess and her lips are swollen. There's a red mark on her neck I'm also responsible for.

It's not until we're both partially dressed and are in the kitchen that either of us speaks again. Harper takes a seat at the counter, watching me rummage through the fridge.

"Eggs okay?" I ask.

"Yeah, sure."

Harper watches me closely as I pull out a skillet and turn on a burner, finally sliding off the stool and walking up behind me as I crack the eggs. She presses a series of warm kisses down the center of my back as her arms slide around my waist, humming deep in her throat.

"How long can you stay?" I ask, dreading the answer.

"Not long enough. Monday. I'll call in sick, but I'm short on vacation days from the wedding."

I nod, grabbing a whisk and mixing the eggs. Her hands move higher, tracing the lines of my abs.

"I can't cook while you're doing that." My voice comes out thick and husky. I can't get enough of her.

Harper laughs lightly and steps away. "Do you have any tequila?"

"No. There's some whiskey in the cabinet, I think."

She opens three before she finds the right one, returning with a bottle of amber liquid and climbing up on the counter with it. My shirt rides up, reminding me she's not wearing anything underneath.

"Want some?" I take the bottle from her, keeping one eye on the pan of eggs.

After a sip, I hand it back. Harper swallows some and then makes a face, looking out at the city. The Space Needle shines in the distance.

"I like Seattle."

I smile at the sight of her sitting in my kitchen, wearing my shirt. Part of me can't believe she's here.

All of me hates how soon she'll be gone.

CHAPTER TWENTY-NINE

HARPER

"What do you think?" I ask for probably the thousandth time.

Drew finally closes the computer. He leans back, looks up, and grins. "It's good, babe."

"Really?"

"Really. It's really good. Pulitzer Prize-worthy."

I roll my eyes and flop back onto the bed. Like everything else in his condo, it's ridiculously comfortable, and it looks obscenely expensive. Staying here is like living in a swanky hotel. "Now, I know you're just trying to get laid."

Drew laughs. I hear the floor creak as he walks over, then lies down beside me. "We've had sex five times since you got here, Sunshine. I promise, I really mean it."

"Really loving the word *really* today, huh?"

He chuckles again before grasping my chin and tilting my face toward him. For a few seconds, we just stare at each other. "I mean it, Harper. It's good. You should send it to some agents."

"I don't know if I want to," I whisper. "It feels like if I put it out in the world, it won't be the same."

Drew nods, his finger running back and forth along my jaw. It's a soothing, calming motion, and I feel myself relax into the comforter.

"I love skating. No matter where. No matter who is watching. It's one of the best feelings in the world—like flying. But there's an extra thrill to sharing something you love with other people. Playing hockey in front of a screaming sold-out crowd is always something extra. Even if there are fans who will go online and bash me or commentators who will pick every play apart. My point is, it can mean something to you and other people, okay? If you want it to?"

"Okay," I tell him. "I'll think about it."

"Good." He leans over and presses a soft kiss to my lips. His hand moves from my jaw to my hair, playing with the strands for a minute. "Do you know who would really, *really* love this book?"

I roll my eyes but smile anyway. "Who?"

"Your dad."

I bite the inside of my cheek, emotion hitting me like a stack of falling bricks. "I wrote it for him," I whisper.

"I know. *The ending doesn't change the beginning or the middle.*"

Hearing Drew quote words I wrote affects me in a way I didn't expect. "And the ending? It made sense?"

"It made sense that it didn't make sense," he tells me.

He *gets* it.

And it's a special feeling, like fireworks and stardust and coziness.

After weeks of debating, I finally came up with an ending to the book I was satisfied with. The alleged victim, Hank, chose to commit suicide, but didn't want anyone to know. So, he had planted a series of clues that made it seem as if he'd been murdered, simply so no one would know. Know he had struggled or know the guilt of not having seen the signs.

I tried to portray his choice as a selfless decision rather than a selfish one. As an attempt to shield loved ones from the ugliness of an irreversible outcome.

I don't know if it's realistic. I'll never know what my dad was thinking when he ended his life. Whether he considered where he'd be found and how it would tarnish so many happy memories for the people he loved.

Mental illness is confusing and debilitating—for those who suffer from it and for those who love those who do. And this—fiction—is my attempt to reclaim that uncertainty, I guess. To say it *doesn't* make sense and it's awful. To craft some type of narrative that makes sense of the insensible.

I grab a handful of the cotton T-shirt Drew is wearing and tug his mouth to mine, savoring the soft brush of his lips and the warm glide of his tongue as he kisses me back. His hand slides into my hair, combing through the strands. I press against him, humming when I feel the bulge of his erection nudge against my thigh.

"Did you read the dedication?"

"What dedication?"

"Last page."

Drew stands and walks back over to the desk, leaning over to look at my laptop. "I read the last—"

He freezes, staring at the screen. I gnaw on my bottom lip, second-guessing my choice to say it this way.

I stand and walk over to him. "I do. Love you."

Drew blinks, the first sign of life since he read the dedication. I put it at the very end, past *The End*, wanting him to read the whole book before he saw it.

"I fell in love with you during your dance routine to that Spice

Girls song," he tells me. "And then again, when I saw you in that pink bikini. When you dropped that lime. When we kissed for the first time. When you caught that fish. When we danced at Amelia's wedding. When you showed up at my game, wearing my jersey. And I'll fall in love with you a thousand more times."

A tear drips down my cheek, and he gently brushes it away before pulling me against his chest. Crying twice in two days is a new record for me.

"I love you," I whisper.

"I love you, Harper."

I think of my mom's words in the car yesterday. About how my dad thought Drew and I might end up together.

I'm suddenly immensely grateful that my dad got to meet Drew. That Drew knew my dad. It stitches the fracture in my heart that will never fully heal a little more tightly together. Because I'm totally certain that Drew is *it* for me. That all the obstacles that looked so large when we were at the lake this summer are actually small and surmountable.

Drew's phone vibrates in his pocket. With a sigh, he pulls it out. "Troy. I'd love to say he won't come up here and bang on the door, but …"

My laugh is watery. "Let me just get changed, then we can go."

I walk over to my suitcase, opening it and surveying the contents before pulling his shirt off. It's all I've worn since I arrived. Drew's eyes are on my body when I look up, his gaze hungry and his eyes warm. Loving.

"If you weren't such a slow reader, we would have had time before lunch," I tease.

We're going to eat with some of his teammates. My first foray into Seattle beyond what little I glimpsed on the ride from the airport to his condo.

"Your book is over four hundred pages, Harper. It would have taken most people all day to read it."

"So, you're saying you *skimmed*?"

Drew rolls his eyes as I pull on jeans and a sweater. "You're impossible."

"You love me anyway," I say, walking over to him.

"Yeah, I do. I'm also really fucking proud of you."

"Thanks," I whisper.

He smiles at me, then grabs my hand and tugs me toward the door.

EPILOGUE
DREW

I roll over, my eyes flying open when I encounter cool cotton instead of Harper. It's rare—more like unheard of—for her to wake up before me. Alarm races through me when I sit up and discover there's no sign of her in the cabin, either.

I climb out of bed, wincing at the cold wood hitting my bare feet as I walk over to the window and peer outside. It started snowing late last night and is still coming down, white flurries blanketing the pines and covering the lake.

There's a solitary figure standing down by the dock.

I pull on clothes, followed by a coat, boots, and hat, then head outside into the blizzard. I'm not sure what is considered a blizzard. We got snow in Massachusetts, growing up, but Seattle has hardly gotten any since I moved there.

The air is crisp and cold, my exhales tiny clouds that linger and then disappear, as I trek along the path down toward the dock. The canoes have all been stored for the winter, the wooden rack completely covered with snow. We got several inches already, based on the accumulation on the roof of the shed.

Snow crunches beneath my boots as I reach the start of the

dock and walk down it, toward where Harper is standing and staring out at the lake.

"Couldn't sleep?"

She glances back at me and smiles, cheeks pink from the cold. "I woke up and realized it'd snowed. I wanted to come out and look at it."

I stop right behind her, and she leans back against me, sighing contentedly. "It's beautiful, isn't it?"

"Yeah."

It feels like standing in the center of a snow globe, flurries floating down around us and turning our surroundings into a winter wonderland.

"Okay." Harper steps out of my arms. "I'm cold. Want to come warm me up?" She winks.

"Wait."

The word is out of my mouth before I consciously thought it. There's some part of me that just knows. That realizes this is *the* moment.

I thought it would be when we visited Port Haven for a final time this past June, before both of our families sold their houses.

Then, I planned a trip to Germany and France this past August, before I got swept back into the whirlwind of hockey and continued trying to win a Cup. We came close last season, making it to the finals.

But I've always had a feeling it might be back at this lake, where I actually proposed. This is where we really started, this exact spot, where we kissed until our lips were raw, the first time we slept together. A year and a half later, this feels fitting. Right.

Harper officially moved in with me just over a year ago. Empire Records agreed to let her work remotely from Seattle, and she's started pulling her laptop out occasionally to work on her book, too.

"Wait for what?" she asks, looking around like there might be some hint in the snow that surrounds us.

I pull the ceramic bird out of my pocket and hand it to her.

She studies it. "Salt?"

"Yeah. Look inside."

Her forehead wrinkles as she unscrews the head of the blue finch, flipping it upside down so the tiny bag falls into her palm. Harper's eyes dart between me and the bag, her blue eyes brilliant against the white backdrop.

I take it from her and pull the ring out, sinking down onto one knee and ignoring the way the cold snow seeps into my jeans. "I've carried this ring around for months, waiting for the perfect moment to ask you this. Just like I stole this saltshaker from my parents' house in Port Haven because it reminds me of that night where we re-met. I love you, Harper Williams. I want everything with you. The wedding and the kids and a house on this lake. Will you marry me?"

She starts nodding before I can ask the whole question, dropping down in the snow next to me. She's kissing me before I have the chance to slide the ring onto her left hand, the warmth of her lips a heavenly balm from the cold.

Our clothes are soaked and covered with snow by the time I stand, pulling her up after me and finally slipping the ring onto her finger.

We both admire how it looks on her hand, glinting in the early morning light.

"Your mom knows. And Simon. I think your mom told Amelia because she's been giving me these excited looks ever since we got here. If she knows, Theo probably does too. Plus, I told my parents."

"So, basically, I was the last to know?"

"Yep. I wanted you to feel *really* bad if you turned me down."

She rolls her eyes but laughs.

"I also asked your dad when we were there for that Memorial Day cookout."

Harper bites her bottom lip, leaning into me. "You weren't kidding about the months, huh? That was back in May."

"I knew I wanted to marry you a while before that."

"Me too."

"Come on." I grab her hand, squeezing it. "It's fucking freezing out."

We slip and slide up the dock, making a mess of the snow and giggling like little kids.

When I glance up at the main house, everyone is standing there, watching us out the wall of windows. My parents, Francesca, Simon, Amelia, Theo, Theo's parents, Alex, and Theo's aunt and uncle, who own Camp Basswood and were nice enough to invite us all here for Christmas. They're hosting an even larger gathering for New Year's. Troy is flying in for it, and Olivia is driving up from the city. So are Claire, Rowan, Willa, Luke, Silas, Cristina, John, Savannah, and Jared.

"Look," I tell Harper.

She glances around, taking a second to spot what I already saw. "Good thing we didn't just make out for a while and then roll around in the snow, huh?"

"Yeah, good thing."

We share a laugh.

"I'm going to ask Amelia to be my maid of honor," she tells me as we reach the steps and start climbing up toward the deck. I can already hear the commotion inside of everyone running around, probably going to act like they didn't just witness my proposal. "I already talked to Olivia about it."

"Someone was confident a ring was coming, huh?"

"Someone was right," she responds.

I'm smiling as we step inside the house. There are a few beats of silence, where everyone basically freezes in their positions.

Then, Harper holds out her left hand. "We're engaged!"

Celebrations erupt around us, everyone acting overly surprised, as if they had no idea.

My last glimpse of Harper is her wide smile until she's pulled away from me, surrounded by congratulations from my family and hers.

It took us six summers to fall.

And at the end was this. A lifetime of love.

THE END

ACKNOWLEDGMENTS

Jovana, thank you so much for another amazing edit. The extra care and effort you put into each manuscript never goes unnoticed. I always look forward to working with you.

Mary Scarlett, I adore this cover. It's exactly what I envisioned and I loved collaborating on it.

Tiffany, your final touches on this book were perfect. Thank you so much for coming through for me once again. I promise this was the last crazy deadline!

Autumn and the whole team at Wordsmith Publicity, thank you for all of your hard work making sure Drew and Harper reached as many people as possible.

And thank YOU, for reading. I hope you enjoyed *Six Summers to Fall*!

ABOUT THE AUTHOR

C.W. Farnsworth is the author of numerous adult and young adult romance novels featuring sports, strong female leads, and happy endings.

Charlotte lives in Rhode Island and when she isn't writing spends her free time reading, at the beach, or snuggling with her Australian Shepard.

Find her on Facebook (@cwfarnsworth), Twitter (@cw_farnsworth), Instagram (@authorcwfarnsworth) and check out her website www.authorcwfarnsworth.com for news about upcoming releases!

ALSO BY C.W. FARNSWORTH

Four Months, Three Words

Kiss Now, Lie Later

The Hard Way Home

First Flight, Final Fall

Come Break My Heart Again

The Easy Way Out (The Hard Way Home Book 2)

Famous Last Words

Winning Mr. Wrong

Back Where We Began

Like I Never Said

Fly Bye

Serve

Heartbreak for Two

For Now, Not Forever

Friday Night Lies

Tuesday Night Truths

Pretty Ugly Promises

Fake Empire

Real Regrets

Ingram Content Group UK Ltd.
Milton Keynes UK
UKHW010019040723
424490UK00005B/396